Love to T

Stu Jam

The Kode

Steven Jones

Dedication

I dedicate this book to all those who keep us safe, in the world of spying and military might; to those who had to overcome and are overcoming things that happen in their past.

Acknowledgment

I want to thank Tom Clancy for giving me a nudge to finish the book. my friends that I would read it to as I wrote it, Pastor Stephen, Donnie my Sister in Law, Linda my secretary, who spent hours typing when I first started writing the novel. My wife and children who had to hear the saying, "WHAT DO YOU THINK ABOUT THIS" many times. To all TRUE STORIES I have heard from military and Law enforcement friends, and the GRACE of God that keep me safe on many mission trips

Contents

The Kode

Five hours from the 16-point compass in the lobby of the CIA headquarters was a mountaintop farm buried deep in the Appalachian. Unknown to many, it had become a safe house for a highly decorated Medal of Honor recipient, ex-Navy SEAL, and retired CIA agent: the old log house wasn't part of the government's safe houses for working agents. It was a place of serenity for a man who's trying to stay safe from himself and the past.

He was part of an elite group of only a few, the CIA's secret: "THE KODE," known to the agency as "Kill OFF Destructive Enemies": expert assassins who change the name of the KODE among themselves to the "Kiss of Death Enforcers," because each one of the agents seems to have kissed death many times, and even some had been kissed by death.

Each agent was highly trained to protect the USA's interests around the world. But in any group, one seemed to always stand out among its peers; it was Sam Black. With a silver cross, three Purple Hearts, and the Medal of Honor, he was the one that became a legend among the younger agents. The Kode was used in the 70s through late 90s taking out high-ranking officials that posed trouble to America. Many thought that after Congress passed laws to stop assassinations, the Kode had been dismantled. But it was kept and used secretly in the CIA by the Presidents of the United States. With the last four members that worked in The Kode, now dismissed from it for three years.

The four also thought, it had finally been ended: Sam Black being the one that would carry the scar of its operations the rest of his life: The deep scar on the side of his face, left by a bullet from Frankie Morgan's gun. This was slowly putting Sam into a shell of bitterness that could finish what the enemies couldn't, "The death of Samuel Black."

As Sam awoke, a movement in the room startled him, causing him to jump quickly out of the bed. Only to find it was the early morning sun shining through the moving curtains from the morning breeze. It seemed like the days with the Navy SEALs and CIA would always be carved into his mind like a bad New York tattoo. Movement in his life could be a matter of life and death; he chose life. He decided he could live with quick jumps and turns. Could the excitement keep his heart young or one-day kill him after spending 15 years with the Navy SEALs and 20 years in the CIA? Being in his third month of retirement, he would have fewer things to worry about.

The flashbacks of Desert Storm and China and Russia would keep all the excitement fresh in his memory. Trying to keep tabs on Saddam was like hunting squirrels in a fall when there were very few acorns; you just had to hunt until you found one tree that had the bait and then wait for the squirrel. The only problem was, Saddam always sent his look-alikes to make sure if there was going to be a death it wasn't going to be his. All of Washington DC couldn't seem to find that squirrel. But time had its way of getting him. Minding the KGB was much easier. You just didn't trust the same one twice. China was a little different; they were always trying to steal the technology from the United States to better their missile system. It was the greedy hands of the West that always found money in their pockets.

Most of the focus during the end of Sam's CIA career was on China. Russia had very little to offer, and China had become a growing concern over Taiwan. They wanted to test the US president's backbone; they knew the president was not a military man, just a good politician. But all that was past, and now Sam could try to keep up with the small mountaintop farm buried deep in the great Appalachian Mountains. As Sam started towards the kitchen to fix his coffee, Buck, his German Shepherd dog, followed him. His dog wasn't only his companion but had become a listening ear for all of Sam's stories and tales as though he was talking to a human.

As Sam sat down at the table with his dog Buck next to him, Sam began to rub his dog behind the ears. He said to Buck, "You are a real friend, and boy, you sure are a good listener."

As Sam began to pour himself another cup of coffee, Buck began to bark and went towards the front door. "Buck, what's wrong? Why all the barking? Oh, I see dust coming up from the road; someone is coming. Let's go to the gate; it's probably one of the Adair boys going hunting. Nah, it's too new of a vehicle for the Adair boys. It has government tags and dark windows; now that's not a good sign, boy. Stay, Buck, it's all right."

As the driver stepped out of the vehicle, Sam waved his hand in a friendly manner and said, "I'm Sam Black; can I help you?"

"Yes, my name is Jim Logan, and I have heard a great deal about you, Mr. Black. Your file is very thick."

"Yeah, I guess the paperwork does add up after thirty-five years in the government."

"Mr. Black, I'm going to get right to the point; it's China. We are in a spot that we must have your help."

"Sorry, Mr. Logan, I'm not interested in your problem. You see, I no longer work for the government."

"Mr. Black, you don't seem to understand; this is a major problem. The United States and all its allies are at risk."

"Listen, Logan, the United States had big problems before, and they have many men who do more than a retiree. I have read about the Los Alamos spying with Mr. Lee, and it's the government's fault. They didn't move fast enough when the FBI told them of the breakdown in security in 1995. So, Mr. Logan, count me out of your, or should I say the government's stupidity. I was trying to get my life back on track; you see; I am going to be a grandpa this year. I want my daughter to be able to have my time for once in her life."

"Black, hear me out; this has nothing to do with Mr. Lee or Los Alamos. You may never see your grandchild grow up. In fact, you may never be able to enjoy your retirement if China gets the "War Peace."

"War peace, what is war peace, Mr. Logan?"

"It's the part of the puzzle the United States has been waiting on to finalize; it's the Star Wars program."

"Star Wars? Are you crazy? That went out before Ronald Reagan left the office."

"That's what the world thought. It's been the highest-kept secret up until a few days ago. Our top scientist came up missing; his name is William Webb. He was putting together the final touches, code-named 'The War Peace.' It's spelled PEACE because the peace of the United States and the whole world depends upon it. We think China is trying to take him out of the country to put together a Star Wars program to take the upper hand in military power. They were watching the Gulf War closely. They saw the superiority of the United States technology, and they started making their moves to have plenty of high-tech weapons before they try to take Taiwan. You must get Mr. Webb back alive before they can get him out of the country into China. His codename is 'THE WAR PEACE.' If they get the Star Wars program before we do, the world will be at their mercy. Mr. Webb had put together a laser that could shoot down and destroy any nuclear missile as soon as it was trying to be launched."

As Sam looked into Logan's eyes, he could see fear. Mr. Logan wasn't a big man, short in size and about 60 years of age with gray hair and wire-rimmed glasses. He looked like a banker, but by the tone of his voice, it had to be a major deal. As the flashes of the past began to shoot through Sam's mind, he remembered seeing the stone-cold faces of people in the third world countries living under communist and dictatorship rule. Their laughter seemed to be little, and the children's faces blank for lack of hope. How would he live with himself, knowing that he could have kept this from happening to the United States?

As he was thinking of the horrors that might follow, Logan put his sunglasses back on and said, "Sam, the government is offering a five million reward to each of you."

Sam replied, "What do you mean by each of you?"

The Kode

"The secret Kode, Sam, they are waiting for your answer."

Sam replied with a rough tone in his voice, "The Kode? It's been three years since I've seen them, Mr. Logan, and don't forget that we had some problems toward the end. I went my separate way," said Sam, sharply.

"Listen, Sam, they have agreed to follow your orders."

Sam was quick to speak, "For three years, I worked alone; I made all the right decisions. I'm still alive today."

"Sam, the government knows the contention between you and Frank Morgan and how much Dannie and Koon Hee meant to you. They studied the reports; Morgan has admitted his wrongs."

"You mean little Frankie has admitted his wrongs. Wrong cannot take this scar from my face," snarled Sam. "Did they tell you not to stare at the scar, Mr. Logan? I have noticed you have been trained to stare off and not at my face, so take a good look, Mr. Logan. See the deep tear in my flesh? My grandchildren will be reaching for it and not my glasses."

"Sam, listen to me, Frankie didn't, sorry, I mean Frank didn't know it was you; it was just a shot in the dark."

"It was more than just a shot in the dark!" yelled Sam. "He wasn't where I told him to be; he was trying to be a hero. He lives that kind of lifestyle. I have told him again and again, no heroes. Just get the job done, I told him. He wouldn't listen. That shot not only cost me my face, but it almost cost us all our lives. It has taken me three years to try and get this out of my mind, and you come along with this big offer and sad story about the future of the world. You must leave now, Mr. Logan. I must think this through, so I am going to the rock. Come on, Buck, let's go."

"Sam, wait, please. I must tell them something so they can start the mission," pleaded Logan.

"Tuesday I will be in Washington DC, Mr. Logan, and I will let you know then. Tomorrow, attend church, Mr. Logan, and pray that Mr. Webb is still in the United States. Come on, Buck, and don't look back; bad luck just like Lot's wife."

"Tuesday we are counting on a yes, Sam," Logan said as he drove off.

Sam knew that Morgan was nothing but a gambling nightmare to himself and others. "Come on, boy, let's go to the rock where I can think. We can check on the horses later."

"Here she is, boy, the rock, my place of daydreams and quiet times. See that cloud, Buck? It looks like a goat's head! Hard like Morgan's. I'm sorry, but he spends most of his time in Las Vegas gambling. Work again with Morgan? No can do."

The Kode

As Sam sat on the rock that once belonged to his grandfather's farm, he began to remember the stories his father had told him. His grandfather was a preacher who traveled by foot and horseback throughout the hollows and the mountains, preaching the gospel of hope. Many childhood memories of that time filled Sam's head.

The old road coming up the mountain was loaded with happy days from the past. Sam's dad would take the children to the mountaintop farm every week when he was free from the coal mines. That farm was almost like religion to him, a place to be free. It always felt the same to Sam.

About three miles from the farm was the one-room school that Sam had the pleasure of attending for one week. It was the last one-room school of its kind. Halfway between the farm and the school was where Sam's aunt lived. She was the teacher and the principal at the school.

Sam's dad, being an old Navy man from the Second World War, felt Sam needed just to get a glance of the past from his childhood. Sam remembered the one week he attended the school during the fall when he was in the fourth grade.

The school looked like an old church, with its steeple on top. It had no running water, only an outside pump and outhouse. No Charmin for toilet paper, just a Sears catalog. Sam loved and remembered the days walking the old dirt road for one week to that school.

He remembered making the fire in the old potbelly stove that was still in the mountain house today. Being only about 11 years old, he enjoyed cranking the old wooden spool that would draw the water out of the well. Sam would still smile when he saw the old metal dipper hanging on his wall next to the stove, that everybody drank from and out of the same bucket. If one had a cold, soon everyone would.

His girlfriend, Catherine, knew that Sam had more scars than the one that was on his face. It seemed that Sam couldn't forget Ola, his childhood sweetheart, wife, and the mother of his beautiful daughter. As a child, Ola would come to the mountains with Sam's family. On the journey home from the farm, Sam would wait for the right moment, acting as though he were asleep. When his dad would put on the brakes, he would roll out on top of her. She always laid in the back seat, and Sam would lay in the space above the seat next to the back window. The cars were big in those days.

After going away for the summer of his senior year to his uncle's house in Fredericksburg, Virginia, something had happened. When Sam returned home, Ola had blossomed into a beautiful woman. They were married nine months later. All the extra time he had during his early Navy training was spent loving her with all his heart. She died from breast cancer when their daughter Jennifer was three years old. Sam was left alone in a world of questions with none to be answered. Trying to keep young Jennifer away from all the military crap was one hard job, but with the help of Polly, her sweet nanny, would make the job much easier.

Polly Maggs was of a special kind; she came from the mountain people who were very religious. Maggs was the early pioneer settlers not far from Sam's farm. Sam learned about her when he was hunting for bear, and she agreed to work for him. Polly was a very strong and influential woman. Many people around the base would come to her for answers, even though she had very little education, she had a heart as big as the mountain from which she came. She still lived with Jennifer in the house outside Washington DC. Jennifer and Catherine seem to get along great. They both thought that Sam is running away from all the true meaning of life.

Jennifer had turned out to be a beautiful woman like her mother, Ola. She reminded Sam so much of Ola that he would tear up being around her at times. Now that Jennifer is married and going to have a baby, he may be able to grow closer to Catherine. As Sam begins to look over the mountain, he speaks in a low tone voice saying, "Am I crazy?" He said to himself, "Shake yourself, Sam Black, and get a grip on yourself. Walk! Yes, that's what I need, a walk." Sam yelled, "Buck, come here, boy. Let's go check on the horses."

Sam began to talk to his German Shepherd, "Buck, that big rock when I was young was my place of serenity, it was sacred to me. My mind plays tricks on me, boy, you sure are a good listener always wagging your tail."

Sam began to talk to Buck about members of the Kode Team, you would think he would be talking to a newspaper writer and not a dog. Sam had a lot on his mind and a very heavy heart, just maybe the US Government was making another mistake. Not realizing the condition of Sam Black.

"What do they think I am? A nut? Koon Hee and Dannie, now that's another story. They listen and would lay down their lives for you. The KODE... Kiss of Death Enforcers, that was our nickname. That's what KODE was supposed to be; a solid team with no stupid mistakes but look at this bullet-scarred face. Like the Apostle Paul in the Bible, I bear the marks in my body. When you try to play a hero, something or someone must pay a price. Morgan! Why couldn't he be like the other two? Ice is another form of water, and that is what the team was like. They formed to their surroundings to become invisible to their enemy. We all kissed death many times. But when you want to play hero, it reveals where you are to the enemy."

The Kode

Sam began to think about his two friends, Koon Hee and Dannie Browning. Koon Hee was from an American Chinese background. His father was in the CIA and worked in China when he married a Chinese woman. Koon Hee kept his Chinese name and dropped the Jackson name. He was one of the best in martial arts.

As Sam would often say, "He probably could have given Bruce Lee a fight for his money. He could slide into a place like a black snake in a barn, hiding in the shadows to take his prey with a sudden strike. He only knew death. He had what is called a killer's instinct."

Sam continued to talk to Buck. "I remember a time during the Desert Storm being on enemy lines for two weeks. Three tanks came into view. Koon Hee made us a bet that he could kill the men in the last two tanks without firing a shot. He said he would give the front tank to the Apache helicopter so they wouldn't feel too bad. Just before darkness, we had given the locations of the tanks. Their time to hit would be at 3 AM. It was after ten when they were on the outside. The tanks were about three hundred yards apart. You could see the glow of their cigarettes in the dark. I wouldn't let Koon Hee go alone, so I told him I would go along as a backup. However, in my heart, I knew he didn't need me. We approached the last tank first like a wolf after a stray. I watched from a short distance with the night goggles. There were two men in each tank. Just as he reached the tank, one man climbed up on the tank just above his head. The other one walked off about twenty yards. I put my scope on the one in the distance with my finger at the trigger. He was armed, and I knew the distance was too far away for Koon Hee. But like the black snake, he laid and waited until the other man returned."

"With a swift move he broke the man's neck on the ground. With a bounce flip, he put a knife through the heart of the one on the track quicker than a forty-five bullet. After his return, his only word was 'next'. I think he was trying to entertain himself because he didn't understand the word hero; only Morgan knew that word. Look boy another cloud and that one looks like a poodle dog. I wouldn't let Koon Hee take the second tank," continued Sam.

"He never said a bad word. Just speaking softly as we moved back, he said, 'Thanks for the one tank,' with a half-cocked grin. Morgan was all fired up about taking the tanks, and I told him; no more tanks will be taken because the location coordinates have already been sent. The Apache helicopters will take care of the rest. We are to move out to another location. Morgan spit on his gun and said, 'What do you think these are for?' He sneered when I said to keep the gun in your hand, and not use it until I tell you otherwise. I knew it was only a matter of time when a problem would arise."

The Kode

"You see Buck, a hero is someone who lays down his life for his comrade, not because he is looking for a pinnacle on a temple to sit on so everyone can see him or her. A real heart of bravery and not a look-at-me heart. Frank is all mouth with only himself in the picture. You hear me boy, he is a low-life gambling fool. The only thing the SEALS saw in him was his bomb-making ability. They should have given him some shooting lessons. He's crap! You hear me, Buck? Crap! Frank Morgan! They expect me to work with Frank Morgan. Maybe the next time he pulls the trigger, my grandkids will have one less grandpa or maybe he might plant one of those bombs under my bed. Are you listening to me Buck or are you just tolerating my mouth? Boy, if only you could talk, maybe you could tell me what to do. I am talking to a dog so I must be crazy. I'm sorry boy you are my best friend. Maybe everyone is right; I am just holding a deep grudge. Yeah, probably as deep as this scar on my face."

"I talked to you Buck as if you were a human, maybe I am like Dannie; part of our heart is dead." Sam began to remember what she always told him, that part of her died when her father molested her. She said the part to love a man was dead. Even though she was a beautiful woman, she had only dated once. According to her story it lasted about fifteen minutes. When Henry, the star football player, laid his hand on her leg, she jumped from the car screaming, "I hate you Daddy, I hate you!"

Dannie and Sam were good friends and talked often about things in their past. Even though her blue eyes would shine, you could still see the hurt deep inside. She always brought it up when they would talk, that made Sam remember something his Grand Father would say; 'Out of the abundance of the heart, the mouth speaks.'

He knew she was hurt but didn't know how to heal the wound. He couldn't see, just maybe that's what was wrong with him. Every time he looked into the mirror, he saw the wound.

"Dannie was the computer and lock expert," Sam conveyed to Buck. "She could open any lock or hack any computer. Her long hair almost would touch the keyboard. I told her she should be glad for automatic washers. She almost fell on the floor laughing when I told her about the time I was washing clothes for my mother on an old wringer-type washer and when I got too close, it grabbed my arm. As I was screaming watching myself being pulled in, I thought my life was ending only to be saved by my loving mother."

When Sam stopped speaking to Buck and just sat quietly gazing at the mountain, Sam remembered telling her that one day the computer was going to suck her in. She told him her only peace was opening someone else's private thoughts, and to which Sam told her it wasn't the thoughts, just their information.

The Kode

Sam knew, Dannie just tolerated Morgan. She always thought Morgan was an arrogant smart mouth. He thought all women was to fall in love with him with just one look or his "come to me baby" attitude. He had tried to come on to Dannie when they were in Mexico with the DEA, and she made it clear if he ever tried anything again that she would plant one of his bombs in his underwear drawer. He seemed to enjoy his mirror and, always acted like a smart-mouthed know-it-all.

While staying in Jaltipan, Mexico, Dannie and Sam spent many hours just plain talking as friends. They were staying in a remote area looking for a leader of a drug cartel, staying in a run-down house called Swine Suite. The hog pen next to the old mud hut filled the house with hog perfume. Dannie bedded in the room with Sam because she always felt safer with him, like a big brother.

Dannie always kept in touch over the three years they were separated. The times they would have dinner together, they would get buried in the past and sometimes what they thought would be their future. In a way, Sam was looking forward to working with her and Koon Hee again.

"Buck, you're my hero and my real friend. Come on boy; let's see about those horses. We've got a trip to Washington DC to make. Guess I will have to leave you with Jennifer and Polly. We will give them a call when we get back to the house. They will probably think I am out of my mind to even think about taking the job that the government has offered. But for five million bucks, that's hard to turn down even if Frank has to be a part of the plan. Let me pour this grain in the buckets, boy, and we will head to the house. You probably have an appetite from listening to all my palaver."

"Where in the heck did I put that cell phone? Maybe my memory is leaving me too. Let me see. Where was the last place I used that stupid phone? Toilet, oh Lord, surely, I didn't leave it in the outside John. Here Buck, chew on this bone and I will be right back."

Sam just couldn't let go of the memories, he began to think to himself. "Morgan! Working with Morgan again; that fool is full of himself. Studied chemistry and wanted to be a scientist too. Ended up working in the Navy Seals, making some of the best killer bombs ever. That fool could make a bomb look like a stick of chewing gum. Phone, where are you? Ok, now you are an official toilet phone. Hmm... no one home but my crazy answering machine. I will call back later; I don't talk to my own voice, just talk to myself, aloud.

"Buck, come here boy and let me scratch your head. Boy when you kick the bucket, I am going to give you a proper funeral. I will bury you down next to the rock because you have been a real sidekick and a good listener." As Sam returned to his house to his favorite chair, Buck lied beside him and they fell asleep, only to be awoken by a visitor.

"Hey, what's going on Buck, what are you barking at? It's 3 AM and I must have fallen asleep. What's the matter boy, is something outside?"

Probably just that black bear snooping around in the garbage again, he thought.

"Let's get a light and take a look outside. Oh, I see headlights at the gate, but it's three in the morning. I'll take my pistol boy, just in case. Hey, now they're blowing the horn, don't they know what time it is? Quit blowing that horn, I am coming! Can you see this light flashing at you?"

"Hey Sam! Do you still have that mean dog?"

"Yeah, who wants to know?"

"It's Frank Morgan. Sorry it's in the middle of the night but trying to find this old dirt road is like trying to find a needle in a haystack. My GPS system couldn't seem to help either. This road is made for dune buggies, not Cadillacs. Mr. Logan never told me you lived in the boogie woods."

"Nobody told Logan to tell you or anybody else where I lived. I told him I would give him my answer by Tuesday," Sam said angrily.

Ignoring Sam's anger, Frank continued, "How is Jennifer and Polly doing Sam?"

"I guess you came from Vegas to ask me a stupid question at three in the morning," snapped Sam. "You never did have any respect for someone trying to sleep. Stay Buck! This is the bird I have been telling you about."

"You wouldn't let him bite a man now, would you Sam?"

"No, but I might let him bite a boy that should be a man."

"Is there any way Sam, I could come up to the house and talk a minute?"

"Sure, just leave your toy car there and walk in front so I can see your best side."

"Come on Sam give me a break. I have done everything to say I am sorry."

"Shut up Morgan and keep walking. We will talk in the house."

As they entered the house, Sam gestured for Frank Morgan to sit over there by the lamp.

"Nice cabin you have here Sam."

"Cabin? This is no cabin! This is my grandfather's house."

"Sorry Sam! I used the wrong word, but this is a nice place you have here."

"Cabin! Did you hear that, Buck? Logan sent this hotel suite staying; mommy's boy to tell me my house is a cabin. Why are you here Morgan?"

"They need the KODE TEAM Sam, and time seems to have become a big factor."

Sam replied, "Logan said THE KODE TEAM was waiting on my answer."

"That's true Sam, but it's Dannie and Koon Hee. They won't take the job without you in the middle."

"What about you Frank?"

"I need the money Sam; I don't have a lot of choices. Vegas hasn't been good to me this last month. But you know Sam, it has always been good working with you and the gang."

"Sure Frank, it's been fun working alone and now I have to wonder about your shooting ability again."

"Listen Sam, that night of the shooting—"

"Shut Up!"

"But Sam..."

"Shut Up! I should blow your head off right now." Sam screams, as he pointed the pistol towards Morgan.

"Come on Sam, point that pistol to a different direction."

"Oh you don't like looking down the barrel of a gun. Maybe you don't like the scar on my face either."

"Sam, come on now, you have never acted like this before."

"Acting? I'm not acting! I have looked at this scar for three and a half years."

"Sam listen to me, that night..."

"I told you to shut up," screamed Sam again; "Don't speak of that night to me now or never again or I will kill you."

"All right Sam, have it your way. If you don't want to help in this matter, I will tell Logan. This is the reason why he sent me; to see your reaction toward me. The United States can't afford another mistake because of your mental suffering."

"You sorry slum bag, you have no remorse for what you did to me."

"Go ahead Sam; shoot if it will make you feel better. Nobody can talk to you. You are the one that sees it one way... your way. What about Catharine and Jennifer, how are you treating them?"

"OUT! Out of my house!" demanded Sam. "Sorry Buck, I didn't mean to scare you by slamming the door. Let me pick up this picture; it's Polly and Jennifer and me when we were at Niagara Falls. There was no scar on my face then. I've got to lay down Buck. Oh, my head is hurting, and I know I shouldn't have pointed that gun at Frank. He was right this isn't like me. What is wrong with me? I have to pull it together, but I can't seem to sleep; I can't even think. I don't believe Logan will want me on the Team after Frank tells him of my stupid actions. I just lost it! I lost all thought of everything. I have never done that in my lifetime. I am going crazy Buck."

"They don't even know of my condition or Logan never would have come here or maybe they had an idea and that's why they sent Morgan. Tomorrow we will get the axe Buck." As Sam finally drifted off to sleep.

Frank drove back toward DC, wondering what to tell Mr. Logan.

In his heart, he knew that at one time Sam Black was the best in spying and recovery. Sam could jeopardize the life of Webb and the whole Star Wars Plan. He would have to report the gun pointing action.

As Sam's cell phone rang, it took Buck's barking to wake him from what seemed to be a deep coma. But on the fifth ring, he answered with a low "yeah?"

"Daddy, where are you? I need you to come to the hospital."

"What's wrong, honey?"

"Daddy, it's the baby, he is not waiting and he is coming early. Please come quick."

"You will be just fine, honey. Little Sam will wait until I get there."

"Wait? I told you, dad, there is no wait for this child. You better be here."

"I love you, sweetie, and I'm on my way."

"Buck, we've got to hurry, so get in the truck."

What a night! Frank shows up in the middle of the night, I lose it and point a gun at him, and my first grandchild is coming early. This must be a good time to go crazy. Especially if I keep talking to a dog.

As Sam turned on I-66 in Front Royal his thoughts were cloudy about the visit from Frank Morgan. He knew that his thoughts and actions were not professional. In fact, he was past the point of any logic or reasoning. He had never seen himself like this before. Then a flash crossed his mind and he saw fire; he could still feel the warm blood run down his face. He shook his head and said, "Over and over... why?"

Time moved quickly as he turned onto the Ferry Road to go across the Potomac to Germantown, Maryland. His focus was now on his daughter, his life's joy. *Can I really be there for her when my actions seem to be deteriorating daily?* He began to remember how when she was young, she would swing on his arm, always saying "my daddy is the strongest man in the world." But now she doesn't even know that her daddy is falling apart mentally. But Sam knew that deep down in him is a willpower that will keep him alive for many years. He must roll over that stone and become alive again even if it is for his family. The very thought of giving up could never be in his vocabulary.

As he pulled into the row of clinics on his way into the parking lot of the hospital, he read a sign that said "mental health." "Maybe I should check in there instead," he thought as he bursts into laughter that even Buck ignored. "Buck, you will have to stay in the truck until I can get you over to Polly's. I will come down a little later and take you for a walk."

Sam walked into the hospital. Spotting the information desk, he quickly asked the receptionist where his daughter might be. She looked up and smiled at Sam. "Room 220, second floor. It must be a grandchild."

"Yep," Sam replied, "my first."

"The elevators are down the hall on the right," as she pointed.

"Thank you, ma'am," as Sam moved with haste.

As the elevator opened, Sam's countenance changed. He came face to face with Frank Morgan and Jim Logan. The thought of his rage the night before flashed again in his thoughts.

He knew they were there to say no use coming down to the headquarters.

"Sam, Jennifer is doing fine, and Polly is up there with her," Morgan said with a smile.

"Glad we caught you, Sam," Logan said as he took him by the hand. "Frank told me that he thought you would take the job. He said you and him worked things out last night."

Sam glanced over and stared at Morgan for a moment, wondering what was going on. He knew that nothing had been worked out; it only seemed to become worse.

"Sure," Sam said, "Everything has worked out."

"Good, then your answer is a yes?"

"Listen, guys, I will give you my answer after I see my daughter."

"Sure, Sam, here is my card with my cell number. I will be out to dinner but waiting for your call," Mr. Logan said as he stepped from the elevator.

Morgan stayed on and said, "Think I will ride up with Sam."

Logan smiled and shook hands with both men again. As the elevator door closed, Sam looked straight into Morgan's eyes and said, "Why? Tell me why! You know what happened between us."

"Listen, Sam, I thought it over. If I was in your shoes, my thoughts may be the same as yours. I know you, Sam, as a man of integrity. As for myself, I just try to survive from day to day. No place to go, no one to see."

"What happened to that little chick named Cindy?" asked Sam.

"Well, she got tired of me using her money at the card table. You see, Sam, I'm not taking this job for Uncle Sam. I owe some big money to the good ole boys."

"Who are the good ole boys?"

"They call them the mob."

"You've got to be kidding me. You've got mixed up in the mob?"

"I didn't say in with the mob, and I said I owe them a little money."

"How much is a little?"

"$250,000.00. So, you see, I must take this job."

"What does Logan think about this mob deal?"

"He only knows I like to gamble, and the rest is between you and me."

"Why? Tell me your problems?"

"Because I want you to take this job so we can get started. I am tired of looking over my shoulder."

"So, what do your mob friends know about the job?"

"Nothing! They think it is another Middle East deal."

As the door opened on the second floor, Sam stepped out, looking for the room number. Frank stayed on the elevator. As the door slowly closed, he said, "Later, Sam."

As Sam turned down the hall, he whispered under his breath, *He is such a fool. The mob knows this guy is a nut.*

The Kode

As Sam entered the room, he found his daughter sitting on what seemed to be a large beach ball. Her face filled with a smile, and she said, "You made it. You made it before little Sam, Dad."

"I came as fast as I could, honey. What's the big ball for?"

"It's a new thing they use in birthing babies."

As Sam bent over to kiss his daughter, he saw Frankie out the window talking to a couple of dark-skinned men. He watched as he saw the hand movements. *It must have been Frank's mob buddies.*

As Frankie got into his car, one of the men, the smaller of the two, pointed his finger to look like a pistol, turned, and walked away. Again, he whispered, *he's such a fool.*

Jennifer overheard and said, "Who's a fool, daddy?"

"Nothing, honey, I was just thinking out loud."

"Sure Dad! You were talking about Frankie. He left just before you came up. Forgive him Dad. It's the right thing to do."

Sam almost raised his voice as he spoke the word forgive, only to say sure, sweetie, forgive.

As a contraction made Jennifer groan, Sam held her hand and rubbed her hair. "It will soon be over, honey. Just hold on. It will be worth the pain when you hold that little fellow. Where is Polly?"

"She went down to the cafeteria, but she will be right back."

As Sam held his daughter, his thoughts kept going back to the visit that Frankie Morgan had made to his farm. *Why didn't Frankie say something to Mr. Logan about his crazy actions? Forgive! That's the word his grandfather had used in his preaching for 60 years. But what Morgan had done to me was more than sin; he had carved into my face that which was unforgivable, or was it in my heart?*

As Sam was deep in thought about his past, he didn't even notice Polly as she walked into the room.

Finally, after speaking his name three times, Sam snapped out of the angry thoughts only to smile and say, "Polly, I missed your cooking." Not only had Polly been a great Nannie, but she knew every mountain recipe there was to know.

Polly responded back with a short laugh. "Sam, if you could stand to stay around for a few days, I would fix you some of that good home cook. You looked a little pale, Sam. Guess you'd been living on sandwiches and pork 'n' beans again."

"Listen, Polly, I will be in DC for a few days, and I will take you up on that home-cooking deal as soon as this little girl has my baby."

"Your baby? You will have to fight me on who gets to hold

that boy the most."

As Jennifer had another contraction, she gasped for breath and said, "Both of you, remember I get all the first holds."

As the baby fought continually to go back and forth, Dr. McDowell walked in and began to slide the curtain around the bed, asking everyone to step back for a few minutes.

As Jennifer was being checked, Polly looked at Sam and said, "Tell me what's wrong, Sam."

"Wrong, what do you mean wrong?"

"Listen, Sam, I have seen that blank stare in your eyes many times. You can hide it from Jennifer, but you can't hide it from me."

"Polly, I have been asked to do a little mission for the government."

"Sam, you have given enough years to the government. Let someone else do their dirty work. You're not the only man alive who must jump when the government calls."

"I know Polly. This is a little matter that probably won't take but a few days." Sam didn't want to get into details of the danger because he knew Polly would just worry; she was like a mother to him.

"Listen, Sam, you've got a little grandbaby coming. You

hear me son? It's time to enjoy yourself for a change. Tell them no, just for once. Tell them no!"

"Can't do that, Polly, just yet."

The curtain around Jennifer's bed opened, and Dr. McDowell said, "We are going to have to take the baby. He just won't turn right in the birth canal, and we don't want to take any chance. She has been in labor for a long time for him not to turn. But she will be just fine."

"Where is Jeremy? He should be here," said Sam.

"He is here Sam. We were at the cafeteria together, and he was finishing up his meal when I left," explained Polly.

Sam replied, "Well, the General better hurry up." Sam had nicknamed his son-in-law General because his last name was Patton. Although his name sounded military, Jeremy was nothing of the sort. He was a quiet man, mild in manner, and trying to make the PGA circuit. He had gone through college on a golf grant and was now working at a golf course in Aberdeen, Maryland, as a golf pro assistant.

As Sam took Jennifer by the hand, her smile warmed his heart, and he forgot his night with Frankie Morgan. "Daddy, don't worry, everything will be just fine. Remember, I am a Black, and that puts the toughness in my veins," Jennifer proudly proclaimed.

As another contraction hit, she tightened her grip on Sam's hand with a light moaning sound, and just for a moment, Sam remembered a time in Iraq when one of his soldiers had been wounded in battle, and Sam had to pull him from the front. It was as though he was pulling someone from a lake drowning, laying sideways with his arm under the soldier, dragging foot by foot until they were safe in the foxhole.

As he held the hand of his dying comrade, he whispered in his ear that he was going to be all right. As he felt the grip began to tighten as the death angel came close. The soldier looked up into Sam's eyes, and with a gurgling voice, he said, "Sam, you always were a great liar."

"Sam! Sam!" Jeremy shook Sam to bring him back into the real world. "Hey man, if you get much deeper into your thoughts, you're going to fall over."

"Sorry, Jeremy, I am just a little tired."

Jeremy continued, "I could see Buck out of the cafeteria window, and he seemed to be looking for you."

"Ok, I guess I better go down and take him for a potty walk," Sam turned and gave Jennifer a wink, and told her he'll be right back.

Jennifer gave her dad a thumbs up, saying, "I don't plan on going anyplace."

As Sam started down the hall, he saw what looked like one of the men who had met Frankie Morgan in the parking lot. As the elevator closed, Sam rushed through the stairway door, jumping steps as he went down, only to find no one on the lobby floor. Hurriedly, he bolted through the front doors, spotting a dark Mercedes leaving the hospital lot quickly. Sam spat on the ground and swung his arms violently, swearing to kill Morgan if anything happened to his family because of his gambling flings.

As Sam reached the truck, he spotted his faithful dog lying on the floor. White foam was coming from his mouth, and his breathing was short and shallow. "Buck!" Sam shouted. "Hold on boy. I will get you to a vet." Not far from the hospital was Newtown Veterinary Clinic. Sam never even noticed the note lying on the dash as he sped out of the lot. "Hang on, boy, just one mile and we will be there."

As he reached for his emergency flashers, the red light was backed up. Sam shot off the road on the bank with Buck sliding toward his feet. Huge chunks of dirt flew as he threw it into four-wheel drive. Just missing one of the power poles, Sam jerked his Ford truck back onto the road with his horn wide open. Buck, now lying next to his leg, assured his pal would be all right.

As Sam pulled into the lot, Dr. Hayford locked the clinic door. Slamming on the brakes and jumping from the car, Sam screamed for him to wait. "What's wrong Sam?"

"It's Buck, Doc. Something has happened to him." As he opened the door to carry Buck in, he noticed a silver ring with a paper pulled through it. As he carried him in, he reassured his old pal that everything would be ok. Dr. Hayford told Sam to lay him on the table. With a puzzled look, the doctor began to examine Buck. "What has he eaten Sam?"

"Only some dry dog food this morning before we left the mountain."

"Yesterday, he ate the same thing with only a piece of turkey sandwich that I had left."

The Doc instructed Sam to put on gloves as he said, "I don't know what we are dealing with at this point. It could be some of those mountain rabies. Has he been running loose in the woods, Sam?"

"No, only when we go for walks. He stays with me all the time."

Wiping away the white foam from Buck's mouth, the doctor glanced at Sam with a worried look. "His breathing is very poor, Sam, but I will do all I can."

The Doc and Sam had been friends for a long time. He, too, was an ex-GI who served in Vietnam and went to college on a GI bill. So, Sam knew if anything could be done, Doc Hayford would do it. They had spent many hours talking about the waste of men's lives in the jungle of a political war, with the higher-ups always feeding President Johnson with the wrong figures and information. Doc always said the only thing the war gave him was nightmares and the education to become a veterinarian.

As Dr. Hayford drew blood from Buck, he looked up at Sam as if to say we have been friends for a long time, but it looks like time has expired for your friend. As Sam rubbed his old pal's head, he said everything would be all right, and Doc would make him better in a low tone of voice. Just as Dr. Hayford stepped from the side room, Buck began to try to breathe deeply.

The white foam began to pour from his mouth. "Do something, Doc!" Sam shouted. But the fight was over, and Buck was no longer breathing. "Please help him, Doc, please help him," Sam pleaded as tears filled his eyes.

"Sorry, Sam, I did all I could do. I didn't even have time to run the blood tests." Sam turned slowly towards the wall, holding his forehead and rubbing his hands back and forth through his hair as though he were at a loss for words.

Dr. Hayford walked over to Sam, put his arms around him, and shook his head. "I don't know, Sam, I just don't know, I didn't have time to run those tests. I am so sorry."

Sam turned toward the front door and muttered a soft thank you to the Doc. "I will call you tomorrow and let you know what happened," Doc Hayford said sympathetically.

As Sam turned back into the room, he asked, "Doc, will you do me a favor? Put him in a cooler until tomorrow. I must go back to the hospital where my daughter is having a baby, but I want to take Buck back to the mountain so I can give him a proper burial."

"Sure, Sam, no problem," said Doc. Hayford.

As Sam walked slowly toward his truck, he wiped the tears from his eyes again. "Buck, I will miss you, man," he whispered. Opening the door, he again spotted the note pulled through a silver ring. As he reached for the note, an empty feeling came into his stomach.

The note simply read: **Tell your friend to pay up, or many will die. With Love, Pizza.**

The inscription on the ring read Gold Nugget - Las Vegas. Sam angrily threw the note on his dash and slid the ring on his middle finger. As he quickly started the truck, he left black marks on the pavement as he sped back towards the hospital. Slamming his hand on the steering wheel, he shouted, "It's Morgan's fault, and I will get even, Buck, I promise I will get even. I will wear this ring and place it in the mouth of the one that killed you."

As Sam's mind was lost in rage, he sped by the hospital entrance sign, slamming on his brakes, spinning his truck sideways, jumping the curb, and crossing a grassy hump into a vacant parking spot.

Running toward the hospital, Sam spotted the same black car leaving the parking lot in a hurry. He bypassed the elevator and ran up the steps to the second floor. As he turned the corner, Jennifer was taken into the delivery room.

"Daddy, where have you been? You must have walked Buck ten miles," she said.

Sam smiled, "Yes, honey."

"Mr. Black?" the nurse interrupted, "you will have to put on this gown, booties, and head covering if you are going in with your daughter."

"No worries, ma'am," he said, using a phrase he had often used after spending time in Australia.

But the empty feeling he had in his stomach gave him plenty to worry about. He knew that Morgan's dealings with the mob and his job to find Mr. Webb were more than most would want. But Sam had been down hard roads before, and he knew how to survive through tough times.

The Kode

As Sam entered the room with his daughter, the big light above the table caused him to remember Buck lying on that table, gasping for breath. Without even realizing it, he spoke Buck's name aloud. Jeremy got his attention by shaking his shoulder.

"Sam, are you daydreaming again?" inquired Jeremy.

Sam slowly spoke, "Yeah, just a little tired, I guess," and then breathed out slowly as if he had been holding his breath.

Going into a room to change into the clothing given to him for the birthing of his grandson, tears filled his eyes again as he tried to forget the death of his dog. He knew the days ahead were troublesome, like the rivers in the mountains after a spring rain when they overflowed their banks and washed away everything in their path. He also knew that many would die before all of this was over. This could be a river that even Moses couldn't part with.

As Sam started down the hallway toward the delivery room, his attention was diverted to a waiting room television special alert.

"This is a special report from WVAZ channel 5. Live on the scene of a car bombing in German Town, Maryland. A late-model Mercedes has been destroyed by what appears to be a car bombing. Still no details on the driver and passenger of the car, except both were killed in the high-explosive blast. The FBI is working with ATF officials to determine the kind of bomb materials that were used. This could be a terrorist attack against diplomatic officials from another country. The FBI reports the bomber was well trained to cause this kind of destruction, being centralized only inside the car. No pedestrians were hurt. Stay tuned for continued coverage on WVAZ channel 5 news."

Sam felt numb inside as he looked down at the silver ring on his finger. Only three miles from the hospital and a car identical to the one he saw in the parking lot couldn't be a coincidence. It had to be Frankie Morgan's bomb in the car of his mob friends. What came next had now become a puzzle that Sam must put together with lost pieces that would keep death from his family and himself.

He was startled by a voice saying, "Sam, let's go. They are ready for us in the operating room."

As he entered the room again, the light over the table reminded him of Buck, and tears filled his eyes, but he smiled as his daughter reached for his hand and said, "Daddy, I love you, and you are the best Daddy in the whole world."

He kissed her on the forehead and told her that she is the love of his life. "Your son will be strong and blessed and bring you many years of happiness just like you have brought to me. I will always be here for you and him."

Dr. McDowell then pulled the curtain halfway around the

bed, blocking the view, and asked all to stand back about six feet, "It won't be long until we see the new life God has allowed in your lives."

Sam again found himself in deep thought about the news report on the car bombing. He knew deep inside that Frankie had placed that bomb inside the Mercedes. Things were now unfolding that were going to hinder the work of finding Mr. Webb. As he reached for the scar on his face, he wondered what the days ahead would hold for his family and his retirement. He suddenly snapped from the deep thoughts as he heard the first cry of his grandson, Samuel.

Tears of joy filled his eyes, and for a moment, bad thoughts were replaced with a beautiful baby boy with a head full of black hair. As Dr. McDowell handed the baby to the nurse, he smiled at Sam and winked as if to say everything was all right. As the nurse cleaned up the newborn, Polly looked at Sam and said, "He's the spitting image of you, Sam," in her old mountain talk.

"Listen, Polly, you know the boy had to come out looking like me because I am the only one here that has any sense."

Polly reached for Sam's hand quickly to say, "Sam, my boy, you spent your nickels' worth of sense on the government, and they ain't returned no change."

Within Sam's heart, he knew Polly was right; a lot of his years had been spent killing and losing words held in deep secrets in files at the Pentagon and the CIA headquarters.

"Sure, Polly, but you and I now have a baby boy that we can bounce on our knee, and when we get tired, we can give him back to his mommy."

Laughter filled the room, and Sam got to hold Samuel first, but not for long; as Jeremy said, "That's enough. Sam took his turn with the baby."

As Jennifer awoke from the anesthesia, little Samuel was being passed back and forth like a basketball. When the doctor was finished with Jennifer and the curtain was pulled back, Jeremy gave the baby to its mother.

"He is so beautiful," Jennifer said, and Sam was quick to reply that Polly said he looked just like him, to which Jennifer replied, "Remember, Dad, they say I look just like you, too."

Everybody seemed to gather around the bed like an old sitting hen.

Sam pulled up a seat next to Jennifer. With tears in his eyes and a smile, he said, "Honey, as soon as he is big enough to walk, I will take him to the mountain farm and teach him how to rabbit hunt. I already have a gun made to fit him. It's my old 37 Winchester that

Dad cut down for me to fit my short arms."

Jennifer laughed as she pointed her finger at her dad to remind him he must first go to church and be anointed before he touched a gun.

Sam began to tell the story about his first squirrel with the old Winchester. Everybody stopped talking to listen to another one of Sam's old experiences from the past. They had all heard so many, but they had learned to enjoy what they called "Black history."

They also knew it was good for Sam because it kept his mind off the scar and that incident in his life that made him unhappy. So, out of respect, they all listened and acted as though it was the greatest thing they ever heard.

As Sam began to tell how he was just big enough to hold up the gun, about eight years old, he was ready for his first hunting trip with his dad to a place called Moncove Lake.

Sam began, "It was about a three-hour trip, and we would leave around 2 AM. Dad would take off a week from his coal-mining job. We stopped at a small country store that serviced hunters. The little store was called 'The Barn,' although it had no resemblance to a barn. It was in the area of farm country called Sweet Springs Valley."

"By the time we got to the store, it was about five in the

morning. While Dad was inside the store sipping on a cup of coffee, I walked outside to get away from cigarette smoke. I saw someone coming out of the dark shadow from the end of the building. I felt the hair on my neck stand up, or at least I thought it did." With these words, every ear in the room was glued to Sam's next words.

Jennifer spoke first from the listeners and asked if he ran.

Sam quickly gave her a sly grin and let her know he doesn't run from anyone. Everyone knew that Sam was running from himself, but no one dared to make that kind of statement. Sam continued with his story.

"Moving slowly toward me was a crippled man on a crutch. He was young, about twenty years old, delivering papers in the area. Because of his crippled legs, I wondered why somebody didn't help him. I found out later he had no one; his parents were killed in a house fire when he was fourteen years old.

He had tried to get them out when a beam from the old farmhouse fell on him, and he had to drag himself out just in time to watch the house being consumed with fire and taking the lives of his family. The store manager later told Dad the boy just closed himself off from people, just talking enough to collect the paper money, but he talked to me for about fifteen minutes on that trip. I told him it was my first hunting trip, and he offered me a few pointers on squirrel hunting.

He said that when he was able to climb hills, squirrel hunting was his favorite pastime. I remember reaching into my pocket, finding the $1.40 I had saved up for the trip, and as I shook hands with him, I placed the money in his hand. It startled him for a moment, but I was quick to say, please take it. I want to give it to you. A smile filled his face as he turned from me to continue giving out newspapers."

It seemed that tears filled Sam's eyes for just a moment, and he wondered if perhaps he was getting soft in his old age. Sam glanced up and saw the clock; it was 5:55, so he quickly excused himself and exited the room.

He didn't want to miss the news report on the car bombing. As Sam started down the hall toward the waiting room, he glanced down at the ring on his finger. As anger began to rise, he felt the nerve in his face beginning to jerk. It was the side in which Frankie Morgan's gunshot had torn apart. As he grabbed his face, the anger built into a blinding furor that caused him to walk into a nurse.

"Sir, Sir, are you all right?" Her words sounded like deep mountain thunder in a hollow pipe as Sam saw the white dress come into view and the face of the woman he had almost knocked down.

Looking down quickly to check her nametag, he said, "Sorry, Miss Lewis, I haven't had much sleep, and my daughter just gave birth to my first grandson."

"Well, sir, I can understand that," she replied, "but if you're leaving the hospital, you should take it easy driving out and consider walking instead."

As they both laughed, Sam looked around, still in a daze, as he spotted the waiting room. He made it just in time to hear the newscaster come on to bring the updated story on the car bombing.

"Good evening from WVAZ channel 5. This is Gary Patterson. A little while ago, a car bombing took the lives of two men in German Town, Maryland. We will go to the scene of the bombing with a special report from Cindy Burgess."

"Cindy, have the FBI or ATF officials given the names of the two victims, and who may be responsible for this attack?"

"Gary, it seems like very little has been said by either agency, but we do have some information from anonymous sources that these two men were linked to the mob. The bombing could have been from another crime family. The question in almost everyone's mind is if the bombings were done to kill only the occupants of the car. The bomber had to be well-trained and experienced. One official did say he had never seen a bombing so contained as if to say the bomber hand-picked his victims without hurting anyone else."

"Cindy, we know that nothing like this has ever happened in or around German Town before, so how are the people reacting?"

"Gary, we have talked to several people here at the mall parking area, and most are shocked, but some believe the crimes of DC are moving into outer areas. This is Cindy Burgess reporting live from the scene of today's car bombing in German Town, MD."

"Thank you, Cindy. Now to the President's news conference early today at the White House."

Polly interrupted and asked Sam, "what's on the tube?"

"Oh, Polly, sorry I didn't see you come in. Nothing but trouble, Polly, nothing but trouble."

"Sam, my boy, you can't hide forever from the past or the future. I can see it in your eyes, Sam; you need to think twice about this government job."

"You keep saying it's the last, but that worried me, Sam. It might just be your last at everything. And no one is going to care, son, when they plant you on the mountain, six feet deep; no one but your family."

As Sam took Polly in a hug, tears again filled his eyes. "I love you, Polly, you are just like a mother sent from heaven."

As Polly patted him on the back, she told Sam in her

mountain words, "If I could, Sam, I would hog-tie you to the fence post, but son, you have to live with the choice. You will have to drink from the water, bitter or sweet."

As Sam glanced back at the TV, a nurse spoke from the doorway, telling Sam he had a phone call.

"You can take it at the front desk," she said.

"Thank you," Sam replied. "I'll be right back, Polly."

"Just remember what I said, Sam, bitter or sweet," Polly reiterated.

As Sam reached for the phone, he spotted Frankie Morgan at the door talking to Jeremy. Sam's voice seemed to change as he answered with a rough hello.

"What in the world are you mad about, Sam? Has that new grandson stolen your little girl's heart?"

"Oh, Dannie, I'm sorry, it's so good to hear your voice. I'm so tired, Dannie. I've not had much sleep lately."

Dannie knew something was wrong, but she replied, "I am just about at the hospital, and I wanted to see that new grandson. What floor are you on?"

"If you don't mind, Dannie, just pull into the back, by the ER, and pick me up; we can have some dinner. I need to talk to you about something. We can see the baby afterward."

"Sure, Sam. I should be there in about four minutes," assured Dannie.

As Sam hung up the phone, he told the nurse he would be at the cafeteria if anyone was looking for him. He only said it to throw off Frank until he could get away from the hospital. Going toward the opposite set of stairs, he found himself grinding his teeth as he tried to get away from facing Morgan again on the same day.

As Sam saw Dannie's red Camaro pull into the ambulance area, he jumped in and told Dannie to move quickly because he didn't want Frank to see them leave. His conversation quickly turned to Frank Morgan.

"Dannie, do you know where Morgan is staying?"

"What do you have planned, Sam, a little friendly visit?"

"Well, just say we need to know what is going on in the mind of a child."

"Yeah, sure," exclaimed Dannie. "He's staying at the Hilton close to the Dulles Airport."

Speaking at a fast pace, Sam continued, "We need to move quickly and have dinner at the Hilton while Frankie is at the hospital looking for me."

"I will pull over, and you can drive Sam. I will go onto the computer system and find out his room number. We don't need any desk clerk giving away descriptions of his admirers."

Intrigued, Sam asked, "What can you do with that toy Dannie?"

"It tells secrets of the past, present, and future." Dannie began to speak as she read: "Yeah, that's their code. Yep, he is in 623. And I just so happened to have a bunch of key cards that I can program to open the house to the mouse."

"You mean rat," snarled Sam.

"Sam, you know how I feel about Frankie. Maybe not as bad as you do, but I would rather work with a snake."

"OK, we will park here at the steak house and walk across. We will go through the side entrance."

"Here, Sam, hold this while I make a key."

"What is that gizmo?"

"Just watch it; it makes doors open and can even give you a credit card. Slide this in, wait until the light blinks...slide your hotel key through this slot, and in we go. Let's take the steps...nobody walks steps anymore."

"Well, my legs should be in shape after climbing the

mountains, chasing deer..."

Dannie interrupted, "Number 623 to the left...should be on the left... Wait, someone was opening the door across the hall from Frankie's."

Dannie grabbed Sam, pulled his body next to hers with his back next to the key maker in the door, and kissed him toward the checked side of his lips until the woman had turned the corner. Dannie turned quickly, made the key, and entered the room. She reached and pulled Sam in, as he stayed in shock over the kiss.

"Sorry Sam, had to think quick... she couldn't see our faces, and we didn't have to say good evening."

As Dannie smiled, Sam looked a little blushed.

"Ok, Sam, what are we looking for?"

"Anything we can find that might link him to that bombing in Germantown."

"Well. Look here... he left his laptop. I'll download all his files... should be something on here that you can use."

"How long will that take?" Sam inquired.

"Not long, Sam, just keep looking. I'll have it in a couple of minutes."

As Sam looked through Frankie's suitcase, Dannie was stealing all his files and found his passport.

"Let's see where he has been... Bogota, Columbia, Jamaica, France, Italy, Columbia, Italy, Columbia, so our boy has been up to something between Italy and Columbia. Got it all, Sam, let's get going."

As Sam turned to leave, he spotted a silver ring lying on the nightstand. As he picked up the ring slowly, he glanced down at the one on his finger... the same kind he found with the note in his truck when his dog was killed. As he felt numbness on the right side of his face and pain rushing to his brain, Dannie's voice faded away.

When Sam came to himself, his vision blurred; he saw a Coke machine coming into view with Dannie's hand over his mouth, whispering in his ear.

"It's all right, Sam, don't talk. Someone was going into Frankie's room."

Dannie had just got Sam out and into the concession area before a lady with a key entered Frankie's room. Sam didn't speak. Just followed Dannie. Dannie held Sam's hand and pulled him like a mother would her child across the street. As Sam was still in a helpless daze, Dannie pulled him to a side exit out into the parking area.

The Kode

Sam was breathing hard as though he was hyperventilating. Dannie opened the car door and pushed him into the seat. She shifted gears, quickly exiting the lot and sliding sideways. Sam leaned forward with both hands rubbing his head, murmuring dying words of what was wrong with him. "Am I dying, or am I just crazy?"

As Dannie pulled into Baskin Park, Sam slowly snapped out of the state of mind he was in. Dannie brought the car to a stop under the big oak, where she and Sam had come so many times to talk. She reached over and softly rubbed Sam's hand.

"You'll be all right, Sam; I will help you through this. We have been through a lot worse in the past."

"Dannie, I think I am falling apart. If anyone finds out about this, I am history."

"Listen, Sam, you are a strong person. I know that you must go back and see yourself as you dragged yourself through swamps and gunfire... You spent numerous days at sea on that raft with no water, and you were the one that held us together. Listen, Dannie, I'm not that person anymore."

"You are Sam, and you are, someplace down inside, you still have what it takes to push beyond the pain and the past. And I am going to be behind you pushing... I know you can make it...."

"Listen, Dannie, I must find a way to get over Frankie;

whatever it takes, I have to be able to shake him out of my mind. If I thought I could get him out of my life with his death, I would kill him myself."

"Sam, you must push past this hate that you have for Frankie, or it will turn on you and eat you like a cancer," Dannie urged.

"I am trying to blot this out of my mind, but it is like a bad dream that has been put on video, playing over and over daily," Sam replied.

"Listen to me, Sam. A wise man once said, 'as a man thinketh, so is he.' You need to look in the mirror of the good in your life and see what you taught us about self-surviving," Dannie advised.

"That's not easy to say now because every time I walk by a car, I see the scar in the window. Every time I walk through the malls, I see the scar in the glass reflecting back, that night when he disobeyed my orders," Sam lamented.

Before Sam could speak again, Dannie slapped him across the face, the deep scar a stark reminder of past events. As Sam looked puzzled, she leaned over and put her forehead against his, whispering softly, "I need you, Sam... We all need you... Please come back to us. You can beat this; I know you can beat this, Sam."

With tears in her eyes, she leaned back into her seat, wiping them away. Sam took her hand, and for a moment, they sat in silence.

As Dannie started the car and began to leave the park, Sam heard his cell phone. Slowly, he looked to see who was calling, then put it on his side, leaned back, and closed his eyes. The song his grandfather used to sing when he was a kid in church began to fill his thoughts, "It will be worth it all someday." Sam began to hum the tune, knowing that his tomorrow would be shaped by either his love for the future with his family or his hate from the past. Dannie didn't speak until Sam stopped humming.

"Where to, Sam?" she asked.

"Drive north on 95; we will stop above the beltway at the Holiday Inn. We need to look through the files you downloaded. If we are going to get back the package from the enemy, we want to make sure Frankie's problem won't get us killed. I need to make sure there are no mistakes on this mission," Sam responded.

"Who called, Sam?" Dannie inquired.

"Oh, that was Catherine," Sam replied. "Call her back, Sam. You know she worries about you," Dannie suggested.

"Yeah, I know, I'm just not in the mood for talking. We must find out about Frankie..." Sam started to say, but Dannie interrupted.

"Enough about Frankie, Sam. I worry about you. You're

special to me. Call Catherine; she loves you and cares about you, Sam. It's only right."

"Yeah, I know, I shouldn't be so selfish," Sam replied.

As Sam talked to Catherine, Dannie found the exit to the Holiday Inn and turned into the parking area.

"Okay, Dannie, let's do some digging," Sam said. "I will go and get the room, while you gather up your equipment. I will wait for you in the lobby."

As Dannie walked into the lobby, her eyes searched for Sam. Puzzled not to see him, she walked slowly by the check-in, asking if her husband had gone to the room.

"I saw him go into the bar, Mrs. Jameson," the receptionist informed her.

As Dannie reached the bar, she was caught off guard by an unexpected scene. Next to one of the bar tables was a man lying on the floor, with Sam's knee on his chest and a steak knife to his throat.

Dannie shouted at Sam using his check-in name, Jirah. "Stop, Jirah, stop! You need your medication.... this man has done nothing." But Sam seemed to be deaf to Dannie's words. As he stared into the man's eyes with large beads of sweat dropping from his face, Sam spoke, as though anger was locked up in his lips. "Take your finger now and put it in the scar on my face."

The man tried to apologize, "I am sorry mister, I've been drinking, didn't mean to laugh at your face. I am telling you one more time take your finger and put it in the scar on my face, or I will leave a scar across your throat."

The man slowly moved his finger toward Sam's face, placing it in the scar. Sam demanded him to move his finger up and down in the scar. As the man obeyed what Sam said, fear filled his face as he felt the knife blade pressed into his neck. His words became choked from tension from the blade, as he tried to apologize again.

Dannie didn't make any sudden move toward Sam; she was trained to move slowly, speaking to Sam that she was coming toward him, and that it was her hand that was being placed upon his shoulder. She spoke softly to him to let the man up. Dannie slowly moved her hand up toward the man's hand on Sam's face, removing his hand and placing her hand upon the scar. "Come on, Sam, he's drunk, and we don't need this."

Sam began to remove the knife from the man's throat and, with a burst of anger, slammed it into the floor next to his face.

As Dannie picked him up and started him toward the elevator, she knew the police had been called. She pressed the 1st floor button and pulled Sam toward the stairway closest to the car. As she exited the building, she saw the patrol car pulling into the front of the Holiday Inn. She waited until the officer went inside, and then she pulled Sam again at a run toward the car. She left the parking area toward Interstate 95 South; she drove for about ten minutes before Sam spoke.

"Care if I turn on the radio?" Sam asked.

"Sure, Sam, nothing like music on a star-filled night," Dannie replied.

Dannie knew that Sam was in a bad mental, depressed state of mind. As she tried to figure out a way to help him through his self-made battle, with himself being the enemy, Sam began to hum the song again, "It will be worth it all someday."

Soon, Sam broke the silence between the two by commenting on Dannie's perfume. Dannie knew that her remarks toward Sam's mental actions would have to be soft because she knew the Sam of the past, the one who had no breakdowns before being shot by Frankie Morgan. She started off with a little blonde joke.

"How did the blonde die from drinking milk?" Dannie asked.

Sam smiled, knowing that it was Dannie's way to dig into his heart and steal his secrets, but he always left her an open door. "All right, Miss blondie, how did she die?"

"The cow stepped on her," Dannie replied, and they both laughed.

As they were laughing, Dannie's cellphone rang.

As she plundered through her purse to find the phone, Sam sank in his seat and hummed his favorite tune. "Hello Dannie, it's Polly. If Sam is with you, don't speak my name or say anything about this conversation."

"Sure, Mom, what do you need?" Dannie replied.

"We have a big problem at the hospital," Polly said urgently. "Jeremy has been shot! He was with Frankie Morgan in the cafeteria. It doesn't look good. Can you take Sam to your apartment until I get some more information, and I will call you? I don't think Sam can deal with this at this time. They were trying to kill Frankie, and Jeremy got hit. I think Frankie has gone to the motel."

"Sure, Mom, just let me know, and I will take you to your appointment," Dannie replied.

As she put her phone back into her purse, Sam asked if everything was all right. "Yes, Sam, I must take Mom to her doctor tomorrow. She will call me back and let me know the time. We will go to my apartment and work on this, Sam... I have more equipment there that will do a better job."

"Whatever, blondie, I will just take a nap," Sam responded casually.

As Dannie picked up her speed toward Fredericksburg, she

looked over at Sam as the moonlight hit his face; the deep scar seemed to speak to her about Sam's ordeal. It was as though she could feel his heart's cry for help, distant like a mountain. As tears ran down her cheek, she whispered to herself, "I need you, Sam, you are all I've got. You're the dad I never had."

Both Dannie and Sam were in need of healing from the inside out, even though Sam focused only on the scar on his face. It seemed the scar was somehow connected to his heart, filling him with bitterness against Frankie. Dannie knew the task ahead would be a difficult one, but she held onto the past knowledge of Sam's strong will to survive.

As Dannie pulled into the driveway between the two old stone pillars that held oil lamps, she wondered how to give Sam the information about the shooting at the hospital. Coming to a stop by Big Willie, the huge willow tree she had named as a child, the car lights showed the deep carvings from knives that her friends and cousins had carved into the bark; hearts of love with names. It had held her while she swung from its vine-like branches day after day, playing as a child. It was still standing strong, ready to hold her again. Somehow, it reminded her of Sam.

Sam awoke with a sudden jerk, placing his hands on the front glass, wondering where he was. Dannie quickly spoke, "Easy, Sam, that windshield won't bite you. I decided to go to Mom's." Sam laughed as he lay back again in the seat. "Yeah, yeah," he said, "must have been the moonlight reflecting through the glass."

"Come on, Sam, we'll try not to wake up Mom. She likes her sleep and can get mean without it."

"Sure, maybe that's where you get it, Blondie. I've seen the tiger in you too when your sleep was disturbed."

"Listen, Sam, the only disturbance I can remember was when I was sleeping next to a snoring bear, and I would have to use rifle range earplugs to blot out that ungodly sound that came from you."

"Listen, Blondie, it kept the wild animals away."

"That's for sure," laughed Dannie, "but better than that, it kept Frank away too." As they laughed their way toward the house, they knew the mission for the KODE TEAM was no laughing matter.

Dannie knew the call from Polly may put Sam over the edge because Jeremy was close to Sam and they enjoyed fishing together. Many times, they slept in an old van at Smith Mountain Lake where they fished for striped bass. They always joked about smelly feet, and how Sam could outsnore a grizzly bear. Jeremy was more like Sam's son than son-in-law. Even though Dannie didn't go to church often, she prayed in her heart that Jeremy would live while she quoted Psalms 23 over and over, hoping the next call from Polly would be good news.

Dannie lived with her mother most of the time in an old three-story plantation house that was built before the Civil War, although she had an apartment in Fredericksburg where she did most of her computer work. The plantation house had belonged to her mother's family for generations, and she had spent most of her summers there as a child, playing in the long hot Virginia days.

It was about ten miles south of Fredericksburg, VA on some country road close to a town called Ginny. The dirt road was about a mile to the house crossing the tracks where the freight train and Amtrak came speeding through the night. You could hear the train's whistle for miles. Every summer soybeans grew in the fields on both sides of the road. The dust would cover the green plants until a fresh summer rain would come and paint them clean and green again. It was a place of peace with old gravestones because it was a perfectly quiet place to unwind. Sam and Dannie would take walks from the old house through the pines to the Beaver Lake and sit in the Jon boat talking sometimes for hours. It was a way for Sam to get back to his love for nature and Dannie's way of talking to someone who really cared for her, and always took time to listen. Her father was never brought up nor his death at the hand of her mother who shot him as he tried to rape Dannie again. It was his last attempt.

So, Dannie had to hold up Sam, who held her up; they were like each other's crutch.

Dannie knew that Sam was no laughing matter, and that she had a bigger mission to keep her friend safe from himself, than to get back the United States scientist from the Chinese. As they walked toward the door, Sam stopped suddenly, looked up, and stared at the moon.

Dannie turned back, laying her hand upon his shoulder, and they both stood silent for a moment. "Listen, Sam, if a man can be sent to the moon, walk on it, and come home safe, you can walk on this problem and overcome all that is trying to stop you from being who you really are."

Sam looked back into Dannie's eyes and asked softly, "Why are we here? I thought we were going to your apartment to get into Frank's files."

Dannie, quick not to stumble for words, said, "I have to pick up some documents I left here, and I thought you might want to spend the night, rest, and go down to the beaver dam. I can work from my laptop with these downloads, and we can run by the apartment about noon and finish up there."

Dannie knew Sam loved the beaver dam; it was a small lake about half a mile from the home place, down a narrow sandy road through the tall Virginia pines.

"You can row me around the lake while I work, might ease some of the stress."

But really, Dannie was stalling for time until she got word again from the hospital about the shooting. She knew her mother had no TV because she was old-fashioned Church of the Brethren, and one thing they preached against was no television. So, Sam could not get any news about the shooting from the media. She had already, by phone and text, informed Polly to be strong, and to tell Frankie not to tell Sam about Jeremy.

"I will get my documents for the meeting tomorrow at The Nest, and we will be on our way. I work better by the moonlight; it brings out the evil in me," Dannie said with a smile, trying to ease Sam's anxiety.

"Okay, Dannie, you win. I will just wait over by Big Willie because I don't want to face Mom if you wake her up," Sam replied.

Sam had always addressed Dannie's mother as mom. Both had a respect for each other and talked about Bible verses and old hymnbook songs. You would almost think Sam was called to be a preacher.

"Tell you what, Dannie, I will wait by old Willie while you pick up what you need. If you can work by the light of the moon, I will row you around the lake, but I remind you I just might howl at the light of the moon," Sam proposed.

"That's a deal, Sam. You howl and wake up the forest, and I will find out which one of you is the craziest, you or the government," Dannie responded with a thumbs up. She turned to enter the house as quietly as possible, leaving Sam to himself. Down inside, she hoped to wear him down so that he would sleep most of the day until she could find out the outcome of the hospital shooting. She knew that the meeting at THE NEST may not go so well. If Sam got word beforehand, he would probably kill Morgan. She would have to try and get Sam to the meeting before going to the hospital. This might allow her to save the KODE TEAM from destruction.

THE NEST was a secret part of the CIA to which only a few had access. Its location was south of DC toward Fredericksburg, on old Route 1. It had been a gravel pit year before and was located near Fort AP Hill.

Chambermaid to Blind Man, will meet you at pick-up, 1800 hours, all goods to go, bring the surprise package, party set 1930 hours, subject will be waiting.

Dannie stared at the date of travel Frankie had scribbled down—it was the day before the killing of the defense minister from Columbia. She'd seen it on CNN. A bomb had torn through a section of the country club he was staying at, taking his life and that of two men later identified as businessmen in natural gas drillings. No one had claimed responsibility; reports hinted at Columbia's drug ring's involvement

As Dannie sifted through the files, she stumbled upon the second one titled "Chambermaid to Blind Man."

"Boy Scouts moving to Vegas," she muttered to herself, scanning the cryptic message. "Dog pound has retrievers, pick-up Friday 1100 hours. Watch your back."

She furrowed her brows, the tension in the room palpable as she continued reading. The message continued, "Message has been picked up from Pizza, thinks you are working with Carlos, repeat watch your back. See you at THE NEST."

As Dannie stared at the word "Nest," she knew someone on the inside was working with Frankie in whatever he was doing. She pondered on "Chambermaid." As she went through all the files, it was the same between "Chambermaid" and Frank. Each one ran through areas of heavy drug trafficking. Three times it went back to THE Nest. As Dannie looked at the last file, she felt the boat move as Sam began to stretch.

"Are you awake, sleepy head?"

"No, Blondie, I'm trying to get this pain out of my neck. Did the bear come into the boat?" inquired Sam.

Laughingly, Dannie said, "No Sam, you didn't snore, you just breathed deeply."

"What time is it, Dannie?"

"It's about 5:30; the sun will be up soon."

"What have you found in Frank's grab bag?"

"Well, something I am not sure of, but whatever he has been doing goes back and forth with someone from THE NEST. Have you ever heard of the code name 'Chamber Maid,' Sam?"

"Nope, can't say I have," Sam said.

"Something is going on Sam that we are not aware of. Those bombs were Frank's work, the one in German Town and Columbia, we have to play dumb, you know that or Frank will not make a mistake."

"Sure, Blondie, we played dumb, and Frank got us all killed."

"No, listen Sam, it's not just a gambling debt. Frank is either moving drugs with the help of the CIA, or he is into money laundering. I need to do some more digging on the mainframe. Sam, maybe the girl that went into Frankie's room when we were there is Chambermaid. I didn't get a good look at her, but she had a key to his room."

"Dannie, I don't think I am able to be part of this War Peace project."

"Come now, boy, put a smile on your face, Blondie will be there to take care of you."

"You know why the blonde nurse took a red marker to the hospital? They told her she had to draw blood." With Sam laughing at her joke, Dannie puts her folders back into the backpack with her laptop. She reaches over and takes Sam's hand and puts her finger on the silver ring. Tapping it with her nail, she said, "Sam when they attack you, they attack me, and I will be there when you return it to Mr. Pizza. Now row me around the lake so I can watch the sun come up."

As Sam rowed Dannie around the lake, she closed her eyes only to see him in her thoughts, laying on the sand road shaking out of control. In her heart, she knew that this could be his last journey with The Kode Team. As she pondered how to referee between Frankie and Sam, her cell phone broke the thought, as it began vibrating against the metal boat seat.

"Hello Polly! How is Sam, Dannie?"

"Sam is doing just fine; he is rowing me around the pond. How are things at the hospital?"

"Jenny is doing great, and Jeremy is doing all right too. Let me holler at Sam!"

"Here Sam, Polly wants to holler ATCHA."

Dannie loved to use the mountain words that Polly used even though you couldn't find them in the Webster. She didn't do it to make fun of Polly, because they were close friends, she only tried to change her eastern Virginia speech, to Appalachian slang. She would catch Sam in front of people at the Airports or in restaurants where people didn't know them, and try to embarrass him. But Sam would always come back speaking Russian acting as though he never knew her. They seemed to know how to light up each other's lives, even when their life was a second away from death. Polly assured Sam everything at the hospital was all right and she would meet him there after his meeting. Handing the phone back to Dannie, Sam started his storytelling. Dannie knew she had a father in Sam, and a second daughter called his friend.

As Dannie placed her phone back in her pack, Sam began telling a story about Polly's family. He had told so many he could have written a book, but Dannie would always listen as though she had never heard it before.

"Did I ever tell you about the time her dad took me to a chicken fight?"

"You mean people fight chickens, Sam laughs, no blondie, chicken fights chickens."

"Oh, come on Sam I know what you meant, I'm not that blonde."

"He talked me into going one Saturday night down by the river, it was called one-mile curve. It was a place where the river and railroad made a curve together for about a mile. They had a big sandbar that had washed up from a past spring flood. About 100 mountain folks would gather, mostly men, a few women came from the beer taverns, they were about as tough as the men. This fight had been talked about for weeks, a lot of illegal moonshine was going to be there, along with money to bet on the cock fight. Somehow the word got out to the county Sheriff who had just been elected, and he wanted the voters to know he was going to stop crime, even if it meant crossing over to the mountain folks who mostly minded their own business. There was only one road in and it was blocked by some trucks about 3 miles back from the sandbar. The sheriff, with the help of the State Police sent by his governor friend, came in from the opposite direction on a coal train, hanging from the sides of the cars. They had two officers posted out of sight to signal with a light when to jump from the train."

They came up on the upper side of the track and used the train to hide them as they spread out above the sandbar cockfight. The crowd was into the fight about 40 feet from the big fire they had made from driftwood. People were drunk and placing their bets on their favorite rooster. When the train went by, 30 officers were standing spread out about 25 feet apart above the action. When someone saw a flash of a badge from the light of the fire, the old man pointed and said, "Ha, lookie yonder," in his deep mountain voice.

The Kode

As the crowd got silent, turning looking uphill toward the tracks, a rough hand grabbed me at the back of my collar and before I could use any self-defense, I was in the river. "Swim boy," Polly's dad screamed, "they ain't going to catch me."

I found myself following him into the dark of the night, being pushed down the river by the current. Every so often he'd say, "You with me boy."

I would reply, "Right on your heels old man." When we came out of the water on the other side, he reached in his mouth pulling out a handful of chewing tobacco, spat a couple of times, and washed his mouth out with river water and said, "Dog gone it, come oh Ace swallowing that chaw."

The moon was out like tonight, and looking back toward the fire, you could see some people moving around. They only caught 23 and most of them were too drunk to run. The governor and the sheriff knew it wouldn't bother them. These people didn't vote.

"Come boy, we're going to spend the night at the hotel."

As we started up the edge of the cliff by the moonlight, I thought, what hotel. As we made it to the top of the cliff, overlooking the riverbed and sandbar, Walter sat down next to a red oak and reaching for his tobacco plug, said to me, "Hunt you a bed Sam, it's going to be a long night."

I laughed, "They got room service here."

The next morning, we looked at the rock from another hill, and I found out that was its name, Hotel Rock, because it did look like a hotel on the hill. It took us about four hours of hiking through the woods to get back to the hillside farm.

It reminded me of my SEAL training. It felt good to be in a place that was tough, but you knew that you just whipped the enemy, even though it was just running from chicken fights. Sam pauses, "I can't fight anymore Dannie, something is dead inside me."

"Don't talk like that Sam, you have people that love and need you. Your grandkids are going to need you. So, I don't want you to think about what's dead, because you are going to climb this mountain and we are going to have an old fashioned picnic on top of it."

As the warmth of the sunrise began to come across the lake, a big white-tailed buck caught Sam's attention, as the deer came out of the woods to get a drink. He slowly took the oar out of the water and put it to his shoulders as if it was a rifle. "Got him in the sights blondie, just got to squeeze the trigger."

"Don't shoot my deer Sam," Dannie replied, pointing her finger at him.

As Sam laid the paddle back in the boat, the napkin ring on

his finger caught his attention. Flashing moments of his dog running through the apple orchard at the home place, walking by his side, and laying next to his bed seemed to put him in a trance. As Dannie stared at him, she knew he was in deep thought, but wasn't expecting what was about to happen. Suddenly Sam jumped to his feet screaming, losing his balance falling into the water.

Dannie quickly grabbed a life jacket, putting it on as she saw her friend about to go under the water. As Dannie jumped next to Sam's body, grabbing for his head to hold it out of the water, she could feel his body shaking as if he were having a seizure. Holding him up out of the water, backstroking with one hand toward the bank, she pulled his body upon the side of the pond. Sam had stopped breathing. She quickly started CPR, speaking loudly Psalms 23 over and over.

As she placed her mouth over Sam's mouth, breathing in, her mind raced back to the time at Frankie's motel when she kissed him, trying to hide them from being seen by the woman while they broke into his room. Now she was trying to revive her closest friend. As Sam began to cough, Dannie turned his head sideways, allowing the water to run out.

As Sam rolled back over on his back, looking up into Dannie's eyes, he knew he had put his young friend into the part of his life that he never expected to happen. He took his hand and rubbed his forehead, speaking softly to her as he tried to apologize. "Don't speak, Sam, just rest a moment. I've wanted to take a swim in that pond for a long time," Dannie said, smiling down at him with tears in her eyes.

Sam reached and took her hand, pulling it toward his heart, laying it upon his chest. "There is something inside here that is destroying me, Blondie; I have got to get it out."

"You will, Sam, I know you will," she said assuredly, reaching down and patting him on the cheek.

Dannie smiled at Sam and said, "I'm going into the pond for the second time. I have to get our boat and my computer stuff. I'll be right back." Sam raised up, watching as Dannie swam towards the boat, took hold of the rope on the front, and began to bring it towards the old dock. He knew in his heart that she was a close friend and an extra daughter.

As she returned to the dock, she took out some of her things but hurried back over to Sam to check on him, forgetting to tie the boat up. As she knelt down, the pain in her heart for her friend and her own problems moved her emotionally. As the light breeze moved the boat away from the dock into the lily pads, they never even noticed.

As one of the tears fell from Dannie's eyes onto Sam's cheek, he touched the tear and began to laugh. "Have I turned yet, Dannie?

Am I a frog or a prince?"

"Neither, Sam, you're the best friend a person could ever have. A prince is not always a friend," Dannie explained.

"How can you have that much confidence in me, Dannie? You just saw what happened."

"I have seen a lot of things, Sam, but that doesn't make the person. A person is made up of character, and sometimes things or people that cause mistakes or tragedy alter it. But the real person somehow seems to reach down and pull from within the truth of who they are, and real character will always win out. I know the real you, Sam, and it can't hide forever."

"Thanks, Dannie, but you know we have a mission to go on, and I am someone that I don't even know. I am dangerous to the team."

"Sam, I have already told you, I will be by your side, and it will probably be a couple of weeks before we move because of planning. By that time, you will be strong, holding your daughter and grandson. That will be the therapy that you need."

"Yeah, sure, maybe you're right. A change in my life will help me get this bitterness out of my heart. I heard my grandfather preach that bitterness would cause death to come much quicker. My family needs me, I know that. And death, I have seen and have known for many years, that's not my cup of tea. I've been drinking from a bitter cup, Blondie, and for the first time, Sam Black fears death."

"That will make you more cautious, Sam. It may even save your life. You're a leader and always will be. But now we need to get that boat back because my backpack is still in it, and my cell phone."

The boat had drifted across the lake next to the lily pads. Dannie suggested she would swim over and pull it back across to the dock. But Sam knew that the lily pads were a bad place for water moccasins, a poisonous snake. So he had a better idea.

"Blondie, are they milk jugs with sand in them still tied to the dock?"

"I guess, Sam, you were the last one to use them for an anchor. I think the rope is long enough for me to throw it into the boat and drag it over the pads."

As Sam walked toward the dock to get the rope and sand jug, Dannie watched as her friend kept rubbing the side of his face where the scar was. She knew that the wound was deeper and buried in Sam's mind, just like her dad was buried in the deep woods. But she remembered how her mother had overcome the killing of her father to go on in life and raise her by herself, even though she never dated or remarried. Keeping it hidden in her heart what she thought was a secret.

The Kode

Dannie wanted to ask her many times about that night, but she didn't want to hurt her mother and bring up the past, even though the past had scarred her life just like Sam. Many times Dannie started to tell Sam about the killing, trying to get it out of her consciousness, thinking she was the reason for his death, but she held it to herself only to keep the scar open in her own life.

Sam shouted back to Dannie as she sat on the grass waiting, "Ha, blonde, let me show you how this is done. It's like roping a cow. Ha!"

"Sam, don't forget my laptop is in that boat, and if that milk jug full of sand hits it, you will be on my blonde joke list," Dannie reminded him.

"Girl, I am not that dense. Maybe losing my mind, but not real blonde," Sam chuckled.

"Yeah, sure, Sam. I just figured out what's wrong with you. It's me, I am rubbing off on you," Dannie teased.

"You have a point there, Dannie. All I need to do is dye my hair blonde, and then I can tell them jokes. Let's get the boat, Sam, so we can get out of these wet clothes. Watch this throw, and you will see how it is done."

Sam took the rope in his hand and marked off 15 feet. Then, he tossed the milk jug into the front of the boat.

"Did you see that, girl? Just like pitching horseshoes?"

"I thought it was like roping a cow, Sam."

"Listen, Blonde, both are the same. You have to be on the mark."

As Sam pulled the boat through the lily pads towards the side of the pond, Mr. Farley pulled up close to the dock in his old Willies Jeep. He had leased the fields for many years on the property from Dannie's mom to raise soybeans. He used the pond to trap for furs and would check his traps each day that he set below the spillway.

He and Sam were friends and would sit next to Big Willie and talk for hours about their hunting adventures. He never would ask Sam about the scar, and when Sam would try to bring up Morgan, Mr. Farley would change the subject with another hunting story. He was wise and knew it had deep roots of hurt in Sam.

Dannie got her things out of the boat and started up the hill towards the road, trying to avoid being seen wet. But Sam waved and started toward the jeep to speak to Mr. Farley.

As he reached the jeep, Dannie could see him and Sam talking and gesturing with their hands, laughing as though they were laughing at her. Finally, Mr. Farley waved at Dannie and said, "Better watch those bullfrogs, they eat pretty girls." Sam then patted him on the shoulder and started up the hill toward Dannie.

Sam was laughing as he came up to Dannie and said, "Had to tell him a little lie. Just what did you tell Mr. Farley that was so funny?"

"I told him that we were getting into the boat and a bullfrog jumped toward you, causing you to lose your balance and fall in. Of course, I jumped in to make sure you got out safe."

As Dannie pulled her wet hair toward her face, she began laughing at what Sam had told Mr. Farley. As Sam began to laugh with her, he reached out and took her hair away from her eyes, holding it in both of his hands as they both stared and laughed at each other. For a moment, the scars that are in both of their lives were hidden in their friendship.

As he put his arm around her and started walking up the hill, they both knew that what's before them wouldn't be hills but mountains. Reaching the sand road and starting through the pines, they saw Dannie's mother coming toward them. Dannie quickly reminded Sam to stick to the same story he told Mr. Farley. Dannie's mom began to point her finger at them like she was mad at the world, "You have worried me to death, Dannie! All morning I was wondering where you were and if something had happened to you."

Dannie grabbed her mother and kissed her. "Sorry, mom, I was working at the pond and I didn't want to wake you."

"Wet, Dannie? What are you doing wet?" Sam told his frog

story, giving her a kiss on the cheek.

"You two, I can't believe you didn't wake me up. Sam, I haven't seen you in a long time, have you forgotten me?"

"No, mom, we came in late, and I wanted you to have your beauty rest." Sam hugged her again and started singing the song he had taught her, "It Will Be Worth It All Someday."

"Okay, okay, Sam, I forgive the both of you. Come now and get out of those wet clothes, and I will fix you a good old country Virginia breakfast."

As they walked toward the house, she asked Sam to bring Polly by to see her. Sam was quick to tell her about his new grandson. "That's wonderful, Sam, but remember you are getting older. So why don't you bring the whole family by for a good Sunday dinner?"

Sam assured her he would as soon as Jennifer gets out of the hospital and has time to rest. As they walked by the woodshed, she took off some coveralls that had been hanging on a nail and threw them to Sam. "Here, these should fit until we get yours dried. And by the way, Sam, after you get them on, you might as well cut up some of that wood for me; winter's not too far off."

Sam knew that the breakfast was well worth the wait and the work. "Listen, mom, for one of your meals, I will chop up all of your wood. Just chop until you get real hungry, and I will have plenty to fill you up."

After they had changed their clothes, Dannie took and put them on the clothesline. Sam started busting the wood while breakfast was being prepared, and all things seemed to be back to normal. But at THE NEST, things were happening quickly, and the days of preparation would have to be only a few hours.

As Dannie entered the house, she picked up her backpack and started toward her old room. Her mother called for her help, "Honey, do you want to help me make the biscuits?"

"Yeah, mom, I will be right down. Let me get some files so I won't forget them." As Dannie entered her room, she moved toward the window, where she had seen her mother take the body of her dad into the deep woods in the farm truck. Her thoughts raced back to that night when she heard the gunshot. As she looked out the window toward Big Willie, she could see the truck covered over with honeysuckle vines next to the barn.

Hidden under the beautiful smell of the flowers was an image in her mind of her dad's limp body being pulled into the back of the truck by her mother. Just a few feet away, her soulmate, her dad Sam Black. As she stared at the truck and then back at her soulmate, tears began to run down her cheek again. She took the curtain and wiped her face. As she turned around, her mother standing in the doorway startled her.

"Honey, what's wrong? Why the tears?"

"It's nothing, Mom. I'm just tired, and Sam has been going through it again with that scar on his face. It seems we are coming down to a final act in a drama play, and we are forgetting our lines. The story that should have ended a long time ago seems to go on without any end in sight."

"Listen, Dannie, Sam has to forget the things behind him and reach for those that are before him, or else your past can destroy your future. You know how much I love Sam; he is like a son to me, and I know you love him too. But he has to find forgiveness in his heart, or it will eat at him until he hates himself."

"I know, Dannie. Because one time I had to forgive."

"Who? Mom? Was it Dad you had to forgive?"

"No, honey. I had to forgive myself."

With those words, her mom reached out and touched Dannie's lips and said, "Be still now, honey, and let's go fix Sam a good breakfast." Dannie hoped that maybe her mom would speak about the night of the murder, when she killed her dad, hoping it would be a way that she could talk about it and free herself from it, or like her mother said, forgive herself.

As her mother left the room, Dannie put the file into her

laptop case and just for a moment stared into the mirror and said, "You have to be strong for Sam, Blonde. He needs you more now than ever before." She took her hand up to her forehead and saluted, "Will do, soldier." As she turned to go down and help her mother with the biscuits.

Walking down the steps, she stopped and turned and went back to her room. Walking into the room slowly, she looked back into the mirror and stopped and stared for a moment. "I forgive you, girl. It wasn't your fault." As she spoke softly, she turned toward the window and said, "I forgive you, Dad. I forgive you." Looking again at the old truck, she could feel herself being renewed with life. A smile filled her face. Mom was right, she thought, you have to forgive yourself.

As her mother called for her help again, she turned and walked with a skip in her step like a little girl. Going down the steps whistling, she grabbed her mother, hugging her and kissing her on both cheeks and the forehead. "I love you, mother, you are the greatest."

"What's wrong with you, girl? Haven't seen you this happy in a long time."

"I just found out, mom. What's it like to be a bird out of the cage?"

"Okay, sweetie, go get Sam. I will fix the biscuits." As

Dannie hurried out the door, she ran toward Sam singing his song, "It will be worth it all someday." As Sam turned with a surprised look, Dannie jumped into his arms like a child, with her legs wrapped around him, squeezing him with a bear hug. As she held him, she started crying tears of joy. "It's over, Sam. Finally, it's over."

As Sam was still puzzled, he didn't speak, only waiting for Dannie to tell him what her excitement was all about. Finally letting go, Dannie looked at Sam with a smile he had never seen before. "I am free, Sam. For the first time in years, I am free."

Something just happened in my bedroom, I can't explain it, but I have some things I want to tell you," Dannie said.

"Did you see a ghost?" Sam laughed.

"No, Sam, I just got rid of a ghost that has haunted me. Come, let's go eat breakfast, and I will tell you later," Dannie said, grabbing Sam by the hand and pulling him toward the house, jumping and laughing and clenching her fist as if her team had won the game.

"Not so fast, blonde. I haven't slept all night, still puzzled about Dannie's actions," Sam remarked with a laugh. "What is going on with this blonde? I will get to the bottom of this later, but for now, I want to enjoy my breakfast."

As they began to sit down at the table, they heard a knock at the door. To their surprise, there stood Sheriff O'Neil. He was a long-time friend of the family. To his regret, he was not there for a friendly visit. He was there on official business.

"Mrs. Miller, sorry to bother you at breakfast. Some hunters seem to have stumbled onto an old grave down next to the railroad tracks, at the old sand pits. It's probably a slave grave, but we may be down there a few days. Didn't want to worry you with our presence," Sheriff O'Neil explained.

"Ha, Sheriff, how's the deer hunting going to be this year?" Sam asked with a grin.

"Sam, you rascal, where have you been keeping yourself? Haven't seen you in ages," Sheriff O'Neil said with a chuckle.

"Oh, I stay very busy taking care of my old home place. I guess that's all an old retirement guy like myself has time to do. You will have to come and go hunting with me whenever you have some free time," Sam replied.

"I will take you up on that. I've been hoping to take some time off. Sorry again to have bothered you so early in the morning," Sheriff O'Neil said as he left.

Dannie turned to see the reaction of her mother. She watched her go to the kitchen sink, staring through the window as Sheriff

O'Neil left in his police cruiser. As she stood silent just for a moment, Dannie worried about how her mother would react. She knew she was a strong woman, but as Sam would say, an old can of worms had been opened. Mrs. Miller pulled the curtains and took the biscuits out of the oven. As she turned toward the table, Dannie and her mother locked eyes, as if trying to read each other's minds. Both had kept their secret for years.

Dannie broke the ice, saying, "Don't put the biscuits on Sam's side; he will devour them all." Sam laughed as he reminded Dannie, "There are only three great cooks in the world: your mother, Polly, and Mrs. Clayman, especially their biscuits. They're like expensive artwork; you collect as many as you can." Dannie felt somewhat relieved as she heard her mother laugh at Sam's remark. As Sam reached for a biscuit, Dannie placed her hand on top of his with a giggle, "Ladies first."

"Okay, blonde, just make sure I get some of that homemade canned jelly," Sam replied. As they settled in eating their breakfast, Dannie glanced at her mother again, wondering about what might happen if the body in that grave was her father's. Just when she thought she was free from the past, it now seemed to cry out of the ground. But even with the worry over her mother, she still felt something happen to her in that bedroom, a peace that passed understanding.

"Sam, I got some fresh buttermilk from the Mennonite farm. I believe I can spare one cold glass full," Mrs. Miller said.

Sam was quick to accept, knowing it was some of the best around. "Only one catch, Sam," Mrs. Miller added.

"Okay, mom, I knew you were holding back something from me."

"It won't hurt too much, Sam. I want you to bring Polly, Catherine, and Jenny down to see me and eat Thanksgiving dinner with me."

"You've got yourself a deal. In fact, I might just bring the turkey; might be a wild one, but it will get the job done."

"Here is the milk, Sam. Let's shake on it."

As the deal was being made, at The Nest, another deal was being put together. In the office of Criss West, senior adviser over CIA rescues, a discussion was going on with Mr. Logan. "We have to act fast; our days of planning have to become but a few hours."

"That's impossible, Criss; you know what's at stake here."

"Yes, I do, Mr. Logan. We have a major problem on our hands. You see, I just got word that our intelligence has picked up a call from San Francisco. Yuan Wang, who is over a shipping company in the Bay area, has been working for us for about 12 years, but he seems to be jumping the fence with the Chinese. We have known this for about 2 years, but we were still using him for information. There has been a container at one of his loading docks, which was moved in from the metal fabricator. That may be the place that Mr. Webb will be shipped out on. We went to the metal shop and got some info on this container. It seems odd to build a shipping container with special air condition units and humid climate controls. This thing was wired for lights and everything that you would need to live in it. We have been monitoring the shipyard and the container with the FBI; we can't make a move until we know that Webb is there."

"What was in the call that makes you think Wang has something to do with Mr. Webb?"

"We intercepted a call between Wang and the Chinese embassy concerning a woman named Lynn Ming. She works at the embassy. We believe she is part of the kidnapping and was used to seduce Webb into a place of capture."

"What about the tracking device that Webb had?"

"It was the old TRK33 version; the heat of the skin charged the battery, and his was working part of the time. He had planned to change it to the new TRK33A, which the Special Forces are using. That's how we have linked him to Lynn Ming. The night of his disappearance, he was picked up by satellite at the Hyatt in Springfield. Come, let me show you some surveillance tapes from the motel. Watch on the right of the screen. That's Miss Ming over by the check-in. Now she is going toward the elevators. She receives a phone call on the cell. Turns and goes back toward the check-in. Now you see Mr. Webb coming through the main lobby and going toward the elevators. She follows him into the elevator as though she doesn't know him. Watch the view from inside the elevator."

"Is that a hot scene from an old man? What? I thought he was married, Criss."

"He is married, but his desire for the younger women put us all in this predicament. Here they get off the elevator on the 9th floor, go to room 916. Time is 8:45 PM, and they leave separately at 11:15, two minutes apart. Here is a tape from the front parking area. Miss Ming leaves the building; a taxi is waiting to pick her up. Watch closely as Mr. Webb gets into his taxi. A man approaches the car from the other side, getting in the back quickly. Watch his hand; it has something in it, pointing to the driver's head. We traced the action of the two taxis that night. Both showed up at the Regan National Airport. Only one problem: a dead taxi driver was found in the parking lot the next morning. There was a leer jet on log that night to L.A. It was a jet used by the China's embassy. So Mr. Webb is between L.A. and San Francisco.

"Why the hurry then, Chris?"

"Look at these photos taken last week. You see Mr. Wang

talking to some of his dockworkers. Look in the background, sitting in the car, that's Miss Ming. The man that's driving is Manchu Wan; he is also a worker at the China's embassy in DC. We pick up the call between Ming and Wang; it was coded but spelled out: *The Fishing Boat would leave port 2 AM Thursday.* That gives us only about 52 hours to try to intercept the transfer of Mr. Webb without him being killed. Also, we need to keep this from the news. We don't need another ugly incident between the US and China, like our Spy plane they picked apart. We have to make some adjustments in this rescue operation. If there is any killing, it must look like a robbery. The President has informed the top guns at Langley this has to go down as a TOP SECRET mission. The war on terrorism is only a small issue now that Mr. Webb is missing. If the WAR PEACE gets into the hands of Beijing, we are going to lose our status as the world's number one superpower. The Taiwan conflict will be a sure deal in the hands of China. I have already taken the liberty of putting part of the Kode Team into play. Koon Hee has been working on the load dock for two weeks. I have sent Frank Morgan to San Francisco; he will be setting up all the equipment needed on a fishing yacht."

As Sam finished up his last biscuit, Dannie sat and pondered how to get Sam past the shooting at the hospital and how to keep her mother from going back to the past, the murder of her father weighing heavily on her mind. She now knew in her heart that the freedom she needed had come that morning. But the task at hand was daunting—she had to figure out how to break out of a high-security prison, bringing Sam and her mother along.

What if the sheriff turned up with a positive ID confirming the body was her father's? Would she lose her mother to the justice system? And Sam—what would it take to erase his memory of the scar on his face?

Dannie was so deep in thought she couldn't hear Sam and Mrs. Miller laughing about the gravy on the side of her face, not until her mother reached over and wiped it off with a hand towel.

"You're a messy girl, Dannie. I may have to get out one of your old bibs," Mrs. Miller teased.

Dannie smiled at her mother and assured her it was only because of how good her cooking was.

"Well, Mommy, we've got to go," Dannie said, snapping back to the present moment.

Mrs. Miller was quick to ask if Dannie would be coming back later that day. "Don't know yet, I will call and let you know what my plans are," Dannie replied.

Sam walked over and put his hand down on Mrs. Miller and gently squeezed her. "Love you, Mom, and thanks for a wonderful breakfast," he said warmly.

"You know that you are always welcome in my home. Don't stay away so long, and remember the deal, you have to bring the family down for Thanksgiving dinner," Mrs. Miller reminded them.

"We will be here, I promise. By the way, it's not easy to pass up one of yours or Polly's Thanksgiving feasts," Sam said with a grin.

As Dannie got into the car, she looked back at her mother standing and waving in her old flannel granny gown. "I love her, Sam. I love her a lot," she confessed.

"I know you do, blonde. She's a special lady," Sam reassured her.

Driving down the road toward the railroad crossing, a sheriff's car turned across the tracks down toward the old sand pits. "Guess that will keep O'Neal busy for a few days, Dannie," Sam remarked.

"I know he hates that when deer season is just coming in," Dannie agreed. Then, with a deep breath, she said, "Sam, I need to tell you something."

"Listen, blonde, I've heard all your jokes," Sam teased, but Dannie insisted, "No, Sam, really. I have been waiting to tell you something for a long time."

"Ok, girl, let's have it. I know you're tired of putting up with me," Sam said, breaking the silence.

"Come on, Sam, you know that's not true. I haven't been able to put some things into words because it's the ghost that you thought I saw back at Mother's. It's the ghost of my past, Sam. Something happened when I was young and..." Dannie trailed off as her cell phone rang.

"Hello? Oh, hello, Polly," Dannie answered. "How is Sam?" Polly inquired.

"Well, he's sitting here beside me looking real full from Mommy's big breakfast," Dannie replied with a chuckle.

"Good, that's great. Let me holler at him," Polly requested.

"Don't holler too loud, Polly, you might hurt his hearing," Dannie teased, and Polly laughed in response. "You know what I mean, city girl," Polly retorted.

"Sure, mountain woman. I love you, Polly," Dannie said affectionately before handing the phone to Sam. "Here, Sam, Polly wants to holler at you."

Sam took the phone with a smile. "Polly, my loving and caring nanny and friend, what can old Sam do for you?"

"Well, Sam, just to hear your voice with a little laughter in it is all I needed for today. I'm glad you're feeling better, Sam. I worried about you, boy. Couldn't even sleep last night. You're like my own youngin', Sam," Polly expressed warmly.

"Thanks, Polly, you're like my mother, and that will never change," Sam replied gratefully, feeling the warmth in Polly's words.

"Okay, Sam, you've buttered the bread pretty good," Dannie remarked, and Sam chuckled, knowing in his heart that he meant every word of it.

"Sam, I know you had a rough night and Jenny is doing fine. Why don't you rest at her place until later on this evening, and I will be here at the hospital until you get here. You're not as young as you once were," Polly suggested with concern.

"Now, Polly, you know me better than that. That little girl is my heartbeat. We'll stop at Dannie's apartment to pick up some disks, and we should be there about 2:30 this afternoon," Sam assured her confidently.

Ok Samuel let me holler at Dannie, Sam knew when she called him Samuel she was upset at him. Dannie you gottie keep Sam away from the hospital until late tonight or tomorrow. You know if he finds out about the shooting he will go after Frank Morgan and it won't be pretty. I will do that for you Polly if any way possible, I promise. Bye Polly, we love you. Sam was quick to ask what Polly had requested. Ah Sam, you know Polly, she wanted some of mom's homemade jelly. She is a good person Dannie, she has been a mother to Jennifer and her wisdom far exceeds her education. Listen to me Sam, what Polly has cannot be taught in any school. Love is a powerful source of education within itself, it teaches how to hold and how to let go, it also teaches us how to forgive others and ourselves.

With those words, Sam grunted and rubbed his hand across the scar. Dannie knew that what she had felt at her house was the only thing that could free Sam from the bondage of hate. "If you can't forgive, you will die from the inside out," she mused silently. And even though Sam's scar was on the outside, his real scars were deeply rooted in bitterness in his heart.

As Dannie pulled into the Mountain Oaks Apartment complex, Sam was fast asleep. She tried to open the car door softly to allow Sam to rest, but he jumped forward like a cat on a mouse, hitting his knee against the car's dashboard.

With his bloodshot eyes, he turned slowly toward Dannie and winked. "Just practicing my kickboxing," he joked.

"Sam, if you keep hitting and kicking my car, I'm going to have to charge you abuse fees when you ride with me," Dannie teased.

Sam snapped back with a grin, "It's your fault. You know in our profession; quietness can be a killer."

"Let's get these disks, and I want you to run some more checks on Frank Morgan's South American adventures, Ms. Blonde," Sam instructed.

"I can do that, Sam, but you have to promise to sit in the big chair and sleep until I gather up the info. That way, if you jump because of the quietness, you'll only hit the old coffee table," Dannie bargained.

"Well, I suppose that sounds like a fair deal. Afterwards, we can go to Mrs. Clangman's and have that special lunch," Dannie suggested.

"You must be trying to fatten me up, girl. After that breakfast, we shouldn't eat for a couple of days," Sam joked.

"That's right, Sam, but remember, going after Mr. Webb may keep us away from some good food for a long time," Dannie pointed out.

"Yeah, you've got a point, Dannie girl. I may need some extra energy just putting up with Frank," Sam admitted.

"On that note, I think I will take my nap," Sam declared. As he stretched out in the lounge chair, Dannie hoped he would sleep for several hours, buying some time before he went to the hospital. After seeing his reactions last night, she knew that Sam was walking on the edge of a major breakdown. But she had set in her heart to stand behind her friend through it all, whatever the cost. Being in the spying business had a big price tag.

As Dannie began the search, hacking into one of the mainframes at the Nest, she covered her tracks by using a computer she stole from an embassy in Hong Kong. She knew they would lock onto her in a short time, but her skills would beat their best efforts. As the disk was being filled with work done between Frank and the Chambermaid, she glanced over at Sam and smiled. Whispering softly, "Sleeping like a baby, are we, Sam?" she observed, looking at the scar on his face. She wondered how long it would take to see him back the way he was before that night.

Dannie began to sift through the information on the desk, trying to find Frank's connections to the Chambermaid and if that had something to do with his mob problems. She started to notice codes about a place called The Cathedral, and names began to appear that she remembered from years before.

As she worked to put the pieces together, time slipped by quickly. She heard the Saint Mark's Church bells going off and glanced at the grandfather clock in the corner next to Sam. 12 pm... As she looked back over at Sam, he was sound asleep. The information she had received began to take her in circles, particularly concerning The Cathedral. As she began tracking down key names in the file, she heard her pager vibrating in her backpack.

Someone from Langley Headquarters had left her an urgent call-back number.

Dannie went into the bedroom to make the call, hoping that Sam would stay asleep. As she dialed the number, she wondered why she was receiving the call from Langley and not The Nest. Only a few calls had ever come in from there. "Surely they didn't pick up on me pulling Frank's files," she thought.

As the voice on the other line answered, he greeted her as Ms. Miller. "How is your day?" he asked.

"Just fine, Sir. And who is this inquiring?" Dannie responded.

"I am James McCall; I work with Mr. Logan from this side of Washington. I am the adviser to the President on what is going on in the world of espionage," he explained.

"That's fine, Sir," Dannie replied, "He is the man in charge."

"Well, Ms. Miller, the man in charge is extremely concerned about our missing scientist. We have a major world crisis on our hands, and we need to end it quietly and as soon as possible," McCall stated.

"We are guessing that Sam Black is with you," he continued.

"Good guess, Mr. McCall, and he is asleep in the living room," Dannie confirmed.

"I don't care where he's sleeping in your house," McCall spoke with a blunt, rough tone. "You have one hour to be at the Hospital emergency helicopter pad on Barker Ave. We will have a bird there to pick you up."

"One hour? Are you crazy?" Dannie shouted aloud. "There have been no planning stages. And just what did you mean by 'I don't care where he's sleeping'? Are you suggesting something, Mr. Adviser to the President?" Dannie shouted again, her voice filled with anger.

"One hour, Ms. Miller," McCall repeated calmly, and as Dannie heard the phone go dead, she shouted again, "Just who does he think he is?" She slammed the phone down in frustration.

As Dannie turned, she found Sam leaning against the door, staring at her, and froze in her place. She made a gasping sound, pointing her finger. "Don't sneak up on me like that, Sam."

"Don't suppose that was a bill collector, was it, blonde?" Sam replied as he stretched and yawned.

"It was a lot worse than that, Sam. It was a smart mouth from the Presidential side of the CIA," Dannie explained with frustration.

"So when did you get direct access to that side with the big boys?" Sam inquired, curious.

"When you came back to this side from retirement. They

somehow knew you were with me," Dannie answered.

"Well, blonde, don't keep me guessing. What did the old boy have to say?" Sam pressed for more information.

Dannie paused before answering and then posed a question to Sam. "If I wanted to go climb Mt. Everest this week and I knew I hadn't trained for it. But at the top was a button that I could push that would save the world. Would you go with me and see that I made it to the top?"

"What kind of question is that, girl? I just asked what did he want?" Sam replied, shaking his head in confusion at her sudden inquiry.

He looked straight into her eyes; it was like this blonde. "If you really believed that the button was on top of Mt Everest that could save the world, I would be at your side all the way to the top. Then you must believe me now, Sam. You don't need this assignment. In fact, I have been thinking about changing jobs and working for one of the computer companies."

"Blonde, that don't even sound like you. You are the one that always loved this job of hide and seek."

"Yeah, Sam, I used to. I have lost my interest." Dannie knew she was lying through her teeth, but she was willing to do anything to protect Sam from sure destruction.

"Oh, I see," Sam blurted out, "I see a little clearer now. Old Sam is over the hill and last night just proved it. So now you want me to just roll over and die."

"No, Sam, that's not true and you know it," shouted Dannie back. As Sam started back toward the living room, raising his arms and mumbling words, the pain began to surge through his head. Stumbling like a drunk, reaching with hands out trying to catch himself, he fell into the corner, knocking off Dannie's collection of ceramic eagles. Falling to the floor on his side, with his body shaking and mumbling words, Dannie ran and turned him over, holding his head up in her arms. Reaching for a magazine, she began fanning his face and speaking Psalms 23 over and over.

"Come on, Sam, I didn't mean you were over the hill. I just wanted to protect you from death. Please, Sam, forgive me if it sounded that way. We need you, Sam," she repeated over and over.

As Sam began coming to, Dannie was crying over him, holding him close to her chest like a child. Sam's faint voice broke through her tears. Placing her ear close to his mouth, she heard the words, "Sorry, Blonde, didn't see the enemy approaching. This is a tough enemy, Blonde, that can't be seen, only felt."

"I know, Sam, but you will make the kill. He can't get away from the great Sam Black," replied Dannie. As Sam began to hum his song, 'It will be worth it all someday,' Dannie joined in, and for a moment she forgot about the call from the President's advisor. A passing ambulance caught her attention, and she glanced at the clock. Ten minutes had gone by, what seemed like an hour.

As Sam slowly got to his feet, Dannie helped him move toward the sofa. "Sit here, Sam, and I will get you a cold rag and something to put on that cut." A small amount of blood was just above his eye from a cut after falling on one of the ceramic eagles. "This might hurt a little, Sam, but you will get no Purple Heart from this one." Dannie began to wash off the blood and put on the antibiotic cream. "Be right back, Sam, with the cold towel and bandage."

Finding an ink pen, Sam began to draw on a table napkin. His drawing caused Dannie to laugh, and she had a hard time stopping, eventually just putting her hand over her mouth, making soft grunts. Sam had drawn a Purple Heart Medal and used the button on his shirt as the pin to hold it. Slowly, Sam put his hand to his forehead in a salute.

"Thank you, General," Sam replied, "for this great honor and privilege of helping destroy your eagle collection, and most of all, your reputation. You think this could be my last Purple Heart, Blonde?"

"I sure hope so, Sam; it's probably the easiest one you have to date. I'll pay for your collection and help you get some eagles."

"Forget the eagles, Sam. It was just something that gathered dust; I never did have time to keep up with dusting them." As Dannie put on the bandage, she knew the bigger scare was within inches of her hand, the one she would like to remove from Sam's life forever.

"Here, Sam, let me put this cold towel on your head. Just lean back a moment; we have to talk. You and I have a big problem."

"What do you mean, girl? It's not your problem; I'm the one with the crazy head—can't think, can't walk, can't sleep, can't look into a mirror. It all came to a climax when Frank came to the farm. Then to the hospital like nothing ever happened, that sorry piece of dirt. I should have killed him last night."

Dannie placed her hand on Sam's lips. "Don't talk; it's my turn, and I have to get this out. I need your advice." As tears began to run down her cheeks again, Sam forgot his anger towards Frank Morgan.

"It's Mom I'm worried about," Sam asked, "Is she sick?"

"She has a secret, Sam, that she thought was hidden." With a puzzled look, Sam wiped the tears from her face. Dannie paused, then continued, "She killed my dad, Sam. She shot him one night and thought I was asleep. He came back home after... he had... he had."

Dannie began to weep, emotionally sobbing. Sam took her

and held her the way she had just held him. "Don't say it, Blonde. I know what he did to you, and death wasn't good enough."

"I saw her, Sam," Dannie whispered, her voice trembling. "She put his body in the farm truck and drove towards the railroad tracks. Sam, she went down towards the sand pits where Sheriff O'Neil is looking. I'm worried he's in the grave they found. What will I do, Sam, if they take her away? I'm all she's got, Sam."

"Dannie, look at me," Sam said, cradling her chin in his hand. "Even if they find his body, years have gone by. There's no evidence, no blood. The law knows how your dad was—a drunk, a troublemaker in the towns, fighting in the bars. Your mom's secret is safe, Blonde. They will only think someone he owed money to or had fought with had killed him."

As they both sat in silence, holding each other, a helicopter was in the air on the way to pick up two broken pieces of "The Kode."

Another ambulance going by toward Memorial Hospital made Dannie jump up. "Sam, that call I got from Langley was about the mission. There had been no planning stages. We were to be at the hospital in 35 minutes. They were sending a chopper and they gave no details," she explained urgently.

"You don't have to go, Sam; you have done enough for our country."

Sam shook his fist in frustration. "No planning stages? Are they crazy?" he exclaimed.

"People could get killed and the whole mission could go up in flames. Sam, listen to me," Dannie pleaded, her voice tinged with worry. "It's already starting off as a bad deal. You stay with your daughter and I will walk away from this job with you."

As Sam looked back at his friend, he felt a pang of gratitude for her concern. "You went back to that room many times, Dannie, and your last trip back was the one that set you free," he reminded her gently.

"I have to, Dannie. I have to face Frank without hostility," Sam continued, determination in his voice. "And one more thing, we have to push that button together on Mt Everest so the world will be safer. I'm tired of running in circles; you only end up at the same place you left from."

Dannie's eyes welled up with emotion as Sam spoke. "Listen, Dannie, I'm better off dead than for my daughter and grandchild to see me in this condition," he admitted, his voice breaking slightly.

As Dannie listened to Sam, she sensed the fighting spirit within him, the determination to survive. Memories of the old farm truck nestled in the honeysuckle weeds flooded her thoughts, reminding her that there might be a rainbow after the storm.

"Okay, Mr. Black, why not," she said with a newfound resolve. "We've been down before, and we always seem to come storming back."

Reaching out, Dannie took Sam's hand firmly. "We'll ride this one out together."

"Dannie, I need to do something we've never done," Sam said quietly.

"Sure, Sam, I trust you," Dannie replied, her voice filled with faith in her friend.

Sam bowed his head, clasping Dannie's hand as he began to pray. "Lord, I don't know how to ask you like my grandfather. But we could sure use your help," he started, his words sincere and heartfelt. "I guess you've been wondering where I've been. It's no good, Lord, the places where I've been and the things I've done, I am ashamed of. But please, if you're listening to Sam Black, help us through this. Amen."

"That was nice, Sam; I didn't know you had it in you," Dannie remarked, impressed by Sam's sincerity.

"To be honest with you, blonde, I'm beginning to wonder what all is really in me," Sam admitted, his tone introspective.

"Well, on that note, let's go and take back what belongs to the United States of America," Dannie declared, pitching the keys to Sam. "You can drive; it's only about a mile to the hospital. That way, if you change your mind, you can just keep on driving."

"Not this time, blonde," Sam replied with a smile. "I need the therapy. Besides, I know you, and you're like my horse Prince—you're chomping at the bit. You computer people are that way; you hate secret things you don't know about. It drives you forward like a racehorse."

"Well, Sam, I've been called the 'A' word, but not a horse," Dannie retorted with a laugh.

"The 'A' word?" Sam questioned, amused. "You know, Sam, the 'A' word; after that prayer, I feel a bit religious."

"Well, don't forget, religious people are killers," Dannie countered, her tone turning serious. "They blow themselves up along with killing others without thought. Psalms 23 is the only prayer I know, Sam. Here lately, I have been using it often."

"It was the prayer my mother used the night she killed him," Dannie added quietly.

"Miss Blonde, that prayer has some powerful words in it," Sam acknowledged, his voice solemn. "Remember the part, 'Thou preparest a table before me in the presence of my enemies'? I have a feeling the table that is set on this mission is going to be covered with blood."

"Maybe not, Sam, this could be the easiest job we've ever had," Dannie remarked optimistically, echoing Sam's sentiment.

"Like the old saying, Dannie, time will tell," Sam replied.

Coming to a red light, Sam spotted Starbucks Coffee. "Whipping into the parking lot," Dannie commented teasingly, "changing your mind already?"

Sam smiled as he got out of the car. "I have to get some high octane, remember we've been up all night. I love them cappuccinos."

Glancing down at her watch, Dannie reminded Sam of the time. "Hurry up; we can't keep Uncle Sam waiting."

"Well, this Sam can do what he wants; you tell them if I forget," Sam replied casually. "Just hurry, Sam; I'm sure they already know," Dannie urged.

Dannie looked on with a gleam of hope as her friend went into the coffee shop. She knew Sam was right—time would always tell. And just maybe, time would heal all wounds, even the one that Sam carried in his heart against Frank Morgan.

Dannie noticed as Sam exited the coffee shop, observing him as the door closed behind him. She saw him glance at the scar on his face, a habitual action that seemed ingrained in him. With one hand holding the coffee and the other reaching toward the scar, it was as though it had become second nature to him. "Old habits are hard to kick, some would say," Dannie thought to herself. But for Sam, it was like a drunk without his bottle—he had to have it. He had to look again and again, as though he forgot for a moment what his face looked like. Dannie hoped it would be a habit he would soon forget and give up forever.

As Sam opened the car door and entered, he spilled a small amount of coffee on his pants in the crotch area. Gritting his teeth, he blew out of his mouth as though letting off steam. "Hot is Sam," Dannie laughed. "Looks like you we-we'd in your pants, Sam."

"Maybe we should stop and change the diaper. Ok, ok, just keep laughing at me."

"I can tell you this much, Blonde, coffee was meant to drink, not pour on your hide," he continued, shaking his head.

"Oh, come now, Sam, as tough as your hide is, coffee will just run off like a rock," Dannie teased.

"What are you trying to say, Dannie? That sounds like a truck commercial," Sam replied with a chuckle.

"Well, it beats all those blonde jokes," Dannie quipped back. "Just do me a favor, hold this coffee until I put this little red vet in the wind."

Sam eased out of the parking lot toward the hospital with a light foot on the gas pedal, not wanting to get back at his friend for laughing at his coffee spill.

"Thanks, Sam. You could have got me real good," Dannie remarked gratefully.

Sam looked over and smiled, masking his inner turmoil. But both knew the weakness of Sam Black was his own reflection.

Entering the parking garage, Sam stopped to take the ticket from the man in the booth. The man quickly stared at the scarred side of Sam's face. "What are you looking at? What, are you a pervert?" Sam shouted, his temper flaring.

Putting the car in park, Sam reached to get out to confront the man, but Dannie held him back by the arm. "No, Sam, you've got to catch a ride," she urged.

But Sam, dragging Dannie holding onto his arm, out of the car, reached for the attendant's shirt, pulling him up to his face. "How about a close view, pervert? You like a close-up picture."

"Sorry, sir, didn't mean to offend you. I see a lot of bad people, I mean things, coming into this hospital parking garage," the man stammered for words, causing Sam's anger to grow.

"Bad people? You think I'm a bad person? Let me show you what a bad person I really am," Sam threatened, his voice low and menacing.

As Sam tried to get his arm away from Dannie, the man

managed to break free and ran from the booth toward the outside parking lot. By this time, Dannie was on Sam's back like a child with a piggyback ride. Sam caught his breath and dropped to one knee, breathing heavily. Dannie held him close, repeating over and over, "It's all right, Sam."

Finally, Sam dropped both hands down on the pavement, looking up toward the parking ramp as though preparing for a 100-yard dash. "What now, blonde? Are we going to pretend that nothing is wrong with me again and again and again? Until I lose all control and kill some innocent bystander to take Frank's place?" Sam questioned bitterly.

"You're getting better, Sam. This time, you didn't go out in the shakes with your body jerking as before," Dannie reassured him. "You have to see yourself complete. It's like the time you redid your kitchen in the old home place. Remember what you told me? You said everything was so out of place that nothing looked right. But you could see the work finished. That's you, Sam. I see the work finished. I won't give up on you now."

"Dannie, come on. You know how far I have unraveled, and you are lying to yourself," Sam argued.

"I have lied to myself for a long time about the rape and the death of my father, but I'm free, Sam. And this one thing I believe: you can pull out of this and put it in the grave with my father like I did. I looked in the mirror this morning, and for the first time, I saw Dannie, the real me, Sam. It was the real me," Dannie asserted.

"You lost yourself, Sam, in anger over a stupid move by Frank, something that you couldn't control," Dannie continued calmly.

"I could have controlled it!" Sam shouted back. "Frank was hard-headed, selfish. He was the one that was out of control, and I knew it was just a matter of time. He wouldn't listen."

As Dannie helped Sam up and walked back toward the car, she could hear the chopper making its landing at the emergency pad. "If you let it, Sam, time can heal all wounds," she remarked softly.

"What about scars, blonde?" Sam asked, his voice tinged with uncertainty.

As Dannie put Sam into the passenger seat, she noticed the booth attendant peeking around from one of the parked cars. She held up both hands and used Sam's line from Australia, "No worries." Picking up the crumpled parking ticket, she put the car in gear and smoked the tires.

Sam turned his head sideways on the seat, staring at his friend, as he held the now-empty coffee cup. As Dannie parked the car, Sam offered her a drink of coffee. Dannie chuckled, holding her hand to her mouth. "Sorry, Sam, in the excitement, I forgot. Watch your head while I put up the top. I promise you, Sam, I will get you another coffee. Not from a cafeteria, I want a Starbucks."

"Okay, okay, I will make sure you get two cups, Sam, on me," Dannie reassured him with a smile.

As Dannie and Sam made their way to the helicopter pad, Koon Hee sent word back to the nest that the container had been loaded onto the ship and placed at the top. He mentioned that some new crewmen had joined earlier, who didn't fit the mold for a typical seaman. They were Special agents from China, most likely, six in all. One of them, he noted, looked like a businessman from Wall Street.

Koon Hee was looking forward to working with Sam again. Sam had always treated him like a son, and they had shared many stories. Even though it was Koon Hee who had given Sam his ear more often to listen to his stories, just like Jennifer, Polly, and the rest. Sam was the great storyteller. Koon Hee never interrupted Sam; he simply sat and listened.

Koon Hee had spoken to Sam many times about growing up in the US, how at an early age many of the students laughed at him and called him "slant eyes." Being not very big, they pushed him around until he took up martial arts and became a pro at the sport. Afterward, he only had to defend himself a couple of times, and they stayed clear of him. Being well-disciplined by his instructor, he never sought revenge.

Sam knew that Koon Hee was a solid team member and would die for his country or comrades.

Koon Hee respected Sam as a leader and knew that his friend was a wounded soldier from the inside out. He had been briefed by Mr. Logan before flying to California to watch Sam and report any unfavorable actions immediately. But all were unaware of the real condition of Sam Black; only Dannie knew, and in her heart, she blotted out the real truth.

As Sam and Dannie approached the pad to enter the chopper, Mr. Logan was standing outside to greet them. "Glad you decided to give us a hand, Mr. Black," he said, reaching his hand out to shake Sam's.

"Ye', sure," Sam replied with a quick handshake.

As they entered the chopper, a woman was seated next to a dark-skinned man who looked Asian. Dannie stared hard at the woman until Mr. Logan introduced the couple.

"Dannie, I want you and Sam to meet Miss Mary Martinez and Dr. Ramhya," Mr. Logan announced, gesturing toward the couple seated in the chopper. "They will be working from a field office with our satellite people. They will be sending you messages on locations of all people on board, including your team."

"That's great," Sam replied, nodding. "I want you to keep a

close watch on Frank Morgan. Let me know if his weapon is pointed the wrong way."

With those words, Sam leaned back in the seat and closed his eyes. Logan glanced at Dannie, then back toward Sam. Dannie laughed, trying to break the ice. "Don't worry, Sir. He's been up all night fishing; we didn't expect the team to move this quickly without several days of planning."

Mary was quick to reply. "We have no time for planning; it is an emergency situation. A lot is at risk. That's the reason we wanted this KODE TEAM."

Dannie responded, "You're not going to be the one that's getting shot at. We always go into a planning stage so that no mistakes will be made."

"I know, Miss Miller, but sometimes in a crazy game of spying, you have to create your own plans as you go along for the ride," Mary countered.

Logan pulled out a file and handed it to Dannie. "This is some computer info from the dry docks and the shipping company. There are some codes also that we just intercepted; you will have to break. This disk will bring you into the mainframe with us at the nest."

Dannie smiled at those words, knowing she didn't need a

disk. In fact, she thought, "I just got off the mainframe."

"You will have Mary and Dr. Ramhya working with you. We have developed a new computer that you will be carrying with you. I hope you like its design; it cost us about 100 thousand dollars," Logan added.

Logan handed Dannie a small black case about the size of a Cracker Jack box. As Dannie pulled the computer from the case, her face lit up like a kid with a new toy. "Wow, I like it," she exclaimed.

"It's an X7V," Logan explained. "You see, we have developed what the satellite is using now, receiving signal messages by voice. All you have to do is speak into this head mic any control path, and the eye in the sky, in less than a blink, will be putting information for you on the screen."

As Dannie looked over the new computer, Sam began snoring with what seemed to be short grunts.

Dr. Ramhya looked at Mr. Logan as if to say, "You're sure you have the right man for the job." Dannie laughed at Sam with a little girl giggle but was glad to see her friend resting. As she loaded a smart drive into the new computer, she began, for the moment, recalling the events of the last 12 hours. After seeing the smart drive in her pack that she had downloaded Morgan's files on, she remembered the unexpected kiss she had given Sam. Then, with a quick look, she stared again at Mary. She began seeing herself holding Sam next to the Coke machine, looking toward Frank's room at the Hotel. The woman going into Frank's room, it was Mary. She must be the "chambermaid." As Dannie continued staring, Mary's eyes met hers, and for a moment, they stared at each other.

Dannie said, "I was admiring your black hair. It's so long and shining. All my life, I've had to put up with blond jokes. I often wondered why people spent so much time and money bleaching their hair blond." Mary laughed at Dannie's words and assured her that her long blond hair was to be desired.

"It must be a women thing," Sam said.

"Explain yourself," Sam said.

"Hair, coloring it, teasing it, fixing it, always takes women hours to get ready to go anyplace, just because of hair," Sam replied. "And by the way, Sam, I thought you were asleep."

"What gave you that idea, blonde?" Sam retorted. "Well, unless you got a bear in your front pocket, I would say you've been sleeping." All those in the chopper laughed at the bear comment.

As Dannie glanced back at Mary, she wondered how she was involved with Frank's dealings and what she had been doing in the agency.

"So, Mary, how long have you been working for the Agency?" Dannie asked.

"About two years," Mary began, but her sentence was cut off by Logan's reply.

"Mary has been in intelligence for a long time before coming to Langley," Logan assured. "She worked with the DEA in South America for 10 years, tracking down Drug Lords."

As Mary looked away from the conversation, she began running her hand through her hair, as if she were in another world. After a few minutes had gone by, she turned to Dannie and said, "The drug lords had my father and mother killed. My father was the chief of police in Colombia. He refused to be polluted by drug money. Drugs had killed his younger brother. Shortly after he was given his position, they tried to bribe him, to pay him off. He secretly worked with the US until someone in the Colombian government gave knowledge of him to the Cartel, that he was working with the Americans to destroy their factories. I had just gotten out of the vehicle at a local restaurant when they drove by and opened fire on our car. The last words my father spoke to me were, 'I'm sorry I had to fight them, for they are killing nations. I love you so much...' "With those words, she closed her eyes for a moment as though she were going back in time. Then she opened her dark eyes without tears and said, "As I saw my father and mother lying in that pool of blood, that is when I decided his cause would not be forgotten as long as I lived."

Dannie reached out and touched Mary, saying, "I'm sorry for your loss." As silence filled the helicopter, it seemed that each person began to reflect on the events, some from that day and others trying to foresee the outcome of Mr. Webb's capture.

Dannie drifted back to the lake where she had witnessed Sam's breakdown as he fell into the waters. She tried to push out of her mind how he could jeopardize the lives of the Kode Team and even Mr. Webb's, if he had another serious flashback. Then, as she stared at Mary, she tried to piece together her connections with Frank Morgan. Was she the Chambermaid? Why was she on this assignment? How do you go from drugs to rescue and recovery in one of the highest-profile cases since the JFK assassination?

Sam was lying back with one eye half-open, looking over Ramhya and Logan, trying to forget the torment in his head that seemed to drive him against his own will. Remembering his daughter in the hospital holding his grandson seemed to act like a nerve pill, holding in check his outburst over the scare in his face.

Mary appeared lost in deep thoughts of vengeance over the death of her parents, seemingly hoping to make someone pay. Logan wore a worrisome look, not liking the quick movements that Langley had to make. Knowing that Mr. Webb was a vital key to the military and not having enough time to plan the operation, it looked grave, but he hoped for some luck. Perhaps Ramhya was studying

Sam Black, observing how unprofessional he seemed. But for whatever reason, as the chopper made its way to Ft. Bolivar, an unseen cloud of impending death seemed to ride with them.

As the chopper descended to the airfield, a van awaited to take them to the jet's hangar. When the door opened, two men from Langley stood there, each holding a silver briefcase with updated information. Dr. Jim Farris, a heavy-set man with dark hair and heavy eyebrows, was one of the best satellite imagers with the agency, and Mark Brown, nicknamed "Shorty" because of his 5 feet 5 inches' height, was a computer voice analyst with an IQ higher than most people at NASA. Both men would assist from the boat Code Name "Park Bench".

As Sid Logan stepped off the chopper, he began to introduce the passengers. Sam knew "Shorty" from a trip to Austria and immediately took him by the hand, patting him on top of the head.

"Shorty," Sam said, "I swear you have grown about three inches."

"Yeah, right Sam," Shorty replied, "the only place that got three inches was around my waist." Both men laughed, and the mood shifted from distraught to more smiles and handshakes.

Getting into the van, Sam felt a flash of pain that seemed to send fire racing across his brain. Trying not to be seen, he moved to the back seat, pulling on Dannie's sleeve. Aware of what was going on, Dannie moved into the seat beside him and took his hand. Sam placed his hand on top of hers and tapped with his finger on top of her knuckles as he squeezed the side of the seat. With his head leaning backward, he closed his eyes and gritted his teeth, holding as still as possible as he tried to think of his daughter and grandson.

Dannie began singing Sam's favorite song, "It Will Be Worth It All Some Day," which she had memorized. The riders in the van became quiet as they listened to her unusual song. As Sam began to come out of his attack, he stopped tapping on her hand and, after taking a deep breath twice and slowly letting it out, he joined in with her singing as the vehicle sped toward the Gulfstream Jet.

As the song ended, they started clapping their hands and cheering for the singing pair. Logan commented on the entertainment, "Sam, you and Dannie make a good duet. We at Langley didn't know you had a singing talent."

Sam nodded his head, "Well, you see, I always thought I was in the wrong business. I have figured this way, if the rifle doesn't get them, I can always sing them to death." They all seemed to agree with Sam as laughter filled the van again

Dannie looked at Sam and smiled, whispering softly, "You'll make it." Sam shook his head, but his self-confidence was locked in bitterness, like a hidden terrorist bomb waiting to explode when no one was expecting. Sam Black could be the bomb that takes out the bomb maker, Frank Morgan. Time was now ticking, just like the mechanized device to set off the blast. Each second gone by brought a grave look to the CIA's Kode Team.

As the jet was being loaded inside the hangar, Logan introduced Sam to Phillip Castle. He was part of the frog team that would be used to transport Mr. Webb by water if necessary.

"Good to meet you, sir. I have heard a great deal about you, Mr. Black," Phillip said.

"No need to be formal, just call me Sam," Sam replied as the two shook hands. "How long have you been a frogman?" Sam asked.

"About twelve years, Sir, most of it with the Navy Seals," Phillip replied.

"Well, it's good to meet a fellow wetback; it's the only one that's legal," Sam joked. Both men laughed, and Sam assured him he didn't envy his job after spending many days at sea trying to survive the heat and saltwater.

"I heard about you, Sam, from some of my instructors. You seem to have put your mark on a lot of them," Phillip remarked.

"All Seals are brave men," Sam quickly replied. "It's only a few that can take the pressure and be squeezed out into a fighting machine." As Dannie overheard Sam's remark, she patted him on the shoulder and smiled. Sam was able to find words from within but couldn't put them into action. Maybe the saying "half empty" was at work. Something seemed sure; part of what was in Sam was revenge. That notion may work against your enemy, but in a team, it was like having a flat tire without a spare.

As Sid Logan gave the final briefing, he reminded everyone of the importance of the mission. "We have a world at stake, and China—I repeat, China—cannot get Mr. Webb out of the country. We cannot afford for them to have the knowledge of our space wars program, which is also locked up with Mr. Webb. Nor can this become an international news scene. And may I remind you that Mr. Webb must be alive after all this has gone down. The WAR PEACE, ladies and gentlemen," I added to the list, "this is one of the most important top-secret missions you will most likely ever face."

With those words spoken, Logan slowly took off his glasses, looking toward the ground as if to have a silent prayer. He looked up without a smile, simply saying, "Good luck."

As the team walked on board the jet, Sam turned to Dannie and whispered, "Luck's good in a poker game, but we're not playing Texas Hold'em, more like China's checkers, don't you think?"

Dannie pushed Sam toward the back two seats in the plane because she knew it was possible that Sam might have a flashback, and they didn't need everyone on board knowing Sam's real condition.

As the plane traveled down the runway, gaining speed, Dannie stared out the window toward the railroad tracks that ran next to the base. The tracks reminded her again of the sheriff's cars. Her thoughts went back to the area where her mother had buried her dad. Was the body found by the officers her father's, and if it could be traced back to her mother on that chilling night?

Turning westward and now in the thick white clouds, Dannie turned to speak to Sam, who was now asleep. Looking at the deep scar in his face, she knew her friend was in denial of the truth about himself and how the bitterness toward Frank Morgan had now become rage. Like a storm out of control, she hoped it wouldn't make rescuing Mr. Webb a national disaster.

As she peered at the clouds again, her thoughts raced back, this time to the women at Frank's motel. Was she the chambermaid? Could this be Mary? Was she connected with Frank's mob deals?

As the plane slowed down, the drop in altitude caused Sam to jump forward. Dannie reached her arm across his chest, holding him like a child at a stoplight. Sam smiled, knowing his friend was watching over him like a mother hen.

"I better buckle my seat, Blondie, in case I get the jumps again," Sam grunted as he spoke. "Or we could do it like the old days, just strap on a chute and jump."

"You said that wrong, Sam," Dannie replied. "The word is not 'we'; it's 'you' and those other senseless Seals."

"Oh, come on, Blondie, leave us ole Navy boys alone. You know why we keep on fighting and never quit."

"No, Sam, tell me."

"It's **NAVY**, Dannie; it's what **NAVY** means."

"Okay, Sam, whatever! Let me just tell you what it really means as an acronym:

Never give up,

All the way,

Victorious in battle,

You can't quit now."

"Who made that up, Sam? The Naval Academy?" Dannie asked.

"No, Dannie boy, I did," Sam replied. "I would always write it on the insoles of my shoes with a paint marker or on the heels of my boots. Every time I would pull off my shoes, I could read the four commandments that I lived by. It just seemed to keep me in hard times."

"What's written on them now, Sam?" Dannie inquired.

"Nothing," Sam replied quickly.

As Dannie reached down, she pulled off one of her white Nike's. Reaching into her computer case, she pulled out a black Sharpie marker and began to write Sam's four commandments on the inside of her shoes.

"I like it, Sam; it seems fitting to write down such wisdom," Dannie said. As she blew on the ink to make it dry quicker, she handed the marker to Sam. "It's time, Mr. Black, you need to write them again before these wheels touch down in California."

Sam slowly took the marker and stared at it. "Sorry, Dannie, if you can't keep the commandments, why live a lie? My granddad preached the ten commandments and said live by them all. Here, take it," he said, handing her the marker.

"No, Sam, put it in your pocket for later," Dannie insisted.

Sam nodded his head. "Confidence," he said softly, "you seem to have a lot of it about my future."

Dannie snapped back, "Yeah, that's right; I do because it was you that grounded that into us. It could be that first commandment, never give up." As Dannie spoke, her voice took on an angrier tone. "Or maybe it's the fourth commandment; you can't quit now," her eyes now looking fiery.

Sam put the marker in his pocket and said, "Yeah, you're right, maybe later," and closed his eyes, leaning back. As the plane dropped again, Sam turned to Dannie, "Glad you are on our side, Blondie. Best of all, I am glad you are my friend." At those words, Dannie smiled and patted Sam on the hand. "Thanks, Sam, real friends are hard to come by."

As the pilot broke into the conversation, "We will be landing shortly at Port Loma, please buckle up, and by the way, the weather is great in San Diego." As the plane touched down at the Naval base, Sam and Dannie knew the mission was planned too soon, but they had been trained to improvise in every situation. The training could be thrown out the window when the mental capacity of someone is broken and their way of thinking is full of despair and bitterness. But Dannie knew that with Sam, even on a cloudy day, it was possible to have a rainbow. Her hope was that something would rise up in Sam, pushing out all the inner demons that haunted his mind, like the demons of her past that were lost that morning before breakfast. She knew freedom came with a price, sometimes years of fighting a battle with oneself or at the price of something loved.

For whatever reason, she knew that Sam's debt had been paid. He just couldn't accept the pardon. Being locked up in a prison of which you are the warden, with the keys, but not knowing what to unlock, or how to release yourself from the hell from which you had made your bed. With the screeching of the wheels on the runway, it seemed that most of the passengers were eager to start the mission, all but Sam.

"Boy scouts, Dannie, most of these boys are boy scouts to the real battlefield."

"What do you mean, Sam?"

"Look at them! Most of them have worked at a desk, learning espionage with computer experiences from the field men. That's us! We are the ones who have crawled through the blood and guts, making notes to fill their computer files. Some are planners and some are pain barriers. If you have never been there before, how do you know just how much someone can bear?"

"One of my petty officers told me one time when he was boxing as a youth for Golden Gloves, his corner man had never boxed. Sitting in the seat between rounds, he kept telling this young fighter, 'Why didn't you hit him with a hook? Why don't you hit him with an uppercut?' On and on. The young fighter told him after the fight, 'It's easy to sit on the outside of the ring and see all the punch possibilities, but you weren't the one on the inside of the ring hitting and trying not to get hit.' He told me that was the day that he quit boxing. He said, 'I knew the YMCA corner man who had never fought before didn't have a clue of the pain inflicted on the boxer.' He said, 'That's the reason why I will follow you into battle because you know pain.'"

"Yeah, that's right, Sam, but you know it takes all of us working together. The planners are important. Look at this mission,

Sam. Mr. Webb was never in the military or with the agency; he is only the man with a high IQ, yet it's because of him that we are risking our lives. WHY? Because he is a planner putting together a program that will plan the future of nuclear attacks. So you see, everyone can't have mud under their nails and calluses on their hands. Look who's paying the bills for his return, the Space Source Corporation? The whole company is made up of planners of military equipment for the US government. Look at it this way, Sam, for the first time, the planners are giving us a payday. That will help pay for a whole lot of grandchildren's toys and Starbucks coffee. Just leave the boy scouts alone; they will come in handy as they have before."

As the plane was being unloaded and the passengers were moving toward the door, Dannie noticed that Sam hadn't mentioned Frank's name on the trip. With a smile at the thought, perhaps Sam was moving toward commandment number three, Victorious in battle.

Greeting the party in Port Loma was Matthew Marx, an agency specialist working out of the Naval Airwarfare Center in China Lake, CA, and with the Seals Beach Naval Weapons Station.

"Ok folks, I know you have heard this before, but this mission has a very historical meaning. Even though it may never end up in the books, and in fact, we hope it never gets past the file at Langley.

No. 1: You know what's at stake; The Star Wars program, The WAR PEACE, it's a must! Mr. Webb is our source. Not dead! I repeat not dead!

No. 2: Our relationship with China, they must know that the US has the only program that can stop all I.C.M.'s from touching anywhere on planet earth.

No. 3: Highly top secret. This must go down out of the sight of the news world. No mistakes! I repeat! No mistakes! I have a folder for each one of you. We will be doing a briefing at Seal Beach.

No. 4: The clock is our enemy. Our planning efforts must be to the tenth of a second.

No. 5: I repeat again, this is not a dead or alive mission. He must be kept ALIVE! That's all!

"This van will take you to the briefings and your time of day now begins," Marx concluded. As he shook hands with the members of the team, he gave them each a file, Sam being the last one. Looking at Sam while shaking his hand, Marx repeated, "No mistakes," then turned and walked away.

Sam gave a salute, and Dannie punched him in the side, saying, "Don't judge the book by its cover; the van is waiting for us, Sam."

"Sure blondie, let's get it over with." Sam replied.

KODE June 21, 2010:

Everyone in the van knew that in the business of spying, all is uncertain. The one thing that most intelligence groups believed: they are the benefactor or even victorious when they know what their neighbor is up to. It's the FEAR FACTOR, known as the lack of trust. Most all say they trust in a GOD, but it is each other that they don't trust, or even hate.

As the van moved toward the destination, most of the occupants seemed to be at ease, as if they were at a church supper. That is all but Sam Black, as he lowered his sun visor with the mirror looking over each face. He noticed Frank, who was staring out the window, and Sam bit his lip on the side just enough to feel a slight pain. Trying to measure one's ability by reading their faces was something he had done many times. He knew the percent rate wasn't perfect, but he had been right a lot of the time.

Seeing Marx with a pen and pad in his hand, in deep thought with the notes he had written down, reminded him of a man he had met on a flight to England. A Harvard Professor and teacher of world economics.

The man seemed ignorant of common things but had a brilliant mind on world governments and trade communications. Sam had passed himself off as a machine operator in the coal mines.

But during the conversation with the man, Sam knew that in a nation without a safety net of military might and good intelligence, there would be very little money or trade, but rather blood and death, which he had seen plenty of.

Sam could see the wrinkles around Marx' eyes from many late nights in planning operations. He also knew he had judged him wrong. The man was dedicated and real when it came to the love and safety of the American people.

As he glanced over the other faces, all seemed to be occupied with the briefing papers or in thought. Then he saw Dannie staring directly into his eyes in the mirror. As he stared back just for a moment, he could see a frightened little girl hiding in the corner of her bedroom, hearing the footsteps coming up the stairs, thinking it was her dad coming to abuse her sexually again. Sam bit his lip again and closed his eyes. He knew Dannie's thought was to look out for her emotionally crippled friend. It was a good thing to have a friend who would pull the knife out of your back rather than put one in.

As the noise of the van going down the road settled in, the Chinese on the cargo ship were hard at work preparing for their nightly departure. Koon Hee was moving as quickly as he could with what seemed to be a million eyes watching him.

He had located the container that had been built for the

transporting of Mr. Webb, the US scientist. As he continued on doing his work duties, he cautiously marked in his mind every part of the ship's exits and Black Zones, known to the KODE as a place that could potentially hazard their lives. Most of the exits that would be used by them wouldn't care to be posted with the EXIT SIGN.

Everything seemed to be coming into place even if the timing was shortened. The true test was coming in only a few hours. Soon, the phone of Matthew Marx brought everybody back from their worlds of thought, knowing that each call was putting together the operations.

"Yes, I have the road name," Marx replied, "which is OAKS COUNTRY CLUB LANE. The motel is Radissons. Yes, Sir, got it, yes, fifteen minutes."

As Matthews continued his conversation out loud, the team in the van waited for instructions and details.

"Ok, thanks," Marx replied as he turned toward the driver. "Alright, in about fifteen minutes you will see an Exxon station on the right and a Shell station on the left. You will turn right just past the Exxon onto Oaks Country Club Lane. There will be a Radisson Hotel on the left one block after you turn. Go to the right side of the parking area, and you will see a white Hertz Rental van. You will pull in beside it and we will move from one van to the other as quickly as possible. They don't want a Government Van going to the

Marina where we will be picking up the fishing boat."

"Yes, sir," answered the petty officer.

As each of the 15 minutes ticked off, the occupants of the van were moving more, shoveling papers together and readjusting their posture, all but Sam. He seemed to be in one of those deep tunnels of thought, still reclining backward with his eyes closed. As Dannie put away her computer into her backpack, she looked up toward Sam. She could see his papers laying folded next to the windshield on the dashboard. As she leaned forward to nudge him, she decided to wait for the van to make its stop, hoping he would get a few more minutes of rest.

But rest wasn't on Sam's mind; he was traveling back in time with his daughter. Years of memories flashed in his thoughts as though he was looking at a picture album. He remembered staring into the eyes of his grandson; it was as though it was bedded deep into his memory. He remembered the soft skin of the baby, which he knew was part of him. He could see himself holding his grandson's hand walking down the dirt road from his cabin, the way that he had done with Jennifer, his daughter. But the hand now was calloused with war and death. It was as though Sam could smell the freshness of the baby oil, like a perfume from his grandson, and even caught himself chuckling out loud, leaning forward slightly as the van was coming up on the turn to go to the motel parking lot.

The Kode

Dannie leaned forward and said to Sam, "I thought only blondes could have private laughs." Sam grinned with a slight chuckle again and replied, "Blondes only have self-conversations, but grandfathers are allowed to have a private laugh."

As the petty officer approached the turn past the Exxon station, he swerved the van to keep from hitting an elderly man who pulled out in front of him, throwing everyone to the right of the van with Sam's head hitting the side glass. As the van swerved back, Sam jumped and threw the petty officer from the driver's seat toward the center of the two front seats. Jumping into the seat with the van heading toward a delivery truck, Sam pressed the gas, putting the left wheels upon the lane divider. With just inches to spare, the van made it between the truck and the lamppost.

Quickly U-turning the van and turning into the Radissons' Motel, Sam brought the vehicle to a quick stop beside the pickup van. With no one moving in the van and the petty officer still lying sideways between the seats, Sam turned slowly and looked down with a glance, reaching down and taking hold of the petty officer, pulling him up toward himself.

As Sam looked into the petty officer's eyes for a moment, he could see fear and a distraught young man. "Sorry, son, didn't mean any harm," Sam said earnestly. "Again, I'm really sorry. I guess my survivor skills overreacted." Taking the petty officer's other hand and patting him on the shoulder, Sam continued, "Again, I'm sorry, man. I will take you and your wife out to a special dinner when all this is over, I promise."

As the young petty officer gained his composure, he replied to Sam with a laugh, "I didn't think an old man could move that fast." The petty officer's comment about Sam caused the van to erupt into laughter, and the doors started opening quickly as if the passengers were escaping from a plane wreck. Sam leaned towards Dannie and whispered, "Don't repeat this, but I didn't think an old man could move like that either."

Then Matthew Marx walked over and put his hand out, saying, "Let me shake your hand, Sam. I thought the doughboy was going to eat the grill of a delivery truck." With a gracious laugh, Marx seemed to bring in an overweight problem. "No need to thank me," Sam replied. "If I had left the petty officer alone, he probably could have done it much smoother than I."

The young petty officer seemed to blush, but he knew Sam was trained to take on all problems that he found himself in. As he walked over slowly, he said, "Mr. Black... No, Mr. Black," Sam repeated quickly, "it's Sam to you. And again, I want to say I'm sorry." But the officer smiled and said, "No more apologizing, Sam. I've heard about Navy SEAL training. Just thought I would offer you the opportunity to drive the remaining portion of the way," holding up the keys with a grin.

"No thank you, son," Sam replied. "I can only drive during extreme situations when I don't think clearly." Then he winked at the young officer and said, "You're the man, let's get this wagon on the trail." As the officer turned to walk toward the van, the purple mark on his face seemed to catch Sam's attention again. And for a moment, it was as though he could hear people laughing at the young man and his Amish wife. Sam knew the scars were permanent, but the outcome of one's life depended upon their will of purpose and what truly made someone happy, and yes, the Almighty Father God of his grandfather's preaching.

After the adrenaline rush from the van incident, Sam seemed to feel the military vitality moving into his system again. Frank Morgan's voice speaking Sam's name put Sam back into his second world, the one of hate and bitterness. "Ha, Sam, have you ever thought about being a NASCAR driver?" Morgan said with a laugh.

As Sam turned to answer Morgan's question, he grunted, thinking of something to make Frank look childish. He could feel a slight tingle in the area of the scar on his face. Sam was slow in response to the answer, reaching toward the scar. Dannie had moved in closer as if she would be the referee.

"NASCAR," Dannie replied as she pushed Frank back as a friendly gesture. But in reality, she didn't want him that close to Sam. "NASCAR," she repeated again, "you mean mountain moonshine racing, don't you? That maneuver Sam made back there was one where you've missed the neighbor's cow while out running the sheriff."

Dannie had now moved in between Sam and Frank as Sam stared at Frank with what seemed to be the eyes of a serial killer. With the eye above the scar slightly closed, Sam walked over to Frank and put his arm around him, pulling his shoulder towards him.

"Frank, we've been through a lot together. You are probably the best bomb builder I know, but I still think you are dumber than a box of rocks. But look at it this way, people don't expect much from a dummy! That is the reason I brought my own little bomb."

As Sam reached into his pocket, the loading of the van stopped. It seemed like time froze, and the look on Frank's face was one of terror, unable to move. As Sam's hand came out of his pocket, in it was a small round white plastic box. It was Bomb-Mint chewing gum. As Sam opened the container, he took out a mint and put it in his mouth, then reached the box towards a startled Frank Morgan.

"Here, Sam says with a smile, have a bomb mint." It seemed Frank, for the first time in his life, was speechless.

Dannie started laughing so hard, she bent over, holding her stomach. The van occupants seemed to forget their near accident and their call to duty for their country. Even Matthew Marx was laughing out loud, pointing toward Sam's plastic box of bomb mints.

Frank, still not speaking, walked and got in the back seat of the van. Appearing across the top of the van was the petty officer standing on the running board, laughing at Sam's bomb joke.

Sam walked over and placed his hand on Matthew Marx' shoulder and said, "It's never too old to have a good laugh at someone else's expense." He turned to see Morgan sitting in the back of the van looking like a scolded kindergarten child after his teacher slapped his hand with a ruler. But Sam laughed within and used the moment as a goodwill gesture for his own emotions. Laughter was said to be good medicine, and Sam needed anything that would blind his past until the mission work with Frank Morgan was over. A team divided against each other cannot stand! This mission was one that cannot be put on hold.

While finding their positions in the second van, the President of the United States was being briefed on all aspects of the operations to free the US scientist, Mr. Webb. He and his advisers knew what a critical mission this was because the president of China would soon be making his journey to the United States for three-day talks between the two nations. He would also be traveling to Chicago for talks with business leaders for their support that the two countries continue in business trade. Everything seemed to be a ticking time bomb with no one able to diffuse it. It was only at best a guess that the mission would go as planned without any news media or loss of life. With the heavy burden of recession lying upon the shoulders of the American people and billions of dollars in debt to the Chinese government, this would be at most a stroke of luck.

As the van was leaving the Radisson's motel, Petty Officer Johnson pointed to the steering wheel, giving Sam the opportunity to do the driving. "No thanks," Sam replied. "I am going to lay back, close my eyes, and dream good dreams."

Dannie leaned forward and whispered in Sam's ear, "While you're dreaming, Sam, dream one for me because I'm still worried about my mother."

"Your mother will be just fine," assured Sam. "She is a very strong and courageous woman, and you are a chip off the old block."

"Thank you, Sam. We can support each other. It usually takes more than one pillar to hold up a bridge."

"Well, with the way things are, it is going to take a lot of pillars because I feel like the Golden Gate Bridge."

"Well, remember this, Sam," Dannie said, "the Golden Gate Bridge has been here for a very long time."

"That's because no one has tried to steal the gold," Sam replied. "Sometimes something just seems to be golden, but in reality, it's just been painted over."

"Not so, Sam," Dannie countered. "The sun makes it appear gold. Remember how you always talked about the sunrise in the mountains, how you said it made you feel resurrected? Well, in the morning, you will get to see the sunrise from the fishing boat on the face of Mr. Webb, and then you can do that little mountain dance you learned, and I might just join in."

Sam laughed with a grunt as Marx spoke up, "Yeah, Sam, and I am going to join in with a belly dance." The van burst with laughter again, all but Frank, who still seemed to be embarrassed by the bomb joke.

As the team began the journey in the rental van, Operation Park Beach was in full swing. Special Forces had prepared explosives for the decoy ship. They hoped that the decoy ship would cause enough havoc to close the harbor. Satellite images from Langley had placed photo imaging directly on Park Bench, so every move in the harbor and surrounding areas was covered and monitored on high alert. The President and his staff, along with military advisers, were planning to watch the mission from the viewing room. It looked as though everyone had a front-row seat, including Sam Black and his Kode Team. The only difference was the Kode Team had to wear a triangular medallion that made them enemies to the country they were working for. It always seemed in the game of spying that someone had to be the fallen man or the scapegoat to help the president or country avoid tarnishing their image. Sam Black felt it was a way to escape his scarred face and hoped to rehabilitate his mind. Rehab on this mission might come with a price, the death of Sam Black.

Sam reached over and touched the petty officer on the shoulder again. "I want to say I'm sorry, didn't mean to cross the line."

"Sorry, Mr. Black, don't know what you're talking about," the petty officer replied with a smile.

Sam patted him on the shoulder again, and he nodded his head. "I can appreciate that."

As Sam began looking for his cell phone, he didn't know that Dannie had taken it to keep him from calling his daughter. She had informed Polly to talk to Sam's daughter to keep the information away from Sam about Jeremy being shot. Sam turned to Dannie, asking her if she knew what he did with his cell phone.

"It's hard to keep up with my own stuff, Sam, much less keep up with yours," Dannie answered.

Matthew Marx reached into his pocket and handed Sam his cell phone. "Use mine, Sam."

"Thank you," Sam replied, "I just want to check on my daughter. She just gave birth to my first grandson."

"Yes, I know, Sam," Matthew said, "I am a proud father myself, just wished I had a daughter instead of three mean boys."

Dannie was quick to reach and take the cell phone from

Marx's hand. As Sam twisted more to the left, trying to figure out Dannie's intention, those in the van who were watching seemed to focus on the skin that was moving in the scar on Sam's face. Dannie was quick to put up the palm of her hand toward Sam. "Wait, Sam, let me call Polly for you. I need to ask her to drive down and check on my mother."

But Dannie's real motives were to guard Sam against gaining any information that might cause a breakdown. And Sam took the bait because he knew the predicament that her mother was in. In reality, the Kode Team had become two instead of four members because Dannie was addressing only the well-being of her friend Sam Black, and Sam was only a question mark.

As another call came into Marx's phone, Dannie reached him his phone and turned to see Sam slowly turning a triangular medallion in his hand. He felt his years in the service of his country were where his last mission would help the most, but yet it seemed he was without them. He was now aware that he had become a disposable individual who loved the country and its people more than the government did.

"There is nothing fair and balanced," Sam muttered under his breath, catching Dannie's attention.

"You need something, Sam?" Dannie asked.

As Sam looked down at the medallion again that he held in

the palm of his hand, "Nothing is fair and balanced," Sam replied. "Well, I take that back, Blondie, only Fox News."

Sam's remark seemed to get the van laughing again, all but Frank Morgan and Matthew Marx, who was on the phone with an intelligence update from Langley. Frank Morgan seemed to be staring out the window with a blank look, as though his eyes were fastened on a roadside.

The petty officer driving the van called out Frank's name for the third time, speaking his name. Frank responded, "How may I help you?"

"Well," replied the petty officer, "I wonder if you have any more of those bomb mints?"

This time Frank laughed, and the van burst into laughter again. Sam just smiled as he turned to see if Frank had an answer.

"Okay, okay," Frank responded, "he got me good, I admit. Sam had me frozen in place," Frank gestured with his hands as though he was choking himself.

Marx raised his hand to signal quietness, and the laughter in the van went silent. "Okay, folks, it seems everything is a go. There will be two diversions instead of one. A military tanker will be involved in an explosion on the freeway before the Navy ship explosion that will block the harbor. We are trying to divert all local news teams and their helicopters toward that diversion before the harbor decoy is set to go off. The reason being, the less coverage we get, the better off for this mission. A big event is at stake here; the world's two superpowers at the height of economic disaster are facing each other at a standstill that could alter history forever. Remember the Bin Laden mission; China desired our technology in the stealth industry. That mission still holds a taste of Washington and Langley. We cannot afford to leave behind a tail section of anything. This mission has to look like a robbery being made by a militant group. The news services have been informed from a White House briefing about the M.A.G. terrorist group, which is already being aired on most news networks, about two hours ago. So, we are at full throttle to go."

Marx reached Dannie his phone, saying, "Hurry, never know when you'll get a call from Langley. They might be a little nervous about now."

"Thank you, sir," Dannie answered. "Yes, I think we all might be a little nervous."

As she quickly dialed Polly's cell phone, she was very much aware of a mission gone badly; she was reminded every time she looked at the scar on her friend's face. And the one that used to be in her heart, and maybe still was in her Bible-reading mother's heart.

As Polly's cell phone rang, she knew to answer any call,

regardless of what showed up on her ID. All the years she had been with Sam; it was clear a call could come from any phone number in any place in the world.

"Hello," Polly answered, in her deep mountain accent.

"Polly, it's Dannie."

"How's Sam doing?" Polly asked.

"Just fine, Polly," Dannie replied, speaking in a whisper, knowing Sam was nearby. "The flight was good."

"Take care of my boy, Dannie. I love him like a son," Polly urged. "You know I will, Polly," Dannie assured her

"I need you to check on Mom for me, Polly. She might need some company about now."

"I will, as soon as I leave the hospital. I'll drive down and take her some homemade jelly and sweet potato pie. She's always loved that."

"Thank you, Polly, you're a sweetheart," Dannie expressed. "Sam wants to talk to you about Jenny."

"Don't worry, Dannie, I won't say anything, and I've told Jenny to say nothing," Polly reassured. "Okay, Polly, we love you, here's Sam," Dannie responded.

As Sam reached for the phone, his voice carried a hint of

anxiety about knowing his daughter was all right. "Polly, how's my little girl doing?" he inquired.

Polly quickly comforted Sam with her wise words. "Listen, Sam, this girl is so much like you; she's tougher than a locust post. And that grandboy, he might be just a little tougher than the both of you," she remarked.

Sam chuckled at the mention of his grandson's resilience as Polly winked and handed the phone to Jeannie. "It's your daddy, youngins," she announced.

Jennifer wasted no time in speaking. "I love you, daddy, you are my hero, and daddy, you will always be my hero," she said tenderly.

Sam's voice choked with emotion as tears filled his eyes. "I love you, girl, you're special in my heart. So, how is my grandboy doing?" he asked.

"He's beautiful, dad, just so perfect. I believe he's going to have Mom's eyes; they look blue," Jennifer replied. "Only time will tell, dad. Eyes and hair may change color, but he's still perfect."

"But his perfect looks come from you, little girl. You're so much like your mother. She was..." Sam paused, his voice choking. "I love you, and I'll see you all in a couple of days."

"I love you, dad," Jennifer responded before handing the

phone back to Polly.

"Sam, I'll take care of her. You just make sure you take care of yourself and get back here," Polly said firmly. "I will, Polly, I promise. I really do promise. Watch over everything for me, Polly; you know I love you like a mother," Sam replied, placing the phone on Marx's notepad and saying thanks.

Marx opened his eyes and apologized, "Yeah, Sam, sorry, trying to rest my eyes."

"Well, Matthew, if all goes as planned, maybe we can rest our whole body," Sam chuckled as he spoke.

"That would be really nice, Sam, I'm telling you, real nice," Matthew agreed.

Sam reached over and touched the arm of the petty officer. "After a little rest, you and I are going to do some hunting."

"I'm looking forward to that, Mr. Black, sir. It will be an honor," replied the young driver.

Sam smiled and nodded his head as he leaned back in the seat and closed his eyes. The rest of the van's occupants went back to viewing the mission material. Frank Morgan, now out of his bomb scare, was talking with one of the Navy SEALs frog teams. The operation was now at Green.

All of the uncertainties that lay ahead would be a challenge for the Kode Team, even though they had faced adversity many times before, never under these orders. Going into a mission as a government hate group, with no room for mistakes or their death or capture, would be a dishonor and disgrace from a country that they loved and honored. There would be only unseen heroes, no badges of honor, no medals, only hope for a safer United States.

Meanwhile, Koon Hee was moving through the Chinese container ship, trying to find all obstacles that may slow the mission or pose a threat to the team. They could not afford the mission to start off in jeopardy. Sid Logan was now briefing the presidential advisers on the mission and all changes that had been made. In the briefing room and throughout the White House, it felt like the calm before the storm. There was an eerie feeling that surpassed the Bin Laden mission, Iran's nuclear buildup, and Iraq's pullback of troops. The stock markets moved up and down on the worries of the euro and the European nations, without a clue that the United States was about to invade the Chinese vessel in a United States Harbor, which could escalate into a global economical meltdown and perhaps a cold war with China.

The green light given to this mission by the White House had become one of the most critical and dangerous intersections in American presidential orders, perhaps matching the atomic bomb on Japan and the beginning of the Gulf War. As the van slowed to exit onto the road into the harbor, the ocean waters seemed to catch the attention of all the passengers but Sam, who was still lying back with his eyes closed.

"Dannie nudges Sam, 'We are here,' she whispers."

As Sam raises his seat, looking toward the boats in the harbor, he takes a deep breath and exhales. "This looks like a very good place to fish," Sam says, turning to the petty officer driver. "What do you think, son?"

"Not my type, sir. I'd rather be on a riverbank with a catfish pole," the petty officer responds.

"Yes, I know what you mean. I am thinking of a good bass lake with a little early morning fog rising up," Sam replies.

"Yes, sir, either one, sir," answers the petty officer.

As the group makes their way toward the boat slip, Sam's attention is caught by the seagulls, watching them dive down towards the water, which makes him drift back to the mountain cabin. There, he would sit on the rock that had been named Indian Point View. As a child, he would gaze far across the great Appalachian Mountains, remembering watching the red-tailed hawk dive down, catching a squirrel or a field mouse. The birds seemed so free, something that Sam had forgotten after the shooting accident that left his face scarred. "Freedom comes with a price," Sam thought, as he slowly placed his finger on the scar on his face.

Dannie saw Sam touch the scar and knew his thoughts might be drifting in the wrong direction. She placed her hand on his shoulder quickly and asked a question about his grandson.

"Sam, are you going to teach that grandson of yours to fish?" Dannie inquired.

Sam lowered his hand from his face and picked up the medallion from the van console. "Yeah, sure am. I am going to teach him to honor his country."

"You mean to be a Navy man like you, Sam?" Dannie asked.

"Absolutely not," Sam replied quickly. "I'm talking about going to college and taking something like political science and becoming a senator or governor, something that can help keep our country on the right track. In fact, I wouldn't want anyone following my steps. I have a lot of memories about death, and for some reason, I feel I will have to give an account for them someday."

"Sam, you did what you thought was right for your country," Dannie reminded him.

"Yes, that is right, Blondie, but many times I didn't think my country was doing right for what they asked us to do," Sam admitted. "Do you see this medallion, Dannie? Why do you think we are being paid by a company? We have become expendable individuals who will lose their country the moment we put these medallions on and enter that Chinese container ship."

"And why are you doing this for, country or pride?" asked Dannie.

just want to live in peace and freedom. That's why, Blondie," Sam declared.

"By the way, why did you take the mission, Blondie?" he asked.

"Because of you, Sam. That's the only reason," Dannie replied, causing Sam to turn and look her in the eye. As he stared, he noticed a tear running down her cheek. At that moment, he realized Dannie had left her mother at a critical time to come with him. He knew she was like his watchman in the night.

Sam smiled as he wiped a tear from her cheek and said, "The other reason I'm on this mission is because of you, Blondie. I enjoy being around you."

Dannie wiped her eyes again and smiled back at Sam, saying, "same here, Mr. Black."

As the van pulled up to the boat slip information sign, Marx reminded the driver that their slip was number 57A. "Yes, sir," replied the petty officer.

After coming to a stop, the team began unloading from the van. The 35-foot fishing boat docked in the slip already had four occupants on board. One was Ms. Martinez, two Navy SEALs, and a lieutenant from the Army Special Forces. Dannie elbowed Sam as Frank Morgan made his way towards Ms. Martinez and put his hand on her back as though he had known her for some time. As they talked and laughed, it was a piece of the puzzle Dannie and Sam had not been able to put together, after they had seen her go in and out of Frank's motel room with the key.

"I hope this is not a monkey wrench in the gears," Sam whispered to Dannie.

"They sure seem to know each other quite well, Sam," she whispered back.

Matthew Marx turned to Sam, saying, "The equipment needed for this mission has already been placed on board by special ops from Langley. Now, all we need is for the Kode Team to go pick up the package and make the delivery safely."

"I lose confidence in the government sometimes too, Mr. Black," Marx continued, "but you and I both know that usually the people are not the government. I think our forefathers started out the country and its government principles with the thought that the people would be the government and they all would be one, not separate. Sometimes our freedoms have caused liberals to take advantage of being free and commit to laws being passed by one's own agenda rather than that of the people."

"I couldn't have said that any better, Matthew," replied Sam. "It seems that a people or country that desires to be free becomes the hate of other countries and people who do not live in a democracy, which allows free voting for its representatives. Hitler proved what dictatorship can do when one's own agenda is to fulfill a craving to be over its people in the world."

Marx patted Sam on the shoulder and said, "Well enough about history, now it is time to make history whether it will ever be recorded in the books or not." As the team boarded the fishing boat, Sam was greeted by the two Navy SEALs already on board.

"It's good to be working with you, Mr. Black," one of them said. "We have heard a lot of things about you."

"If everything you heard about me was good, someone probably lied," Sam replied with a smile as he shook their hands.

"You know, Mr. Black, Navy SEAL Teams have a deep pocket of memory," the other SEAL said. "We always go back to the past comrades who endured the task, and it reminds us that we would endure. And the agenda at hand will not be taken lightly."

Sam agreed with a nod. "You're right, son. The death of one of us most of the time is the chance of life for many. Most of the history with the Navy SEALs, past and present, is our own, recorded among us."

The Kode

Sam shook their hands again and said, "It will be a pleasure working with you both."

As Frank continued his conversation with Mrs. Martinez, Sam was being introduced to Lieutenant Nathan Dash by Matthew Marx. As the three shook hands, Marx pointed out that the boat they were on was being controlled and operated by the Army Rangers, not the Navy boys, emphasizing with a laugh that his family were Army vets who served in World War One and World War Two.

Sam glanced towards the rear of the ship, then towards the front, and replied, "I believe a soldier in the Army could have enough talent to drive this little boat." Lieutenant Dash chuckled and said, "35 feet is the limit; after that, the white hats take over." With a smile, he reminded Sam, "We special forces enjoy a good shower on the massive Navy ships after a good fight in the jungle."

"I don't think I can top that," Sam commented. He reminded everyone that blood and sweat come from both branches. Dannie gave a thumbs up to both branches of service, then suggested slowing down on patronizing and getting into the control room to focus on the real business.

Inside the control room was a command center connected directly to Langley and the Situation Room at the White House. Mission Park Bench was now at full go. Even though the planning stages seemed too short for Sam's liking, he always knew and understood that when planning is rushed, the outcome can fall short. But when called upon to protect your country, time cannot always be a deciding factor.

As Matthew Marx approached one of the computer stations, he began to explain China's spy unit 61398. "Remember, Mr. Webb is a very special person we must get back," he emphasized. "The People's Liberation Army spy unit—they have been busy trying to hack and steal all the secrets from our major industry's databases. Stealing secrets of Americans and the one secret that they really wanted: was the secret of the War Peace. This is one secret they cannot have."

"Not only do they want The War Peace secret, but they wanted the scientists to create their own Star Wars program. Pres. Reagan knew what he was doing when he created the Star Wars program, ladies and gentlemen. We trust that you know what you're doing to retrieve this man from the hands of the enemy. And this is not a life or death situation; we want this man alive.

"At this time, I want to brief again some of the things I feel are very important from the last briefings and show you some of the pictures and faces of China spy unit which are wanted by the FBI. We believe that some of these men are on the ship with the container also. Remember the medallion that you carry around your neck, it separates you from the United States of America. This is not my choice, I apologize. I know it's hard for you to be a traitor and soldier patriot of the United States at the same time.

"It will be hard to forget your tears and your laughs in the past, in your efforts to keep America safe. But with all respect to you, this has to look like anti-Americans trying to start a conflict between the United States and China. Not only do you have to become the best of the best as a rescue and recovery soldier, but your acting abilities have to precede all of Hollywood's actor elites.

"I personally want to thank you for being willing to become a reproach for your country. I know there's money involved, but I believe Mr. Black that it is not money that you're interested in. Dannie, I believe you have a true heart for your country and will give your best picture-perfect computer skills. At this moment in time, it will have to go far beyond China's spy computer ring 61398."

As Mr. Marx spoke, Frank Morgan and Mrs. Martinez walked in. Sam's eyes were cast towards Frank's like an anchor being thrown from a ship. "Little late, aren't you, boy?" Sam spoke with a cocky grin.

"I was looking overboard at the beauty of the waters that are so blue. I have seen waters that are red with blood, and I decided the blues are much better in color," Frank replied.

Mr. Marx began to speak to Frank with an upset tone. "I

know your past, and I appreciate your bombing skills. I pray that your focus is going to be on your skills and not on your rewards. I promise you money can't buy your life; you only think it can."

Frank Morgan coughed and cleared his throat. "Mr. Marx, I appreciate your skills to control the air-conditioning in this center, but don't try to scold me for my past. But I tell you what you can do when this is over, you can shake my hand with a smile and put some money in the hand you shake and congratulate me on the future of the world and for helping to get Mr. Webb back. No matter what you like or dislike about me, I'm still the best at what I do."

At that moment, Sam and Frank seemed to connect their eyes in a deep stare. Sam reached again towards the scar on his face, and Dannie quickly spoke up, "All right, guys, this is it. No longer is a word on paper, no longer words on the computer. In fact, probably after this mission is over, other than the true fact of who we really are, headlines in the newspapers will read anti-Americans storm a ship from China to steal and to try to cause chaos. But we do not need chaos among ourselves; we have a call of duty to make the future peace for the United States and to make sure it is still going to be the greatest nation in the world. And remember, We Are the Secret KODE, that forever will be held secret. But in our hearts, we know we're going to be the ones that help to bring more peace and opportunity to our United States than in the rest of the world. Because the KODE Team is going to give their best, so man up."

Mr. Marx began clapping his hands as though he had been at a concert over Dannie's speech.

"Well said, young lady," Mr. Marx commended. "You amaze me. Those are words of power, and that's what we're here for, to make sure that we have the upper hand and power. Because if China gets our scientist, not just a pillar but a pillar of strength will be removed from our nation. We cannot let the building become weak. I want to thank you again for your service, and I believe we will see each one of you again. I will shake your hand."

As Marx turned toward Frank Morgan, he repeated, "I will shake your hand, each one of your hands. This is going to be a well-kept secret with no heroes that will be printed in the paper, only hoodlums with a heart for their country, and we will be the only people who know the truth."

"Enough of all the mumbo-jumbo," Mr. Marx began speaking from another part of the command center. "I want to show you some flashes from the ship where the container is; our man aboard the ship, Koon Hee, has sent them to us. You see the exits of the entrance doorway, you see how the containers are laid out, and you see the container which contains Mr. Webb. I want you to study them because we only have a few moments of time. This is the time that you must become a computer to record these enter and exit points photographically because you must get in and out with Mr.

Webb. Remember, this mission is a mission of mercy, a mission of must, the mission of peace, and mission of strength."

As the photographic pictures began to come in on the big screen in the room from what Koon Hee had sent from the container ship, all eyes were upon the ship that contained a scientist and the knowledge of the Star Wars program.

As Sam viewed the photos coming on the screen, Dannie walked over and nudged him, saying, "This will be a mission that will rewrite history, and one day when you hold your new grandchild, you will look back and remember how you did have the strength to endure, and the pride that you will feel will be for the safety of the future of your grandchildren."

Sam reached down and touched Dannie on the shoulder, saying, "Your mom will be all right." Dannie smiled, looking back at Sam. "It's good to have a real friend whom we can share griefs and sorrows and even our victories with."

"Victory is a big word, Dannie," Sam spoke in a low tone as he stared at Frank Morgan. Sam stuttered as he began to sing another song that his preacher granddad used to sing, "Victory, oh victory shall be mine, if I hold my peace and let the Lord fight my battles, victory oh victory shall be mine."

Dannie reached up, touching Sam on the lips softly, like a child's mother petting her child's lips to get the child to smile.

"Remember, Sam, what we're fighting for—peace, the War Peace. So I believe in a new Sam that takes comfort and guidance from the songs of his grandfather, and you are going to hold your peace, and Frank Morgan will only be a faded memory that will no longer haunt you."

As Dannie reached to take Sam by the hand, she noticed her hand touching the silver ring that came from the gambling casino. Sam reached down and removed Dannie's hand from the silver ring, treating it as though it was something special, and stared at it, turning it on his finger. Suddenly, beads of sweat began to pop out on his brow, and his face became red with anger from the killing of his dog Buck. Dannie quickly looked around, checking to see if anybody was watching Sam's actions. It was a perfect moment for most; all were occupied with the pictures on the big screen. Dannie took cold water from a bottle in the palm of her hand that was sitting next to her and splashed it on Sam's face. Sam reached his hand upon his forehead and slowly moved the water down his face, wiping it on his shirt. As Sam took his hand off his shirt, he looked at Dannie with a humble look. "Are you trying to baptize me to wake me up?"

As Dannie squeezed Sam's hand, she whispered towards the side of his face. "Maybe you should think twice, Sam, and should call yourself out of this rescue task force. Sam, your face was blood red, and your blood pressure was shooting straight up."

"I believe I will be all right, Dannie, as soon as the action starts. My brain will go into survival mode instead of hate mode. By the way, Dannie, my mother used to have these things; she called them Hot Flashes."

As Dannie looked towards the ground, shaking her head and trying not to laugh at Sam's comment, Matthew Marx announced a new screen with pictures of two men from the Chinese spy unit 61398, the top two hackers.

As Marx pointed towards the picture of the first man, he said, "He is known as a Big Guerrilla in the computer world; his real name is Sun Dong. In the next picture, you see his computer's name is Win Happy, his real name is Wang Kaillang. Having stolen hundreds of terabytes of data from at least 140 businesses and organizations over the last 6 ½ years. They are working to siphon trade secrets, nuclear deals, and all information confidential from emails from companies like US Steel, Westinghouse, Solar industries, and now Steelworker's international unions. Get a good look at these two pictures; if possible, we would like to have these two men alive, along with Mr. Webb. We have sent these two photos to Koon Hee on the ship. As of now, he has not responded back, so we do not know if these men are still on the ship or if they have gotten off. They are on the FBI's most wanted list."

"Remember, we are working in the space of the darkness;

the only light that you will see is a light of the ship that will be on fire as a decoy, which will be off at a distance blocking the entrance and exit in the harbor. This boat will be out in the harbor as though we are fishing. We will be about one mile from the decoy ship. The SEAL team and the KODE Team will be on a small fishing boat that will be about one-quarter of a mile from the Chinese ship. The KODE Team will leave the small fishing boat on a special rubber raft that will make its way to the shipping container. There will be falsified documents left on this rubber raft that would indicate traitors to the United States and some false movement that this group is planning and going to do. It will be what information that will be given to all news agencies. The SEAL team will be a pickup unit only; the rubber raft is to be left behind."

As the lights got brighter in the information room, Matthew Marx asked if there were any questions. "I know that I'm putting a lot on the table, but this is one of those times when the cook has no choice. The Chinese have made their bed; now they are going to have to sleep in it. And the KODE Team is going to sneak into their bedroom, without waking them up, and take their prize possession, just like they entered into our computer systems and hacked them to try to steal the viable information that makes our nation great."

Sam spoke up, "I have a question. When the decoy ship is on fire to block the entrance into the harbor, what is going to keep other smaller ships from coming into the harbor around the decoy ship?"

"Good question," Marx replied. "Hold that question just for a moment, Mr. Black. I will give you an answer."

Matthew Marx walked over to the side and made a call. As he was speaking with someone from Langley, Sam noticed Frank Morgan taking small canisters out of a backpack that seemed to be odd in shape. He walked over and said, "Are you taking some rations along with us in case you get hungry?"

Frank turned to hold one of the canisters in his hand. "These are my own little special decoys, Sam, that I'm going to use. As we get on that ship, I want to make sure we get off that ship safely. You never know when you need a distraction to make someone look the other way."

For the first time, Sam seemed to smile back at Frank Morgan. He reached his hand towards Frank in a gesture to shake his hand. Frank took the bomb from his right hand and placed it in his left hand, then put his right hand in Sam's. And just for a moment, they stared at each other with a smile. "I believe we will get the job done," said Sam.

Frank didn't speak, but he nodded his head yes, as Sam walked towards Matthew Marx to have his question answered. Matthew turned toward Sam and said, "The Coast Guard has already been notified, and they will be used to block any other ship, small or large, from entering the harbor. The fuel tanker will be placed to block the incoming traffic flow from the interstates into the harbor, and the decoy will go off first."

Marx raised his hands and said, "I have one more screen to show you from Langley. This will be the entrance for the KODE Team and the place where they will leave the rubber raft. If you notice on the screen, 200 feet from the rear of the Chinese ship where the anchor is, you will see an entrance into a place that has steps leading up. This comes from some cable units that help operate lights in the harbor. This is being sent from Koon Hee. This ship will still be loading containers, Koon Hee will cause a distraction with one of the containers as it is being lifted up. This will be your ticket to enter the ship. He has the equipment with him to hear and to speak to the team, so everything will be synchronized with perfect timing."

"Now, do we have any more questions, or is it time to go fishing for the big fish?" Marx asked.

Lieutenant Dash responded, "It's time to pull up anchors, Park Bench is ready to go fishing. You have been given coordination from the satellite to the very place we want to be setting. You're in command."

As the boat was being prepared to go out into the harbor, the two Navy SEALs that were going to be working with the KODE Team walked over to speak to Sam Black. "We want to shake your hand again, Mr. Black, before we depart the boat. We're going on the other small boat and will meet you there. The recovery boat and everything will be ready. Pickup is going to be our pleasure when this mission is over. Who's to know, you may teach us a few things that we haven't learned in the past?"

Sam smiled and shook their hands. "An old dog cannot be taught new tricks. So, if you learned anything from this, enjoy living. Life is short, and it passes quickly."

As the two Navy SEALs turned and left the boat, Dannie walked over and touched Sam on the shoulder. "I think I am going to have to take a few bottles of ice-cold water with us, Sam. I saw how you shook the hand of Frank Morgan, and I believe the baptism of that water has changed your way of thinking."

"There is one thing that I have learned, Blondie," Sam replied, "enemies that are fighting enemies sometimes turn on each other, and they both lose the war. I wish that was the case, Sam, but the truth is, I think the government changed all our ways of thinking. Why else would we be taking this assignment? The understanding between you and me, we know why Frank Morgan is taking this assignment. He's in debt to a bunch of gambling mobsters and is trying to save his own neck."

"Yeah," said Sam, "and I'm still wondering why Miss Martinez was coming out of Frank's motel room. I have a hunch that she is up to something, which we may not be aware of."

Dannie looked a little puzzled at Sam's remarks about Miss Martinez. "What do you mean, Sam? You suggest she is working with the mob, to get him?"

"I'm not sure, Dannie," Sam replied, "she knows something that we don't know, and I think she knows something that Frank Morgan doesn't know. Maybe we will find out on this tour of duty, or perhaps afterward if we read about Frank Morgan's obituary in the news."

"The question that I have, Dannie, is this," Sam continued, "why is she even on this mission at all if she works for the DEA and not the CIA? Who does she know that gives her the right to be in this control center?"

"Can I make a suggestion?" Dannie said. "Maybe some of the DEA agents also work with the CIA, trying to get the kingpin's drug lords which are in Mexico, Central, and South America? Remember, she said they killed her parents; maybe she has a crow to pick with them, except she has also a scarred heart."

"I know all about having the scar, Dannie," Sam replied, "it seems like the scar never goes away. I have another hunch, Blondie, that maybe the CIA and DEA have eyes on Frank Morgan, since that bombing in Maryland. No one has ever been charged with the deaths of those drug lords. Well, one of the reasons that no one has been charged, Frank knows how to make bombs that leave no history, but only the history that he wants to show. That's the reason why he is one of the best, and not only one of the best, but that is the reason I believe Ms. Martinez has picked up his trail. I think the government has plans for Frank after this mission. It's not in their best interest to have a bomb maker running around Gambling, making deals with Colombian and Mexican mob thugs and drug lords."

"So just to let you know, Blondie," Sam added, "that little trip we made inside Frank's motel room probably has been recorded with very good US surveillance equipment."

"That is a shame, Sam," Dannie replied, "I don't even think that I had my hair fixed or makeup on yet. If you are going to be on the big screen, you should always look your best." Dannie laughed.

"Well, it's like this, Dannie," Sam said, "when I saw that black government vehicle coming down that dirt road, I knew and have always known that if they want you, they can always find you."

"I have another thought, Sam," Dannie said, "maybe after this mission is over, they will pay us for another mission, since reportedly we are part of a militant group, and in the end, we may have a good retirement."

"Blondie, you're forgetting one thing," Sam replied, "I'm already in retirement. But I never thought about the fact that I could have a little change to leave my grandkids something. By the way, that gives me another idea, Blondie, come with me just for a moment."

The Kode

Sam walked over and began to talk to Matthew Marx, "I want you to do me a favor, Mr. Marx."

"Sure; what can I do for you, Sam?" Marx asked.

"There's something I would like to happen if I don't return from this mission," Sam said.

"You got my word, Sam," Marx replied, "but I'm in grave doubt that will happen. Because I don't think that will be up to me. I really believe she will receive that from your own hand. You see, Sam, you weren't chosen because you are dispensable. They chose you because they knew that you were the best at what you do."

"Will that be the case, Mr. Marx?" Sam questioned, "how come I have to wear this medallion around my neck that says I'm not part of the United States but I'm a traitor?"

"Remember, Sam," Marx explained, "from my Jewish teachings on my mother's side, they always had a scapegoat. So, you see, in essence, you and the KODE Team are the scapegoats. The priest is the government of the United States, which has announced upon you, symbolically, bearing the sins of the Chinese who stole our scientists. And by the strength of the KODE Team, you will carry them back into the wilderness, and the Star Wars program will still be in the hands of the United States. Someone who is willing to bear the blame of others is usually always the stronger person. Like I said a few months ago, I have this feeling everything will be all right."

As Koon Hee followed the man, observing his movements, he slowly took out of his bag of arsenals a paralyzing sleep formula designed by the CIA, known as Dead Sleep. It was a chemical that would paralyze and keep a person from any movement, inducing a deep sleep mode for up to 24 hours. Administered like a diabetes pen, the reaction would occur within seconds.

As Sun Dong made his way through the dining area into the restroom area, reaching for the door, Koon Hee quickly slipped up and injected the Dead Sleep Formula. He then dragged the man into a closet where they kept cleaning supplies, covering him up with used, dirty tablecloths, and quickly exited the closet. He notified Langley, stating one down and one to go, sending them a photograph of the man in the closet. Koon Hee's job working in the cleanup position and in the kitchen area had now paid off.

As he moved back toward the container that held the scientist, Mr. Webb, he took out a listening device and pushed it against the container to ensure Mr. Webb was still alive. The device showed Mr. Webb's breathing and also the infrared outline of his body. All this information was sent to Langley for an update. Koon Hee moved through the ship, trying to find the last man known in the computer world as "Win Happy", Wang Kaillang. He knew if he could complete this task, it would be much easier for the KODE Team to retrieve Mr. Webb and remove him from the ship to safety. But he knew time was not on his side.

The Kode

Back on the command center ship Park Bench, slowly moving down the waters toward the destination, Frank Morgan was going over his list of explosive devices, while Dannie and Sam stood at the rear of the ship, standing next to the railing, watching the waves from the engine's propeller.

Dannie broke the silence, speaking to Sam about the call she had received from Polly. "Sam, you know I asked Polly to go and check on my mother. Polly is a good, strong leaning post, and my mother needs someone at this time."

"I've been keeping up with it on the computer from the local news agencies," Dannie continued, "about the skeleton bones they found down by the railroad tracks. I truly believed it could be the body that my mother disposed of. I'm just wondering if she would talk to Polly about the ordeal to get the weight off of her shoulders."

"Listen, Dannie," Sam responded, "Polly knows how to get the best out of a person, especially to make them feel better about themselves. And to be honest with you, I don't think the truth will ever come out. What is hidden in the sands of that grave will remain a mystery."

"But Sam, what if there's some kind of ID that was left on him, she forgot to remove?" Dannie asked.

"Listen, Blondie, even if that's the case, it doesn't come back to your mother," Sam reassured her. "A few people that are still alive knew the lifestyle that your dad lived. And just maybe it is not the bones from the body she buried; remember the old plantation goes way back to the Civil War... In slave plantations, maybe the bones of a slave, or the bones of the owner's family, could be the bones of anyone."

"Yeah, I guess you're right, Sam," Dannie conceded.

"I think what the government should invent is a medical prescription that lets you forget. Just certain things you want to forget about your past," Dannie suggested.

Sam laughed and said, "It would be worth enough money to pay off the national debt. They do have some CIA tactics called brainwashing, except really a brain doesn't get clean."

"There is so much undercutting from other governments including Russia, trying to cause racial tension in our country that even if we get Mr. Webb back we may be like Rome and deteriorate and be destroyed from within," Sam remarked.

"There is a great saying among constitutional people of the United States," Sam continued, "if the left political group gets control they'll have nothing left, and all of our rights will be taken away. You get it; those on the right have rights, those on the left have nothing left. Foreign governments are not working with the right hand, which shakes the other right hand. The old saying 'let us shake on it,' the left hand was never used. The right handshake was always used in commitment and agreement; it was almost like a written contract in today's world."

"No, you see, Blondie, they're working with the left trying to cause chaos from within," Sam explained. "The old communist regime in Russia made a statement many times, 'we will never have to fire shots.' It's a proven fact they intervened in many of the black civil rights marches in the sixties, and some even believe that Dr. Martin Luther King was killed by Russian operatives. So, you see, Dannie, the enemy always targets good people who are pillars that help hold up the nation or demand rights that have been given to them by the Constitution of the United States."

"So true, political rights will always demand rights for the people," Dannie agreed.

"Wow, Sam, maybe you should have been a history teacher," Dannie remarked.

"Well, Blondie, the thing about history is, it's always that of the past," Sam replied. "Now that I'm going to be a grandfather, I think I'm going to look towards the future. Maybe I should be a future teacher," he laughed at his own words.

"Well, Sam, there is one thing for sure," Dannie said, "what happens in our future will be in somebody's history book in the future."

As Dannie and Sam continued their conversation, an equipment specialist with the CIA emerged, asking them to come inside to see some new advanced military equipment they would be using. Sam looked at Dannie, saying, "This is probably going to be very interesting because I'm sure that technology has surpassed all that we have used in a mission in the past."

As he opened one of the cases marked "Special Ops EQ," the specialist turned to Sam and apologized for not introducing himself. Extending his hand, he said, "I am Zack Mayfield."

"How long have you been working with the government, Mr. Mayfield?" Sam asked.

"I've been working for them for about two years. Before that, I was in Silicon Valley for about 10 years. I came up with some gaming ideas for all the different game boxes that teenagers are playing. In the meantime, I decided to modify this to a greater extent, so it can be used to strengthen our military and surveillance," Zack explained.

"Well, Zack, it's men like you that make our job a lot easier. I appreciate your work and your time for the country," Sam commended him with a thumbs up.

"It just so happens that the country has been really good to me. My family wasn't wealthy, but they were hard workers. My dad was a real patriot; he always had a flagpole in his yard with the US flag flying. He was unable to even finish school and went to the eighth grade. But he grounded in us the worth of a good education, and with that, I got a scholarship in computer science," Zack shared.

"Well, your family should be proud of you, son. That is a good testament to your rearing. Now, you make me more anxious to see some of this equipment you invented," Sam said.

"Here are special glasses that you are going to be wearing. I know they look dark, but they are going to cause the light of the day to shine at midnight. Put them on, and I'll give you a quick show of their ability and what they're capable of doing," Zack instructed.

As Dannie and Sam put the glasses on, Zack began to walk them through the steps. "Push the button that's on the left temple area, and you will see where you will be working. Now, both of you explain to me what you see at this moment," Zack directed.

"I'm above a ship looking down on containers," Dannie described.

"I am seeing the same," Sam confirmed.

Zack began to explain, "What you see at this time are two drones flying above the container ship. If you push the button a second time on the left side, it will magnify the view. Each time you push that button, you're getting closer to the subject. Now push the button on the right side while I darken these lights. Explain to me what you see now."

"That's incredible!" Sam exclaimed. "It's like looking inside the ship with LED lights on. You did quite well, son. When I get old, I may have to have these glasses."

Dannie laughed and said, "What do you mean 'when you get old,' Sam? You're already old!"

Sam chuckled and retorted, "Well, I guess you've got a point there, Dannie."

Dannie's curiosity piqued, and she asked, "What else can these glasses do? I'm very interested."

Zack handed them two small earphones with a small cable on each. "You'll find on the right side of the arm above the ear is a place to plug your earphone. Not only can you hear everything that's going down in the command center, but we also will be watching from the sky with those drones, and you can communicate with each other and with us," he explained.

Sam, intrigued, asked, "What capabilities do those drones have?" as he examined the delicate mechanisms.

"Well, Sam, these little flying machines that you're looking at can speak Spanish, English, Portuguese, Russian, and other languages spoken around the world. This is one of their great features, especially in active battle zones," Zack elaborated.

"So, let me get this straight," Sam replied. "While in the battle zone, you're going to be teaching us new languages?"

Sam turned to Dannie with a smile and remarked, "Maybe this thing can teach us Spanish so we can understand Frank Morgan's new girlfriend, Mrs. Martinez. You never know when she is going to be speaking in her native language, and we would learn to love her conversations, in fact, to whom her conversations are with."

As Sam turned back, it seemed that Zack's look was a blank face in an empty closet. Dannie laughed and said to Zack, "Don't pay any attention to Sam; he still speaks pig Latin."

Zack began to laugh and said, "Now you really confuse me."

Dannie explained, "Let me explain exactly what pig Latin really is. It's a language that you only learn when you live in the big Appalachian Mountains. Every family has their own pig Latin language, and that way, when your neighbors come over, if you want to speak something that you don't want them to understand, you speak pig Latin. All neighbors have it, and know that when you begin to speak pig Latin, those secrets are being spoken behind your back. But it doesn't bother you because your family does the same thing. It's a mountain tradition and a well-kept secret."

With his mouth slightly open, Zack looked really confused. Sam walked over, put his hand on Zack's shoulder, and began to laugh at what Dannie had just said.

"You see, Zack, what you just heard was a blonde comment that makes no sense. That will be spoken on a golf course one of these days as a blonde joke," Sam explained between laughs.

Dannie walked over and touched Sam on the side, saying, "I speak the truth," before bursting into laughter. She then walked in front of Sam, winked, and said, "Sam, speak to this young man some Pig Latin."

Sam turned toward Zack and began to speak some Navajo that he had learned from a friend in the military years before. Zack replied, "Sorry guys, I can't fall for that blonde joke because I studied the language that our military used in World War II to speak code, which the Japanese could not decode or understand their communications, and it was the Navajo language. But good try."

Sam twisted his head sideways with a humming sound and said, "This young man is smart."

Zack smiled at Sam and said, "Actually, I graduated from high school when I was 12 years old, and they didn't use the word 'smart.' They actually said I might be a genius." Then he laughed and slightly pushed Sam, who now had a confused look with an open mouth. Dannie said, "Sam, I don't think that was a blonde joke. I think he's speaking the truth."

The Kode

"So, let's get down to the business of why your machine now speaks languages," Sam suggested to Zack.

Zack then spoke, "Mr. Black, I came up with this idea by watching some of the old movies that were based on military wars where the enemy spoke different languages. In a lot of those scenes in the movies, you can actually see military men hiding when they heard voices speaking in different languages from their own. It seemed that it would identify their enemies who were in proximity to where they were. So, I can actually do that with these drones. If we need a decoy or to confuse someone to have them move from one place to the other, this drone can speak their language with such clarity that they'll think it's their mother telling them to come to dinner, or their boss, or their commander. But in reality, it will be a drone. Always remember in those movies, the soldier would duck and hide or hush his fellow soldier to be quiet when a language was spoken that wasn't theirs but was from the enemy. So, I came up with this idea. Instead of our enemies hiding when we need to see them, we would just speak to their heart's content and draw them out in the open. We have even taken voice recordings from some that we know will be on the ship and have instituted them into the drone, as though it will be them speaking when we need a detour, exit, or decoy."

"Well, now I know where all the Hollywood directors come from Silicon Valley because most of the war movies that are made now portray robotic figures or robotic weapons," replied Sam. "I just hope they are as sensitive as the robot was on the show 'Lost in Space' to the young boy named Will Robinson."

Now it seems like Dannie and Zack were lost for words. Sam quickly reminded them it was before their time. Dannie began to laugh at Sam, pointing down to the ground, "I now know one thing: you are as old as mud."

Zack shook his head, reached into his box, and took out little black clips. Sam was quick to make a remark, "Do we have to wear shirts and ties?"

Zack began to explain what the black clips could be used for. "These are the newest in innovation; they are like the old stun grenades. Let me explain to you how they work. We have a right-hand and left-hand mash vest that is also lightweight and bulletproof, made from material used in NASA spacecraft. If you are right-handed, you will clip 10 of these clips to your vest toward the left side. The same if you're left-handed, you will clip 10 of these clips to the right side of the vest. When these are clipped to the vest, they are activated. When you need one and unclip it from the vest, the mechanism is censored by the heat from your hand, even if you wear gloves, and the quick commotion you throw it activates the explosion, which will stop a bull in its tracks. The secret of these clips is a small piece of atomic material knowledge that has been designed to make the equipment for the soldier as light as possible so that he can move quickly and still have the power to overcome the enemy. So, what you carry is a little piece of the power that was used in the Japanese surrender, to let the enemy know that he doesn't have the ability to win. When you see that all hope is gone, it's much easier for them to surrender without a fight, and that will save the lives of our soldiers.

"There is a pocket in the vest, both right and left, toward the bottom, and in those pockets, you will find six little black cherries, not wrapped with chocolate. These are magnetic because you're going to be working in an area with a lot of metal from the containers of the ship, and the way the ship is built, they will stick to anything. When you stick this cherry to a piece of metal, you will squeeze the two sides, and you will see a small light blinking. You have seven seconds before the explosion. It will help you remove door locks, and they are very light and very powerful.

"And by the way, this is really like when they dropped the bombs in Japan because these weapons will be the first time used in a classified operation. But I want to assure you that I have tried these in many experiments, and they have worked every time, 100% perfection."

Sam began to smile at the young man and said, "Usually, I would doubt things like this in my past, but because of your graduation at 12 years old, I'm all in. You have convinced me that the old school is changed to the new generation of warfare." Sam held up the metal pyramid medallion and said, "One thing for sure, I hope the cherry doesn't get stuck to this.

"Mr. Black, this is not only an operation to get back the scientists who have created the marvel of the Star Wars protection program, but the new innovation that you're going to be wearing is going to make our military a whole lot safer and the enemy a whole lot softer.

"Also, the plugs that you're wearing in your ear to hear and get responses from us will take away the high noise of any blast that is used from the stun grenades and the cherry bombs."

Just for curiosity, Zack," Sam asked, "what kind of special bombs have you given our friend Frank Morgan? Because I have dealt with him in the past, and he is one of the best bomb makers there is."

"Well, to be honest with you, Mr. Black, he is carrying a few items that we have thought he suggested that he would rather use what he is used to, and because of the history of his past, we decided that perhaps he's right. Sometimes in this line of work, the old works well and does bring out the best option."

As the fishing boat came to a stop, it was located in "Park Bench" mode. The SEAL team was getting the transport rubber raft ready to move the KODE team toward the Chinese ship. The SEAL team had been informed that as soon as they got the KODE team to the rendezvous point, the decoy ship would explode. While the KODE team was moving in toward the shipping container, the extra rubber raft and material that would be left behind would be placed there by the SEAL team. The coordination and exact timing had to be perfect because when the explosion happen, every eye from the Chinese ship would be towards the explosion, and that would give the KODE team a small space of time to enter the ship.

Each of the KODE team would be wearing a special black suit designed with fireproof material. Koon Hee had already placed a special climbing cable at the tail end of the ship off of the anchor chain. This cable was made with two handheld pieces and two feet connecter pegs for each member of the KODE team as they moved up the cable. This was a new invention that they had nicknamed "spider cable." Each handheld piece was powered controlled with a special battery system also designed by NASA.

Dannie made a remark to Zack, "Maybe we should call this a Spider Women cable team, then we can catch the evil perpetrators in the web and swoop down and wrap them up?" As Dannie continued to talk, she said, "I could be called THE SPIDER WOMEN, you see boys, I always was a fan of the Spiderman comics. But being a female and a mastermind on the Web, I was always upset. Why wasn't there a spider woman? Never a spider woman? They had a superwoman, they had a batgirl and wonder women; well, I think it's time to change that and I will be called the spider woman of the Web." She paused, "You're right, Dannie," Zack replied, "because most of the time we leave out the site part; so, Dannie, you will be on-site at the Chinese container ship, and there you can create your web, and we will nickname you the spider woman. And I think that would fit you better than the black widow, which was going to be your codename that you would hear in your earpiece because you look too young and beautiful to have been married and lost your husband."

Dannie replied to Zack, "Watch yourself; you may find yourself in the web, and Dannie the black widow spider woman putting a whipping on you." Sam's codename would be Blackbird, and Frank Morgan's codename would be Blackout. Koon Hee's codename would be Blackjack. "As you can see, Sam, we decided to take your last name and make this band of misfits named after you," Dannie explained. "Just leave my codename Black Widow, and I will feel like I'm part of the family."

Sam began to chuckle as he said, "So the great KODE Team becomes THE BLACK FAMILY, which is anti-American, antigovernment, working in guerrilla warfare to tear down nations when actually we are to be trying to lift up the greatest nation in the world. United States of America, this may be hard to swallow, sometimes you gotta go with the flow, and I think the water in the rivers are over the banks at this time."

Frank Morgan, standing close, listening to the conversation and thinking about the handshake that Sam offered, decided to put in his two cents. "Sam, remember this, if you're in the black, you are ahead of the game. People that are in the red are behind, so this may be a good thing. Trust me, I know what it is to be in the red," Frank gestured, "and it can cause headaches, lack of sleep, and that's not fun."

Sam began to twist the ring on his finger again, and Dannie stepped between the two and said, "Well, it's time to get this show on the road," as she nudged Sam to come over just for a moment to look at the equipment that had been laid out, and for certain, everything was in black, even the garments that were wearing.

As everything was moving in full swing, Koon Hee was slipping through the container's ship, looking for the last Chinese computer hacker to take out his target and mark the place of removal. He had been given the location of where he thought the target was by one of the manual labor helpers on the container ship.

As Koon Hee slipped through the food storage area, he spotted his target working with three different laptop computers. Swiftly, Koon Hee took out a ball bearing from his pocket, flipping it in front of his target to catch his attention. Moving quickly, he inserted a knockout medicine into target number two's system.

Next, Koon Hee swiftly gathered boxes of food and

constructed a small crawlspace like a porch or small tomb. Placing the Chinese hacker inside and covering him with the boxes, he then extracted a special design transfer unit from his pocket, provided by the CIA. This unit was tasked with removing all information from the three computers and transferring it to a spy satellite, which would then relay the data back to Langley.

As Matthew Marx approached the KODE Team, he provided them with the updated information from Koon Hee: he had successfully incapacitated the two Chinese computer hackers and placed them in sleep mode, locating them on the ship to be picked up later by the FBI surveillance team, under the guise of searching for the M.A.G. attackers.

With a gracious smile-like gesture, Matthew Marx expressed gratitude to the KODE Team, acknowledging the risk they were undertaking. Saluting them, he emphasized the importance of their mission and the potential consequences they faced, including being labeled as traitors if caught. Moved by the gesture, Sam reflected on his grandfather's wisdom, feeling compelled to turn to prayer for guidance and a positive outcome.

Overhearing Sam's words about prayer, a SEAL team member offered to say a prayer over the team, citing the importance of seeking divine intervention in such critical moments. The team, including Frank Morgan, accepted the offer with gratitude, acknowledging the need for spiritual support. The SEAL member prayed for guidance, strength, and a favorable outcome in Jesus' name, with Sam requesting an additional prayer for Koon Hee's safety.

As the SEAL team leader informed them of their imminent departure from the ship in 30 minutes, he instructed them to suit up in their outfits and equipment. The countdown began for their move towards the Park Bench site.

As Sam walked Dannie towards her dressing area, he was suddenly overcome by a deep thought about the killing of his dog, his fingers tracing the ring on his finger. His shaking and labored breathing caught Dannie's attention, and she quickly led him into her dressing area, guiding him to sit on the stool. Kneeling beside him, she held him close, whispering words of reassurance in his ear.

"Your Sam Black, you're strong, and it's going to be all right, Sam, because I am with you," Dannie murmured softly. "We have one mission to do, Sam. We can get it done, and then you can find yourself resting back in that cabin in the Appalachian Mountains. Remember your daughter, and that young child that needs a grandfather. Be strong now for your daughter. You're strong, Sam, you can overcome this. I want you to breathe deep. Come on, Sam, you can do it. Breathe deep."

Dannie felt Sam's hand tightening on her arm as he began to

take in deep breaths, the shaking in his body gradually subsiding. After several minutes, Sam leaned forward off the stool, taking one final deep breath before slowly exhaling. As he looked around and then stared at Dannie, he asked, "Did anybody see this?"

Dannie assured him that they were alone in her dressing room, and no one had witnessed his episode. She noticed the ring on Sam's finger and gently requested, "Sam, I want you to do me a favor. You are my friend. May I have that ring until all of this is over? I will wear it on the chain with the triangle medallion, and I promise I will give it back to you when this mission is over."

As Sam reached towards the ring, Dannie grabbed his hand, speaking softly. "Sam, let me take the ring off," she said. Sam shook his head and winked. "Yes, go ahead."

As Dannie turned the ring off of Sam's finger, she turned her back and placed the ring on the necklace that had the triangle M.A.G. sign. She then placed it back on her neck and tucked the medallion inside her shirt, before turning back toward Sam.

As Sam eased off the stool to leave the dressing room, Dannie stopped him. "No, Sam, you stay here in this dressing room. I will go to another one, and if anyone says anything, I will tell them that we were speaking about your daughter and your new grandson."

As Dannie opened the door and turned towards another dressing area, she saw Frank Morgan. He was talking with one of the Navy SEALS outside his dressing room. Quickly to speak first, Dannie said, "Hey, Frank, Sam has been telling me about his new grandchild. We just talked about his daughter having her first baby, and after this mission is over, he is going to get to hold him again and start teaching him how to be a survivor."

Morgan shrugged his shoulders as he responded, "Sam does not talk much to me, and when he does, he is always irritable. But I can understand, and I hope someday he will understand. Sometimes everything does not go as planned. This is one time I am hoping for all of us, that it will go as planned. Plans sometimes have a rough way of ending, even when you're building a skyscraper. Sometimes in the middle height, your beam is cut too short... you have time to cut another beam. We have a tall order to be filled and no time to come up short."

As Dannie entered the dressing area, Sam emerged from the room fully suited up in OPS gear. He reached his hand out to Frank and said, "For our country and my family." Frank put his hand in Sam's, speaking in a low tone, "For our country, family, and your new grandson." With those words, Sam smiled and patted him on the shoulder.

As Dannie came from the room, she was surprised to see them talking and a smile on Sam's face. With the SEAL Team ready, they all gave their salute to each other again and boarded the vessel for the drop down.

As the SEAL TEAM moved toward the container ship to drop off THE KODE, Koon Hee awaited them at the front anchor - copy. As the signal came in from "PARK BENCH," all Sam had to do was give them a thumbs up. The drone, flying above, had everyone in sight; even when they went out of sight of the drone, the specially built camera system in their Special OPS Equipment provided clear visibility, voice, sound, photo, and light as clear as the noonday sun.

The decoy ship received a signal from "PARK BENCH," and the Navy SEALS that dropped off the KODE Team pulled the trigger on the explosives loaded on the ship Codename, the Pearl Harbor. As the explosives ignited, the rumble shook most of all of the shipping container industries at the docks. Emergency messages were sent out to all in the docking harbor: no ships were allowed to move or be loaded. The intelligence agency had them pre-planned, sending out high alert signs to all law enforcement and emergency responders. Even the Coast Guard was not aware of Pearl Harbor. The highest secrets about the mission were in play, and now came the task of pulling off the mission-coded Park Bench. The Coast Guard was now placed in command to stop and control all shipping in the harbor.

The Frog SEAL TEAM had now moved into place for the pickup and rescue of Mr. Webb and the KODE Team. The Star Wars Program clock was now ticking; each tick could cost thousands of

American lives in the future. China had become the number one threat to United States security. They had upped their spending on all their military, including supersonic missiles. But their goal was to steal away the Reagan program of the Star Wars technology. At this moment in time, they had the Einstein of the most powerful military weapon, one that far exceeded all nuclear missiles. This program could destroy any missile at the moment of its release, from whatever location or country, bringing judgment upon the nation that tried to launch any nuclear warhead missiles. It had this ability with the laser power technology from outer space. News agencies were now covering the ship Pearl Harbor. Some of the agencies trying to get closer to the ship by smaller boats were stopped by the Coast Guard. The Park Bench plan was to do everything in the dark, and it would be that way with all this planning, even though they had a short time to put this mission together. Some Navy SEALS had already been placed on a Coast Guard vessel to move the burning ship out of the harbor and sink it in the ocean, to be used as a man-made reef. All fuels and oils had been removed beforehand, and a black liquid-looking substance, created to look like an oil spill but with no environmental effect, was now released. Special effect cameras were put in place to show a supposed cleanup; also, several Navy SEALS dressed like regular ship operators were filming for a news release, to make every part of the operation look real.

Koon Hee had given a special update on the container. The

one that contained Mr. Webb. The KODE Team would have to go in the top water side of the container, with only three feet of space to work in, and bring him out. The place where the liquid metal solvent would be positioned to cut the hole, and would remain on the vessel for the pickup and delivery had to be executed without any missed cues. It seemed that this mission had no room for any mistakes. If so, the M.A.G. would be brought out, and the information that had been sent to the news agency for the past days would be executed. A new plan to stop China would have to go into effect, one that the United States didn't want to happen. If any way possible, they had to show strength in the undercover and recovery work to the Chinese Communist Party and all the leaders.

The high-tech lift cables had been dropped by Koon Hee, made ready for the three others in the KODE Team to come aboard. The special OPS cables had been designed by the government to move special agents or soldiers up or down in vertical locations without any noise. All the agents would have to do would be to place one shoe or boot in the foot strap and with an individual remote at the hand on each strap, go up or down. Three members of the KODE Team were waiting with the Four Navy SEALS in the OPS vessel for the go aboard command. With the command given from PARK BENCH and with the cable strap in hand, Sam looked at Dannie with an upward motion of his head and nodded for her to go first.

With a five-second lead, Sam nodded at Frank Morgan to go

up. Before he began to ascend, Frank turned toward Sam with an apologetic look, mouthing "sorry for my mistake." Sam simply nodded his head upward, signaling that it was time to move. With only about five seconds between each of them, Sam started up behind Frank Morgan, reflecting on the finger that used to carry the ring Dannie took. He remembered a saying from his grandfather: "It's better to be up than down." His grandfather often preached that most people never have to fight to get beat up; they beat themselves down with void words of anger and resentment. It seemed as though Sam could hear his voice clearly, as when he was young. As he looked back up, he said to himself, "Sam, you must make the change." Despite all the battles and hellish wars, he had been through, this had been the worst battle of his life.

As Sam reached the top of the ship, Frank was waiting with an outstretched hand to pull him up on top of the shipping container. As Sam put his hand in Frank's, he stared into Frank's eyes and, for the second time since the scar, he smiled and nodded his head. Koon Hee was keeping his eyes on the tail end of the ship with his back turned, as Sam asked, "Where is my son?" All of the KODE Team could hear each member on their OPS ear equipment, even the smallest whisper. Koon Hee turned to Sam with a smile as bright as a rainbow, giving him a big hug. "It's good to be working with you again," said Koon Hee, "but much better just to see you."

Koon Hee had laid out all the directions, container locations, and exits. PARK BENCH could hear and speak into the ears of the KODE Team and watch all movement from the drone. But just in case of a communicational malfunction, he had all the major points placed on the paper that could be read through the visible reality mask they were wearing. Each member of the team viewed the paper, knowing that every exit and place of entry had to be memorized by the marker that Koon Hee had placed at each one, only readable and visible through their glasses. From the container that held Mr. Webb to the point of pickup was crucial. Each place that Koon Hee thought there might be Chinese agents' presence or a place they may show up, he had it pointed out. All members of the KODE Team knew the importance of this mission, or it seemed that maybe only Frank Morgan saw it as a money blessing for his gambling habits.

As Sam felt the triangular M.A.G. medallion next to his chest, he wondered why he would take such a mission. Then he remembered his daughter and grandson. All the mistakes of the government that might have been made dealing with China rested on the shoulders of the four ex-CIA KODE Team members, who could help free the world and the United States from communist dictatorship or even annihilation. Or they could become the front page of each newspaper and the headlines of every major news network: "Militants Against Government" Has Been Captured or Killed. But now was not the time to ponder or regret, because there was another old saying from the Appalachia Mountains: "You Have Come Too Far to Look Back."

As they reviewed all documents from Koon Hee, they began the move in pairs of two. Park Bench had chosen Sam and Frank to work together. Each was given an experimental laser weapon designed by Mr. Webb, that when used against someone, would paralyze them; they would have no movement or even speech that would last for one hour plus. It had never been used in law enforcement and had just finished testing through government security sources. The only blood that might be shed would be that of the KODE Team, because the Chinese agents on the ship most certainly had weapons of blood. Frank Morgan was also carrying bomb material in the form of small golf balls and marbles, which could cause distractions and move objects to make exits where there were none. Dannie was given computer access to jam all voice communications on the ship between the Chinese agents and even change her voice to Mandarin to throw them off track when needed. Koon Hee could already speak Mandarin, and he was ready for the freedom of Mr. Webb because he still had family bound in China under the CCP, and he was all about freedom, not just for Americans but for all. Hopefully, the ship PEARL HARBOR ablaze not far from the Chinese container vessel would keep most of the eyes looking toward "The Decoy." They had time explosions going off to move attention toward the blast; quickness and perfection sometimes didn't work together, but on this mission, time would tell.

As Sam and Frank moved down the harbor side of the ship, they followed Koon Hee's instructions relayed through Park Bench. They were informed that "The War Peace" was in a blue container eight high at the top of all containers and located in row seven from the front of the ship. The equipment needed was left by Koon Hee on top of the blue container, along with the Signal Marker indicating where the entrance hole had to be made. Koon Hee would be going up on the water side of the ship, heading to the rear of the vessel and watching those distracted by Pearl Harbor.

Sam and Frank were given the okay to go on the Quay Crane on the dockside. The crane arm was located just above where Mr. Webb was kept in the container, allowing for only about a 3-foot drop. Dannie would be on the bottom deck, moving by the eye in the sky from the drone. Most of the ship's crew members were toward the back of the vessel, watching the explosions on Pearl Harbor. The decoy seemed to be working, along with all the police helicopters in the area of the decoy. Dannie had her computer listening device on, able to translate voices in Chinese to English or vice versa. Koon Hee was watching the crowd from the containers on the tail end of the ship.

As Sam and Frank made their way up the crane side to the top, they had to crawl across to avoid being seen on the crane arm.

It would take more time, and hopefully, they had enough to spare. As Sam crawled across the crane arm lift, he could see Koon Hee on the container watching the crew. Suddenly, a flash of light hit Sam as he neared the end of the crane lift arm. It seemed to be coming from a police helicopter. Sam and Frank had to lay motionless until the helicopter flew by. Their black OPS suits would also help block infrared detection. Once the helicopter with its light had moved towards Pearl Harbor, they began to move as quickly as possible.

Crawling across the crane's lift arm, they reached the place where they had to jump down to the container holding Mr. Webb and start the rescue. As they made it onto the container, Frank began to use the materials left by Koon Hee on the top side of the container: Power Stripes to start removing a metal plate for entrance into the side. He first had to place a hole close to the top of the entrance of the metal to secure the metal being removed from the container, preventing it from falling and alerting the Chinese agents or the ship's crew to the rescue being done at the top of the container.

As Frank placed the special cutting tape in a window-type square, the chemical smell began to rise. It dissolved the metal like a cutting torch. Frank had to hold his mouth to stifle any sound as he coughed. He had already pushed the round hole inward and inserted the metal straps and hook that would hold the metal plate in place. A small communication voice speaker was pushed into the hole so that Park Bench could speak to Mr. Webb, informing him that the team was coming to rescue him and to ensure he followed their instructions.

Sam began to place the drop lines to take Mr. Webb out on the water side of the container vessel, which had an unusual name - The Edge. It was painted with a yellow background like the Chinese flag, with one big yellow star and small yellow stars above each letter of the word 'Edge'. It seemed the painting was recent, perhaps indicating the CCP's thoughts on the current state of international relations, teetering on the edge of conflict.

If Mr. Webb wasn't rescued from his Chinese captors, the entire United States could face a Pearl Harbor-like catastrophe, without the ability to deter war with atomic or nuclear bombs. The saying 'peace on earth and goodwill toward all men' would become outdated. Sam Black knew that all nations had their spies and intelligence collectors, trying to gain an advantage in case of invasion. The Chinese had become particularly adept at stealing information and important technology from other countries.

It was taught to all intelligence officers in war that they should know the strengths and weaknesses of their enemies and build themselves stronger than the strongest, using every weak point as an opportunity for victory. Some resorted to intelligence theft as a means of invasion. Sam spotted some cars with emergency lights on Navy Way Road next to the harbor and remembered the marker

Dannie gave him to put in his boot.

As he turned his attention from the road towards Frank Morgan and reached up to touch the scar on his face, he remembered himself as an 18-year-old, looking into a mirror at his dark hair just before enlisting. He ran his hands through his hair, knowing he was going to lose it all once he was sworn into Navy Boot Camp. But he hoped the scar on his face would never return. Sam began to see bright flashes in his eyes and felt pressure like pain bulging in his eyes.

Frank spoke quickly, "We have a delay, Park Bench."

As soon as Dannie saw Sam in the glasses, she shut down the drone visibility not letting Park Bench see what was going on.

"What's wrong with the drone?" Park Bench said.

Dannie was known to Park Bench has a hacker but now she had become a liar. She knew she would have to lie to hide Sam's problems; she felt innocent like her mother who had to lie when she killed her father and buried him for trying to molest her daughter whom she loved. She loved Sam like a father, that she never had.

"Don't know, Park Bench. I'm working on it" said Dannie.

It seemed for the first time Frank knew in his heart that he was the reason for Sam's unusual actions. He saw him out of the corner of his eye, rubbing his finger on the scar on his face because of his mistake. So, Frank decided to say nothing to Park Bench, as though his system was shut down. Dannie took one of the drop lines that Sam had put for the rescue and with the remote headed up to the top of the container where Sam and Frank were working to take out Mr. Webb, as fast as she could.

As Dannie arrived at the top of the container, her finger up to her lips, she had cut off all help from Park Bench. She looked at Frank and said thank you for not saying anything. Frank looked puzzled, like what happened, is this what I have caused? "Help hold him, Frank," Dannie shouted as Sam began shaking, not even thinking her voice might be heard by the Chinese agents.

Frank put his arms around Sam to keep him from standing up or falling off the container. Then, she began to speak close to his ear.

"You're okay, Sam Black. Everything is all right. This is Dannie, your crazy blonde friend. Remember how beautiful your grandson is, Sam, and your daughter loves you so much."

Dannie continued, "I just talked to Polly. She is watching over your family. She told me that she speaks the Lord's prayer over you every day."

Dannie knew it was Sam's grandfather who was a minister. He loved and taught Sam the prayer when he was young in the mountains of Appalachia, where his cabin is now.

Dannie began to try to quote the prayer. She had heard it whispered many times in war zones by Sam.

"Remember the first, Sam, 'Our Father'. Remember them, 'Our Father, which art in heaven'. Is in heaven, Sam. He was so big you can never walk out of his presence," his grandfather would say.

Dannie spoke again as Sam seemed to be shaking even more.

"Part of heaven," she repeated, "'Thy kingdom come' and 'thy will be done'. And have a prayer for hope for tomorrow, so I can see my mother."

Sam didn't even seem to know that Dannie was misquoting the prayer, as though he was dead and motionless. As Sam's eyes began to blink, Dannie kept saying, "It's all right, Sam. It's all right."

Sam began to raise up in a stare, looking at Dannie and then Frank Morgan.

Dannie whispered again close to his ear, "We are all here, everything is all right."

Sam, disoriented, said to Dannie, "Park Bench, what are they saying?"

"They don't know, Sam," Dannie replied quickly. As Sam turned and looked at Frank, Dannie spoke up for him, "Frank said nothing to Park Bench. He held you from falling off the container."

Sam knew that he could have destroyed not only the mission

but become a laughingstock; as an old veteran CIA service member, to a dead Militants Against Government crazed old man; thanks to Frank, he was still Sam Black.

At the other end of the ship, a problem began to arise. Koon Hee was about to encounter three men coming up on top of the containers, probably to watch the fireworks of Pearl Harbor. Koon Hee had realized something must have happened in the control room system because nothing was working toward speaking to Park Bench or the KODE Team. Now, he would use the option to try out the new laser weapon designed by the one they were recovering and rescuing, Mr. Webb. The nickname that Webb gave the laser weapon was "Down without Death."

Koon Hee placed the dot from the scope on the man who was furthest from the edge of the container, intending to get all the others coming towards him away from the edge. Only to think something was wrong with their friend. The moment he pressed the button, the man went down to his knees, then rolled to his side in a fetal position. His friends hurried to his side, bending over him, and Koon Hee took out both. Deciding he would test the response, he went over and pinched each one of them on the arm and on the face. They looked in a stare, without a blink, as though their eyelids were frozen.

Dannie quickly turned on the voice command with Park

Bench, and the cameras on the drone were left off until Sam was ready to move. Then she called to Koon Hee, "How is it going?"

"Three down, I'm still watching the rear," Koon Hee replied.

Park Bench came back quickly, "What's happened to the signal from the camera views?"

Dannie was quick to make up a story, that she was trying to change some computer functions after the police helicopter flew over.

As Sam moved over toward the drop cables that he had placed, he said, "I'm ready."

Dannie responded, "I'm dropping back to the deck railing." Park Bench kept asking for an update. Sam spoke back, "Just sit still. We are the only ones that have to move, and talking with you slows us down."

As Dannie moved back to the bottom of the container below Frank Morgan and the door that had been cut with the metal tapping torch, with the cable in the hole, he moved the door past the cutout and secured the cable to the left hook on top of the container. Park Bench from the KODE Team was going in for the War Peace. As Frank held the cable and placed his foot on the cutout, he went in, and Sam was right behind him. They knew that Mr. Webb was over toward the center. They had put him in a 6-foot block area with a battery-powered AC fan unit about 4 feet from him, an oxygen mask taped to his face, and what looked like a needle in his arm leading to a hydration bottle. They had him sitting and kept him from moving any part of his body.

Sam and Frank quickly released him. As the President and part of his military leaders watched from the Situation Room, hoping maybe even praying this would not be another Bay of Pigs. In 1961, after the Bay of Pigs, John F. Kennedy created the Situation Room. He said, "We Need Real-Time Information," and what they were seeing was just that. As Dannie double-checked from her computer signal, which was to block all foreign calls and signals to any device that may have been in the container, to detect anyone or any movement by Mr. Webb. When Sam helped Mr. Webb out of his sitting position, he noticed his legs were very weak. The KODE Team was already prepared for such a problem. After unhooking the needle from the hydration bottle, Sam placed it on Mr. Webb's arm and injector. A development for the NAVY SEALS, it would inject in their body a solution called "Wide-Awake" that creates energy and stamina in an exhausted soldier, to keep him moving or to stay awake and alert. They had learned in the past that recovering someone who had been in confinement could really slow down the operation and recovery if you had to carry or help carry a person. Technology has advanced to make things somewhat easier. Sam noticed the speaker Frank had placed through the hole to alert Mr.

Webb from the "Park Bench" command center, telling him that the team was coming in to get him.

"Park Bench, can I leave the speaker on the seat that they had Mr. Webb strapped in, so you can give them a message for us when you pick up, that they have entered?" Sam asked.

"Say, 'Don't mess with the US.' Sorry, Mr. Black. Return all the goods," Park Bench replied.

"Will do," Sam replied.

Sam took out of his pocket the marker, given to him when Dannie reminded him of his slogan, that the Navy letters meant to him. With the marker, he wrote on the back of the seat, "USA," and on the seat itself, "Don't mess with us." Frank saw the writing that Sam put on the chair as he was placing a black thin strap around Mr. Webb's waist and chest that is bulletproof to most small-caliber bullets and flotationable. Frank turned and asked Sam to add "KT" for KODE Team on the seat also. Park Bench was quick to reprimand Sam for his writings, but Sam never even responded to their words.

Frank climbed up on some of the cargo left in the container and had Sam place Mr. Webb's foot in his hand to lift him upward. Frank took Mr. Webb by the hand to lead him into the crawlspace, toward the cutout. Sam came up from behind as they made their way toward the hole Frank had taken out of the container.

Meanwhile, Dannie spotted two men walking toward her, shining a light upon the containers. The two men stopped for a moment about four containers away. Dannie turned on her translation device and voice pick-up. They were not crewmembers; they were agents with the Chinese government. They were mentioning a couple of things about Mr. Webb. One began to smoke a cigarette as they talked about being homebound for China. They bragged about how they pulled off the greatest kidnapping in all the world. This was going to be more popular than the 'EAGLET' kidnapping, one said to the other, referring to the Charles Lindbergh baby kidnapping in 1932 from their New Jersey home. There was also talk about General Norman Schwarzkopf, which really got Park Bench's attention. It seemed that they knew history because they were speaking about how the New Jersey State police lead investigator H. Norman Schwarzkopf was the father of the Persian Gulf War Commander. Some of the Generals in the Situation Room now were leaning forward because most of them had been around the Gulf War Commander and knew him personally. Some of them didn't even know that his father was part of the Lindbergh investigation.

After John Condon, a teacher, placed an Ad in the Bronx newspaper and offered to act as a mediator between Lindbergh and the kidnappers, he communicated with the agreement of the kidnappers under the code JAFSIE and the kidnappers' secret written messages across New York City. Dannie herself didn't even know about this kidnapping to the extent that these Chinese agents were talking about; the Lindbergh kidnapping in every detail. The agents also talked about how they agreed on $50,000 that was paid to them in gold certificates at a cemetery in the Bronx called St. Raymond's. The note that was given to John Condon and Lindbergh said the baby could be found in a boat called the Nelly located at Martha's Vineyard in Massachusetts. The baby was found dead about five miles from the house with a head injury. The Chinese agent also spoke about Hitler and how the German carpenter who got caught spending the gold certificates at a service station, which the government had all of the serial numbers and was later executed in the electric chair. The strange thing now was how the agents had designed a chair that looked like an electric chair that held Mr. Webb in the ship container. Webb's recovery was put on hold while the agents were talking history. They were too close for comfort. A decision had to be made on how to remove them or hope they would return to the rear of the ship with their other agents.

Mr. Webb began to thank Sam and Frank for their service to the country and expressed great gratitude for keeping him from being taken to Beijing, China. He mentioned that he was looking forward to finding a good secure area where he could drink some ginseng tea, which he loved, and find some chocolate-covered coffee beans that he dearly loved.

Sam then told him about the "Down but not Dead" weapon he had invented and that Koon Hee had to use on the three spectators. It worked perfectly. Mr. Webb smiled and said, "That is the only word I keep in my mind. Perfection means to me free."

"What do you mean by 'free'?" asked Sam.

"Look up the word," Webb replied, "when you get us out of this hole in the wall and on safe ground. To me, it means no room for defects in high-powered military equipment designed by me."

Sam remembered his grandfather preached a sermon about being perfect even as your heavenly father is perfect. Maybe he meant to be free. For whatever reason, Sam was always told in the military that to be free means sometimes you have to fight. Mr. Webb, being in the dark container with only a small glimmer of light from the docks, could not see the scar on Sam's face, which probably was a good thing. For sure, Mr. Webb would inquire of Sam how he received the scar. The KODE Team didn't need another breakdown while taking Mr. Webb off the ship.

Frank and Sam had got Mr. Webb over to the cutout exit hole, waiting for the "Down Command" from Dannie. As soon as the "Down Command" was given, Koon Hee would be moved away from the rear of the ship toward the drop-down point to help in the evacuation. The two Chinese agents started walking back toward the rear of the ship after another loud explosion went off on Pearl Harbor. Dannie gave the "Down Command," and Koon Hee started across the top of the containers toward the drop lines. He would have to move about 500 feet as quickly as possible. Knowing Koon Hee and his ability, it wouldn't take long.

As Frank went through the cut hole, he placed the drop line that was connected to the safety harness around Mr. Webb and over his black wrap for extra security. Mr. Webb would have his foot and chest snapped and secured to the drop lines. As he hooked Mr. Webb, Sam was stepping into the drop line when a major problem occurred, one that no one was expecting. Somehow, the metal cutting acid had gotten on the cable that was holding the metal door, the metal that Frank had cut out of the container. It gave way, and the heavy door would certainly make a lot of noise if it hit the ship first and then the water. Frank called to Koon Hee and Dannie to prepare for agents and workers coming forward due to the noise. Sam dropped quickly to about 30 feet above the deck when he heard the door hit. It slammed into the side rails on the ship decking and ricocheted off, knocking Dannie into the container. Sam could see her lying on the deck. He shouted, "Park Bench, hacker down, hacker down.

As Sam looked towards the rear of the ship, four men were coming toward Dannie. Sam placed the scope dot on them from the new weapon, taking out the first two men, and the other two began to run towards the rear of the ship. Koon Hee took both out. Park Bench called to the KODE Team, "Remove 'War Peace,' leave hacker behind, repeat, leave the hacker behind." That was one commandment Sam didn't want to hear because he knew she didn't have a chance without him. To Sam, she was a friend and a soldier. The one thing that you learn in the military is that no soldiers are left behind.

Sam spoke to Koon Hee, "Keep my backside, we're heading towards the front anchor."

"Will do, Sam," Koon Hee replied.

As soon as Sam hit the deck, he grabbed Dannie. She was still breathing but was knocked unconscious. There was a small amount of blood across her forehead. He took her OPS Mask off and threw it into the water over the ship. He placed her computer device in his OPS suit.

Frank and Mr. Webb hit the deck beside Dannie. Sam looked at Frank, saying, "Use your skills, Frank." Frank told Mr. Webb to stay put, and he moved down the deck towards the rear of the ship, about twenty feet. He took out marble-like materials that were stun bombs when stepped on and placed a handful on the walkway. Sam picked up Dannie and began to carry her. They moved about fifty more feet towards the front part of the ship when Frank stopped and placed more of the marble stun explosive material down on the deck. After placing down the explosive marbles, Frank grabbed Webb's arm and pulled him towards Sam and Dannie. Koon Hee was moving above them, watching the rear and front, as adrenaline was flowing. It seemed Sam couldn't even feel the hundred and fifteen pounds' weight from carrying Dannie. He knew that she probably had a concussion, hoping that she had no bleeding in the brain area.

Somehow the Chinese agents had picked up on the Navy SEALS and their raft under the front edge of the ship. Park Bench called to the KODE Team, "Update, update."

"We are on the move," Frank replied.

"Park Bench to KODE Team, we have another problem," Park Bench said. "The drone has detected a small balloon over the vessel. It looks like a reconnaissance piece being used by the Chinese agents."

As Sam stopped, Frank turned and asked Mr. Webb, "What will that laser gun device you created do to a balloon?"

"I don't know, but don't push the button. Place the dot on the object and hold the button down, and we will see what happens," Mr. Webb replied.

Koon Hee quickly laid on his back, placing the dot on the balloon and holding down the button, hearing what Mr. Webb spoke. The balloon exploded and headed towards the water. Then Koon Hee spotted something happening on crane arm number five towards the front of the ship, with a cable trying to drop something. It seemed the Chinese agents were not giving up on "War Peace."

"Park Bench, this is Koon Hee. We are detected, I repeat, we have been detected. Something's been dropped by the number five crane on the waterside toward the exit point, I repeat, toward the exit point," Koon Hee reported.

Park Bench moved the drone towards the front of the ship and saw a huge fishing net, commercial style, being dropped on the walking deck, blocking Frank and Sam from moving forward.

Several Chinese agents were now at the front of the ship near the anchor drop. Sam wondered how they were able to get a net, a commercial fishing net. Fishing in the LA Port had dwindled, with only about twenty commercial boats left.

"The Chinese agents are using everything they can to stop the recovery of Mr. Webb," Koon Hee remarked. "They should know everything about fishing nets. China produced over seventy million tons of fish last year, using some of my mother's family to do the work."

Sam relayed to Park Bench, "Go ahead, Sam."

"With the fish net catchers, the one mistake they made is, I'm a fisherman also. Unless you got the fish in the net, he's still on his own," Sam explained.

"Park Bench" to "KODE Team": "You need to go back towards the drop line. I have a different plan," Park Bench ordered.

Sam replied firmly, "Sorry, I don't work for you, remember? I have a triangular medallion around my neck that says I am a Militant Against Government. So shut your mic up and listen."

Frank smiled at Sam and said, "I like that. Tell him again."

"Shut your mic up and listen," Sam reiterated.

"Here is what the KODE Team is going to do," Sam continued. "I want Koon Hee to move towards the front of the ship where we were to exit. Stay on top of the container. Get close to crane arm number five. Notify the LA Police Department that a US citizen has trespassed on a Chinese container ship. Let them know that he is part Chinese himself and he wants to protest against the Chinese Communist Party because his family is held in China. Have them pick him up off the container by helicopter. Make sure they pick him up. Copy that, Park Bench."

Sam spoke to Koon Hee, saying, "Put on a good Hollywood act. Rid yourself of the OPS weapons and suit."

"Will do," replied Koon Hee. "Thanks, Sam. I've always wanted to be an actor."

Sam repeated back to Park Bench, "Frank and I are taking our merchandise, Hacker and War Peace, overboard into the water." He then instructed Frank to set up some delay-time explosives on the net. "The police helicopter will work as another decoy for us. But going backward, not so. Someone is going to be playing marbles, and it won't be the KODE Team. We will be in the water. Have the FROG SEAL TEAM come to pick us up quickly to move us away from the ship's time explosions. They certainly will bring in other police helicopters with lights, and we need to be as far away as we can. The fish are not in the net yet, 'Park Bench.' The fish are not in the net."

Some of the planners at Park Bench thought that Sam's plan was feasible, especially Mathew Marx. "Go for a swim, KODE Team. It's a go. Take a swim. It's a go."

Sam handed Dannie over to Frank. She was still unconscious. He stepped over the railing and leaned forward towards Frank, reaching for Dannie. Taking Dannie back in his arms, he told Frank to move about fifteen feet from them.

Frank started moving Mr. Webb to the jump point as Sam said, "We will all go down at the same time. Make sure your OPS Helmet is secured around your neck. It's a pretty good fall." Frank put Mr. Webb against the railing and latched him to himself from behind. "Put your hands and arms across your chest, Mr. Webb," ordered Frank. "It's time to leave China. On three, Frank, we exit on three." Sam spoke, holding Dannie. "One, two, three."

The KODE Team members jumped into the water, holding tight to themselves and the precious cargo. Koon Hee went towards the front of the vessel after he took off his headgear and weapon and put them inside his OPS SUIT to drop it in the water close to Frank so that he could recover the weapons and the mask and laser weapon, which would be floating inside the OPS SUIT. Sam held his hand over Dannie's mouth as they entered the water. The return back up with the floatations on the cold water seemed to cause Dannie to move her legs and some movement in her arms. Sam held her head above water and spoke, "It will be all right, Dannie. Hold on, you will be just fine."

Frank moved Mr. Webb over next to Sam and Dannie, waiting for the pickup. "Park Bench, all is well. Repeat, Park Bench, all is well," Frank repeated.

"Park Bench" to KODE Team, "Pickup is coming your way. Copy, pickup is coming your way," Park Bench confirmed.

"Be sure to keep your head above water, Frank," said Sam.

"Yes, I know," Frank replied. "I never did like the taste of salt water."

"Neither do I, Frank. I don't like the taste of city chlorine water. When this one is over, Frank, come back up to the mountain cabin with me, and I will take you to a freshwater spring. My Grandfather used to take us there to give you a drink of the best water that you have ever tasted."

"You're not talking about moonshine, are you, Sam?" Frank asked.

"No, just water," replied Sam. "They used to use it to make what they called homebrew. But really, it was made under the light of the moon, hoping to see and keep the revenuers from catching them. One moonshiner said he had eyes in the back of his head."

"Thanks for the insight," Mr. Webb interjected.

As "Park Bench" listened to what seemed to be an awkward conversation, their signal seemed to vanish. Meanwhile, Koon Hee was waiting to start his Hollywood acting career.

Sam spotted the FROG SEAL TEAM vessel moving towards them, within inches from the ship. It eased up next to them without making a sound, reaching for Mr. Webb first. Taking Dannie out of Sam's arms into the vessel, then pulling in Sam and Frank, moving away from the vessel quickly out to the waters toward the Navy Way Road. The SEAL vessel could move without sound on electric power, one mile in about seventy seconds if needed.

The Kode

As the KODE TEAM moved to the right to follow the Navy Way Road towards the road bridge, they would go under to meet their pickup at Nimitz Road next to the Long Beach Fuel Pier. Koon Hee began to start his acting show as the emergency helicopter with a SWAT police officer was spotting for him on top of the container. They saw him, and he was jumping up and down and doing weird moves like breakdancing, dressed only in his silky blue knee-high underwear. As a SWAT officer dropped out of the helicopter to arrest him, with orders from the captain to bring him in safely by the way of the helicopter, Koon Hee lay flat, putting his hands behind his head without any resistance. The SWAT officer put his safety belt on with hooks and took him and himself up together. As they entered into the helicopter, the timing was perfect: Frank's distracting bomb went off next to the fishnet on the container ship, causing more helicopters, even the FBI now was on board a police helicopter flying towards the Chinese vessels.

As one helicopter flew close and spotted some of the men who were shot by Koon Hee and Sam with Webb's LASER WEAPON, lying on the container, a major police force of officers started showing up on the deck. They began to question Koon Hee about the seemingly dead men.

"They're probably just drunk and passed out," said Koon Hee nonchalantly. "They must have got bored watching that other ship explode, having nothing better to do."

One of the police helicopters saw two of the men who were lying on top of the container start moving. One stood up, stretching and staggering.

"Those guys are either sleeping or drunken and passed out," reported the police chopper.

As the effect of the laser wore off, they all started to move about. Koon Hee heard the communications coming across the police radio and smiled, saying, "I told you so." It seemed like everything was coming together with perfect timing.

Meanwhile, the military vessel was moving across the water with the KODE Team. Dannie began to murmur words as she opened her eyes wider, staring up at Sam. He held her face on both sides to keep her head from rocking back and forth or moving up and down from the waves. As she regained her mobility, she spoke clearly to Sam, "Who hit me, Sam? Who hit me?"

"Nobody, Dannie," Sam reassured her. "You got hit with the metal door that Frank had to remove from the container. When it came undone from the cable, it came by me towards you like a missile. It barely missed you, Dannie, but ricocheted off the side railing and hit you, knocking you into the side of the bottom of the container."

As Sam kept talking with Dannie, it never dawned on him, or even a thought, that the pickup team hadn't said a word or even mentioned Park Bench. Frank also began to take note of how they seemed to be moving towards another container ship instead of making their way out of the loading area.

As Sam looked up towards one of the frogmen dressed in black suits, with the air hose from the tanks in his mouth and goggles, he remembered there were supposed to be four men, not three. He also noticed the silence; all of them seemed to be smaller in body size than most UDTs, or Underwater Demolition Teams, which were often referred to as frogmen. They were a special group of fighting soldiers, with seven out of ten usually giving up their training to become a frogman. Sam knew size meant nothing; it was those who passed the 16 weeks of training, which concluded with the infamous Hell Week, that truly mattered. Hell Week was the last six days of unimaginable pressure and challenges that would make them understand the term "Hell."

Acting like he was talking to Dannie, Sam whispered, "Park Bench, thanks to these four brave NAVY SEALS, THE WAR PEACE will be delivered safely back." No response came back to Sam. Frank also noticed he couldn't hear Sam through his earpiece as he was consulting Dannie. Sam looked at Frank, and it was as though they were reading each other's minds. Frank moved four fingers close to his chest and then showed three fingers. Sam noticed the same with the mask taken off. Then he blinked his left eye three times at Frank. He would know what that meant. Being in the KODE

Team, he understood the signal code of that winking left eye. When engaged around others you didn't know or trust: "take out the enemy."

The Chinese agents somehow intercepted intelligence from the balloon source or a hacker that Koon Hee hadn't discovered, and they picked up on the rescue and details from Park Bench. But what had happened to the four Navy SEALs at the front of the ship, some of the best that the Navy had? Had China out-advanced our CIA and military special ops units?

As Sam pondered those things, he prepared Frank for the S.A.T. Test, which meant to the KODE Team - Surprise Attack Them. Sam and Frank had passed that test many times, not to get into a college, but to get into and out of the enemy's camp. Frank had also noticed the eye shape through the mask of one of the supposedly Navy SEALs. He had an Asian look, similar to Koon Hee.

Koon Hee was about to cross over Seaside Freeway 719 when it came across their radio on the emergency vac helicopter to check out the front of the Chinese container ship. One of the helicopters watching Pearl Harbor thought they had seen something or someone floating. With the handcuffs being a little loose that the officer put on Koon Hee because of his lack of resistance, he began to work his hands free from the restraints. Using sweat from his back, he folded his hands like a closed salute and with the other hand, with pressure and pain, forced it past his thumb joint. With a little wiggle back and forth, he was free. He respected the police's authority, but he felt his friends were in trouble because the police had no idea what was going on. Light from the helicopter was placed downward and found the ship. Koon Hee spotted what looked like four bodies floating. As the SWAT officer looked out, who was sitting beside him, Koon Hee quickly relieved him of his pistol, putting it to his neck.

"Tell the pilot to drop closer to the water," said Koon Hee. The pilot, thinking that he wanted a closer look, complied. As the helicopter came in from the front side, Koon Hee quickly used the officer's seat as a back-pressure brace, with a double karate kick that put the officer out of the helicopter next to the floating SEALs. Quick as that black snake that Sam said he was, Koon Hee leaped forward, tearing off the mic that was on the helicopter pilot's helmet and placing the officer's gun to his neck. Unbuckling him from his seat, he said, "You have only one good choice." Koon Hee turned the pilot towards the water. "Jump, or you will never see your family alive ever again. Is it worth it? Don't worry about your helicopter. I know how to pilot one, and I will leave it for you on dry land someplace."

Koon Hee had to put up a good bluff because he wouldn't have hurt either of them. The rescue worker pilot had two sons and a pregnant wife; he didn't want to be a dead hero. Leaving behind the loves of his life, the pilot turned and jumped towards the officer in the water, who was holding himself up on one of the floating bodies of the SEALs.

As Koon Hee moved into the pilot seat, guiding the helicopter up above the container ship, he headed towards where he hoped to find the KODE Team, his friends. He knew the officer and the pilot could float on the SEALs, which had flotation devices. It's always been taught in war or rescue; one mistake can cost your life or someone else's. When the Chinese agents pulled in the KODE Team from the water to keep them from being suspicious, they never asked for their strange-looking gun lasers that were hanging around Sam's and Frank's necks. Maybe their black weapon just blended into their OPS Suit, or else they were making their one mistake. Sam acted as though he was easing over his right hand on Dannie's forehead, talking to her as he moved to aim the weapon towards the agent that was controlling the vessel. Frank, at the same time, was moving his weapon, as it laid flat against his chest, towards the one watching them. They knew the operator had to go first, and then Frank takes out the other two men that were in the front. Then Sam could move and take over the controls of the vessel, the laser gun supposedly would penetrate any bulletproof material, and so far, it was working to perfection; Mr. Webb's live-by-word. Frank has his weapon placed towards the front man, without looking through the scope: While looking toward Dannie, not the agent, he could judge the shot. Frank used his peripheral vision on the operator because he knew he would have to push the button within a second of Sam's shot; in case the operator collapsed on the controls, causing another problem.

Sam knew he had to push the button and get to the controls quickly. As Sam pushed the button, he moved over to the controls quickly, grabbing the steering and power forward arm, and turning to neutral, he looked at Frank only to see him removing their weapons and throwing them into the water: when a flash of light was coming from the other container, they knew more agents of the Chinese, were on our home turf. Frank pulled the light from the hand of the agent and flashed it back towards them, trying to throw them off, or anything else they had planned, not for sure which way or what they wanted. Because they had been a lot of mistakes and mishaps.

Sam navigated the vessel towards the channel next to the Navy Way Road, with all communications currently unreliable. Unsure if the other Chinese agents could still hear or listen, even on the Park Bench frequency, Koon Hee raised the helicopter about 50 yards up in the center of the container channel, between the two docks. He turned on the searchlight and moved it quickly, back and forth in a zigzag pattern like the letter Z, to try to spot the SEAL vessel. With the reflection of the water, he saw what he was looking for and turned off the searchlight, avoiding attracting attention.

He knew that Sam and Frank must have everything under control because the vessel was moving slowly away from the containers. To double-check and make sure, he decided to stop just above them and do a quick on-and-off spot with the light. As soon as the light hit the vessel, he saw Sam sitting at the controls. He smiled and dropped down closer without the light, quickly speaking, "It's Koon Hee, Sam. I have our taxi. Go straight to the road, and when you're there, I will sit down and pick you up."

Sam spotted Koon Hee's flashlight on his thumb turned up, indicating he had heard him, and started moving the SEAL vessel quickly towards the Navy Way Road. Moving the vessel next to the bank of the road, Koon Hee jumped out and tied the vessel to a metal stake that held up a sign on the road. Sam picked up Dannie, helping carry her out of the vessel, and turned to Frank, saying, "Shoot them again," thinking it would give them more time to pass on the information and keep the agents incapacitated longer. Frank pointed the weapon and pushed the button on each one, then grabbed Koon Hee's OPS suit along with the head mask.

As Koon Hee set the helicopter down on Navy Road Highway, Sam dashed towards the helicopter with Dannie in his arms, while Morgan helped Dr. Webb. However, as they boarded the helicopter, two men in wet suits, clearly Chinese agents, approached from the other side of the road. One attempted to open the door on Mr. Webb's side, while the other tampered with the fuel tank, trying to sabotage the helicopter. Both agents quickly jumped off as Koon Hee lifted the helicopter off the road. Frank noticed air tanks on the bank of the road, suggesting that the Chinese had removed them.

With communication from Park Bench unreliable, Koon Hee decided to turn the helicopter towards Santa Monica, California, to keep Mr. Webb safe. Sam, holding onto Dannie, discussed the need for a drop-off plan with Koon Hee, emphasizing the importance of not compromising Mr. Webb's life. Unbeknownst to Sam and Frank, they were being tracked by the Chinese, and whatever had been placed in the fuel tank was slowing them down. Additionally, a tracking device had been attached to the helicopter.

As they approached Santa Monica, Koon Hee noticed something wrong with the helicopter's power, indicating possible sabotage. He turned the helicopter north, away from Santa Monica, in search of a safe landing spot. The turbine was malfunctioning, attempting to shut down and restart itself. Spotting flashing lights from an airport, Koon Hee steered the helicopter towards them, hoping to land safely.

As Koon Hee happened to spot Van Nuys Airport, he said to the passengers to hold on tight. "We must go down now; our chances are running slim," he detailed to Sam and Frank. "Hey guys, I see some private jets with what looks like people talking on the outside of one next to a car, probably going to board: we need to borrow their jet. So, have your weapons ready."

Koon Hee saw the pilot and the co-pilot as they entered the jet. "This will have to be quick: a quick takeover, load and go. I just saw the jet that the pilots have just boarded," said Koon Hee. "I will drop the helicopter close to the jet. When you hear the touchdown, jump, Frank."

It caught the passengers off guard when they saw Frank jump from the helicopter with some type of weapon around his neck and rush into their plane. The biggest surprise was the passengers didn't seem to get frightened; they started laughing and pointing at the man still sitting in his car, talking to someone on his cell phone.

As they knocked on his window, pointing at the plane, because he was a film producer and director, and they thought he was the one pulling off a stunt to entertain them. Then came Sam by them carrying Dannie with Mr. Webb beside him, then Koon Hee boarded the plane and closed the door.

The jet engines fired up as the passengers and the film producer began to watch without a clue that the jet was taxiing towards a runway for a quick takeoff. As the film director got out of his car, his passenger friends began to act like they were handing him the Oscar for the best Mystery film. He kept waving his hands back and forth, saying, "No, no, this isn't my doings; someone just stole our jet and kidnapped my pilots."

His friends kept laughing, calling him the Oscar winner as the roar of the engines from the jet takeoff down the runway turned all their heads, watching as the jet lifted off from Van Nuys airport. The film director and his passengers turned toward the helicopter after hearing screeching brakes, to see three Chinese agents jump from a van next to the helicopter, look in the helicopter, and quickly get in their van and head towards the runway area.

Pilots had already been instructed to fly west, toward Washington DC. Sam began to use one of the pilot's cell phones, trying to keep Mr. Webb's landing a secret, but also telling the FAA that this was a government matter and not another 9/11.

Sam called an old friend he worked with in the CIA, named K James Bondi. Finally getting Bondi on the phone, he started their conversation as he always did, "How are you kicking there, secret agent man?"

Bondi replied to Sam, "I can't believe you're on a California phone number talking to me. I thought by now you would be hidden away in that mountain cabin of yours in the Appalachian Mountains."

"Well, I have a problem that has arisen, Bondi, and I need your help—quickly."

"Go ahead, Sam, give me the details," Bondi responded.

"I have with me a very important package for our old employer. They were supposed to pick it up in Los Angeles, but we had some unexpected visitors from China who also wanted our cargo. All communications have been compromised, and now we must come up with a secure drop-off plan through the back door, if you know what I mean."

"Through the back door, copy that, Sam. Let our old employer know we need to deliver the package to Langley Airforce Base and tell them the name on the package is 'The War Peace' and the wrapping is still on. Also, have them let the LA Police Department and rescue team know that their helicopter has been compromised and is located at Van Nuys Airport. Also, Bondi, there are two men floating in front of the cargo ship where the package was picked up. I'll get back to you in a little bit, Bondi. Our pilots are not using their communications as they may have been compromised as well. Their original stopping point is Las Vegas, Nevada."

After Frank Morgan disconnected the pilot's microphones, causing a slight problem at the airport, even the director had a hard time convincing his friends the plane was a return for them. As the film producer was contacting authorities that his jet had been hijacked, the tower also couldn't understand a five-minute early departure with no pilot tower talking, and the FAA had been notified.

"We are heading east but we need to make the stop in Las Vegas that we had planned," said Frank. "Las Vegas, my old stomping grounds."

Sam got into the conversation and said, "We are working to have the aircraft sit down at Langley Air Force Base. Tell your co-pilot friend."

The pilot told Sam, "Sir, this plane didn't get refueled because we had scheduled to do the refueling in Las Vegas, and it just so happens, jet planes don't fly far on empty. In about one hour and forty-five minutes, we can be fully loaded and on our way to Washington DC. Regardless, we must land someplace for fueling."

Sam nodded his head, saying, "No problem. I know Vegas is only a hop, skip, and a jump away. We should be in the clear from the Chinese agents," he thought to himself.

But what Sam and Frank didn't know was that the Chinese agents in the van had also picked up the serial number on the plane and had received information from the control tower on the plane that had just taken off and where it was going. After getting the Las Vegas information, with Chinese agents now working in most major cities in the United States, starting up factories and manufacturing jobs in hard-hit economical poor smaller cities and towns, having their special agents close by, the battle for The War Peace seemed far from over.

The Chinese agents were already having their counter-agents in the Las Vegas area start towards the airport immediately, making plans to take Mr. Webb and remove all those this time that had been with him. The only thing Sam and Frank had going for them at this moment was that they didn't know their jet refueling had been compromised. And the only thing the Chinese had going against them was The KODE Team and Sam Black. Not knowing anything about their opponents, they did feel a little at ease. And that mistake alone could cost them dearly for Mr. Webb. Anytime the package that you are carrying is said to be worth more than yourself, it could cost you your life.

Sam contacted K. James Bondi again and told him to get the message about refueling in Las Vegas. "Keep the message from going in The Park Bench by any air communications, only by word-of-mouth, and make sure that the ear that receives it is Matthew Marx," said Sam. "Let the message to Mr. Marx be that the package that was picked up by the KODE team will be delivered to Langley Air Force Base. Make sure the messenger and Mr. Marx are alone when it is given to him," Sam told Bondi, updating him again at the refueling in Las Vegas.

As Dannie began to regain mobility, she stood and looked at

Sam with a smile. "It's good to have a strong arm to hold you up when you're physically demolished," she said.

Sam smiled back and reminded her of the times she had to hold him and speak into his ear when he would lose all train of thought and just lay and shake. "Sometimes gaining strength from a fellow comrade helps you cross the finish line, Blondie," he remarked.

"Yeah, you're right, Sam, but this race seems to have no end in sight," Dannie replied.

"Listen to Blondie, my granddad used to speak in church, that no matter how good it looks or how bad it seems, all things in this world will come to an end someday. It's just a matter of time."

"Does that include all the pain from your past?" Dannie asked, remembering her hate toward her dad.

"That's what I've been told, Dannie," Sam replied.

"Thanks again, Sam, for not leaving me behind. I'm going to walk a little bit and stretch myself. I will lay your computer here in the seat; the government might want you to return it, since you're too smart for it," Dannie said gratefully.

Dannie repeated her gratitude to Sam. "Thank you for your friendship, thank you for your strong arm, I may have to hold it again someday."

"Anytime and anyplace, Blondie," Sam replied back, giving two thumbs up.

As Dannie went towards the rear of the plane, Koon Hee came over, picking up Dannie's computer and setting it beside Sam.

"Sam, after this mission is over, what are we going to get into? Life was just not the same for me when we were separated," Koon Hee queried.

"Well, Koon Hee, I have to make some adjustments with a new member of my household, my grandson. But I also have been doing some thinking about starting a security business on the side for high-end clients, along with finding and perhaps rescuing their family members or friends; whomever went missing in some of these other countries."

"That sounds like a good plan, Sam," said Koon Hee. "What are you going to call it, the KODE Was Team?" he giggled at the words.

Sam laughed and replied, "I think a good name would be The Black-Out Team."

As Koon Hee slightly tilted his head sideways, looking at Sam, he said, "It sounds like a winner to me, Sam. That takes on several meanings: named after one of the best CIA special KODE Team members, plus he can knock out the power or black-out information from getting out, and we can get our clients out of harm's way with the security expertise and get those family members out of other countries, out of places of confinement. Sounds perfect to me."

Koon Hee was then quick to apologize, "Sorry, Sam, didn't mean to say 'we,' that is unless you will employ me into this new adventure."

"Well, Koon Hee, my boy, I wasn't just thinking of my name Black. I was also thinking of your nickname. I've always thought of you as The Black Snake, how you could wiggle into places others couldn't or wouldn't go into, waiting on your prey to catch the rat off-guard and choking them out."

"That's good, Sam. The Black Snake, he works for The Black-Out Team," Koon Hee agreed.

Frank Morgan didn't hear the conversation as he was talking to the pilots, but Dannie did hear and comes back, standing looking down on both, and said, "I want to be called The Black Widow in this new adventure."

Sam and Koon Hee looked at each other, a little puzzled. "But you have never been married," said Koon Hee.

"I have been married three times," said Dannie.

Koon Hee turned back toward Sam to get a response, but

before he could think up something to speak, Dannie replied, "They were all in dreams I had, and in each dream, I took them out, just like my mother did," she stopped speaking and walked back to the rear of the plane.

Koon Hee turned toward Sam and said, "I just think I heard her whisper as she walked off, 'I hate you, Dannie.' Is something eating at her?"

Sam knew those words were, "I hate you, daddy." "Yeah, Koon Hee, you know how these computer hackers think, they even dream about whatever they hack into or hack off."

"Speaking about hacking, Sam, when I was on that ship, those names came up from the spy unit 61398: Ugly Guerrilla, KandyGoo, and WinXYhappy. The main one, it seems, was called twenty-seven. And as some were on the southeast coast because of some of the conversations I overheard."

"That's strange, Sam said, I just remembered a trainee in the Navy Seals that said he was born on March 27th, and that his daddy was 27 at the time of his birth in Florida, where they lived, which he said just so happens, that Florida was the 27th state that joined the United States."

"I remember another man, Sam, they would mention, a Doctor Phillips."

The pilots were given back the communication gear and felt more at ease after the FAA gave them instructions for Langley Air Force Base after refueling in Vegas, and that the passengers were cleared by the FBI. Frank found out talking with them that both had been Navy pilots and expressed to them how Sam Black was a diehard Navy man and an ex-Navy SEAL. They inquired about Dannie and Mr. Webb, so Frank Morgan had to throw them off a little: "She was a computer science expert for the FBI, and the old guy, Mr. Webb, is wanted by the government and FBI," he never mentioned the NSA, only to make them think Mr. Webb was a fugitive.

The Film Producer finally convinced his party what had happened was real after the airport authorities came with the van to take them to the hangar, where he was hoping to get another private jet out to Las Vegas.

"Who and what were those men that took over my plane?" asked the producer, whose name was John Wiseman, well-known in the Hollywood movie production circle.

"All we got from Mr. Wiseman was they were federal agents with a high-profile fugitive of some sort wanted by the FBI," Frank replied.

Dannie came back as she was listening to Sam and Koon Hee's conversation on the hackers, and she said, "Just for curiosity's sake, did you know when you add up those numbers 61398, it equals 27."

"It does," Sam replied.

"Let's make sure we pass this information on to the FBI, who might need to know about number 27," Koon Hee suggested.

The pilot's voice comes across the intercom, informing them that they will be dropping down shortly to land in Las Vegas North airport to refuel.

Frank came back to ask Sam about the refueling stop. "This will be the first time I've landed in Sin City and didn't get out to go to the tables, to try to win some money," he remarked, "only to see the lights and smell the fuel."

Dannie moved up from the back of the plane toward Morgan, still not sure what Sam might do. Frank told Sam, "When we land, I will step out with the pilot as he checks the plane while they are refueling, just to keep my eye on the lookout for any possible trouble."

"You're not going to sneak out, are you, Frank, toward those casino lights?" asked Sam.

"Depends on what the odds are, Sam," replied Morgan. "And it looks like at this moment in time, they are against me."

Dannie leaned over towards Sam to show him something

about the government computer when the triangular MAG necklace fell out of her shirt. When the ring she took from Sam made a noise, hitting against the medallion, Sam spotted the ring. Immediately bolts of light and numbing went off in his head, and his body began to shake. Dannie noticed the ring on the chain was off her shirt and placed it back inside, telling Koon Hee to sit behind Sam and hold him, that she could sit beside him and speak to him.

Morgan asked Dannie what she wanted him to do. Then she said, "Frank, go toward the pilots and don't look back," speaking in an angry tone.

The pilot asked Frank what was going on with Sam. "He's just a little bit airsick," said Frank, "flying seems to bother him more now than what it used to."

As the plane was dropping attitude towards Las Vegas airport, Mr. Webb asked Morgan, "How long have you known Sam and how did he get that terrible scar on his face?"

Frank replied to his question, "Don't want to talk about it right now; we have to keep a straight line of thought to get you to your safe house."

Frank began to feel his stomach knot up, knowing that he caused a KODE Team Agent to fall from a state of war mind without defeats to a state of mental breakdown and totally defeated. As they began to buckle up for the touchdown, Koon Hee just remained standing behind Sam's seat, holding him tight against the seat.

"Dannie kept speaking in Sam's ear: 'Sam, Polly is with Jennifer and your grandson. She told me they are waiting for you, with your favorite meal from Polly's home cooking: cornbread, pinto beans, and sassafras tea.'"

As the plane was dropping towards the runway, Koon Hee inquired of Dannie what was going on with Sam. He had never seen Sam in that condition before. Dannie told Koon Hee, "I can't explain it all right now; it has been very complicated and hard to understand the line of events in the past few weeks."

"Did someone harm or threaten his family, Dannie? Because you know Sam, he keeps a lot of stuff to himself."

"Between you and I," said Dannie, "just a little bit," and she leaned over and whispered in Koon Hee's ear about Sam's dog being killed by Frank Morgan's gambling money exchangers, but she kept it to herself about Jennifer's husband Jeremy's ordeal with Frank's collectors. She didn't want to talk about the incident, thinking that Sam possibly could overhear her. And she knew that wouldn't be good for his mental incapacity, especially against Morgan, which had seemed to be mending a little from the top of that shipping container on Sam's last breakdown.

As the plane was lowering its landing gear and Sam was still shaking but was coherent with his words to Dannie. "Sorry, Blondie,

I don't think I had enough coffee," he said, putting his hands on his friend that was holding him, saying, "Koon Hee, my boy, sorry I didn't mean to drag you into my lack of coffee problem."

Koon Hee said with a giggle, "Sam, when this mission is over, I will buy you and I two espressos each. We may need three of those double shot espressos for our next job as The Black-Out."

Dannie spoke up and said, "Maybe you just need a cup of Polly's coffee, Sam. I remember my first taste of her mountain brew: I think my hair stood up on my head."

Sam laughed and told Dannie, "Wait until you take her homemade cough syrup: you then can spend all night cutting wood or raccoon hunting after one dose."

"Maybe you should offer that to the government, Sam, for the SEAL Teams when they are exhausted," suggested Dannie.

"Most mountain secrets and formulas are kept secret, Blondie, because their ingredients don't match the government's platform. I will just have to leave it at that," Sam replied as he laughed.

As the wheels of the jet touched the runway and the plane was slowing down quickly, Sam told Koon Hee, "You can let go now; you have been a pretty good seatbelt." Sam's shaking had ceased, and then Dannie patted him on the shoulder and said, "Sam, you're one tough person."

The pilot informed the KODE Team that "we will be going to a private hangar area to get refueled; the truck should be there shortly, and we can get this flight to Langley on its way." As the jet was taxiing toward the hangar at the refueling area, two Chinese agents were also moving towards the hangar after they had spotted the jet turning towards it. Two more Chinese agents were waiting in an SUV not far from the refueling zone.

As the plane came to a stop, the pilots shut down the engine for refueling. Frank Morgan stood up and said, "I'm going outside with the pilot for a moment." Sam got up and told Dannie to go outside with him to get some fresh desert air. Dannie put her government computer in her seat, following Frank and Sam outside of the plane towards the hangar. Mr. Webb was given strict orders to remain in the jet as the copilot is putting in the computer system everything from the flight service and the preflight preparation to Langley Air Force Base.

Koon Hee was standing in the doorway of the jet on the first step with his special ops weapon. No one had noticed the Chinese agents that were hidden beneath the fuel truck as it pulled up to refuel the jet. As the pilot was walking around the jet checking it, Dannie began to tell Sam that she believed the Chinese were gaining the upper hand because of their A.I. program.

"You must speak to me in English, Dannie; I don't understand what you're talking about. I know it's not Chinese, but I think you're speaking in Greek," Sam replied.

"It's their Artificial Intelligent programs. If we don't get the upper hand, they may be able to shut down our planes, trains, banking systems, and electrical grids. Even though their supersonic missiles have advanced far beyond ours, we have the capability of moving ahead of them; we must wake up and wake up quickly."

"Well, Dannie, sometimes it's hard to wake up a sleeping giant, but it has happened in the past when Japan bombed Pearl Harbor. Speaking of Pearl Harbor, wonder how the decoy is holding up."

"Well, Sam, if it is like the rest of this mission, it's possible it could be on the bottom. The other thing about your giant story, Sam, is sometimes a giant can pridefully go into a deep sleep, thinking everything's all right."

As the pilot made his way around the plane back towards the door, Koon Hee stepped aside just for a moment to let the pilot re-enter the plane. As Frank Morgan was walking towards Sam to talk to him about the remaining part of what might happen at Langley, he noticed the Chinese agent at the tail end of the plane pointing something towards Sam and Dannie. Frank leaped towards them, knocking both Dannie and Sam to the ground at the sound of the gunshot coming from the Chinese agent. Frank, now laying on top of Sam, turned himself towards the agent with his special OPS weapon and took him out. As the other Chinese agent tried to enter the plane, Koon Hee took him out.

As Sam tried to move Frank Morgan off his chest, he noticed blood running out of Frank's mouth. Frank was now gasping for breath. Koon Hee was quick to circle the plane, finding the fuel hose still putting fuel in the plane and the man responsible for refueling the plane laying on his side under the tanker. Koon Hee shut off the valve on the fuel truck and carried the fueler, who was unconscious. He came running back towards the KODE Team.

As Frank gasped for breath, he asked Sam, "Did I get him?"

"You got him, Frank. Dannie and I are all right," Sam reassured him. Frank took off the triangular MAG medallion given to him by the government and said, "Koon Hee, place this around the Chinese agent's neck." Sam looked at Koon Hee saying, "Do as Frank says and check with the pilot to see how much fuel has been put into the plane."

After Koon Hee lays the driver down, he walks towards the plane's door. After putting Frank's medallion around the agent he took out, he takes off his triangular MAG medallion and places it around the neck of the Chinese agent that he took out also. Sam turns Frank Morgan over on his back, and he notices a bullet wound around his ribs. As Dannie is trying to put pressure on the bullet hole, Sam is trying to keep Frank from moving. With gurgling words, Frank begins to speak to Sam, "Forgive me, Sam. You took a bullet for me. I'm proud to have worked with you, Sam, and I'm proud to have taken a bullet for you."

As Frank Morgan takes his last breath, screeching wheels from the Chinese agents' SUV vehicle get Sam and Dannie's attention, as it is headed right towards them. Koon Hee begins to fire his special ops weapon into the windshield area of the SUV, causing the vehicle to miss Sam and Dannie and hitting the tail end of the jet, moving the jet sideways and jerking the fuel hose out of the fueling hole onto the ground area. The SUV hits the corner of the fuel truck and explodes into flames.

Then Koon Hee quickly removes Mr. Webb and the pilots from the plane, running over to Sam and Dannie, helping move Frank Morgan away from the burning SUV vehicle. The pilots now help carry Frank as they begin to run toward the hangar away from the burning SUV. When a huge explosion happens, causing the whole side of the airport to light up.

As they make it into the hangar, they find a jet that had just been refueled for a private party going back to Dallas, Texas. Sam informs his pilots who now know some of the importance of this mission. They are told to tell the other pilots they would have to board their airplane and borrow it, and they could come for the ride. As Koon Hee is loading Mr. Webb into the plane and Sam is now carrying Frank Morgan into the plane with Dannie's help, shutting the door behind them, he says to the pilots they will have to exit the other side of the hangar. The pilots work together trying to get the plane out of the hangar toward the runway. They reset over the previous computer work for their preflight preparation to Langley instead of Dallas, knowing that the airport would be shut down.

Sam contacts his friend K. James Bondi to have the FAA notified by the FBI that this plane had to leave regardless of the explosion that had just happened. Sam reminds Bondi also to make sure that they give the information to Matthew Marx only in a private setting, letting him know the package was still safe and on its way to Langley Air Force Base. And to send emergency responders to the hangar where the driver of the fuel truck was, and that he was unconscious and left behind for medical help.

As the plane was making its way out of the hangar towards the only runway that was open, emergency vehicles were coming into the explosion area from every part of the airport. Sam and Dannie had placed Frank's body in one of the rear seats of the jet and strapped him in. They had to use a suit coat that was laying on one of the seats, fitting it over Frank's head, and tying the arms of the suit behind the seat to hold him in place.

All the pilots still thought that Mr. Webb was a high-profile fugitive wanted by the FBI and that the KODE Team were real FBI agents. Sam and Dannie sat in the two seats in front of Frank Morgan, while Koon Hee and Mr. Webb sat across from them.

As the plane was taking off down the runway, Sam looked back towards where Frank was and said to Dannie, "I never could get out of my mind what he had done; that he was no good and was a piece of trash. He wasn't good enough for the KODE Team. Now I realize he had problems like everybody has. No matter what the problem is, sometimes they are hard to solve. He had the gambling problem, I had a problem with forgiveness; but I never thought it would be him, that would be saving me in this stage of my life."

"I guess my grandfather was right, preaching," he said, "sometimes the best is brought out of every one of us, in the worst and hardest situations that we must face." It was as though tears had formed in Sam's eyes, as Dannie patted him on the arm and said, "We will let them know at Langley, that Frank was the true hero." Sam nodded and said, "That's what I was thinking also."

As the plane was now airborne, Sam leaned his seat back and said to Dannie, "I'm closing my eyes a minute, and I need to figure out what I'm going to do with my M.A.D. triangular medallion that the government gave me. There is an old graveyard on the mountain close to the cabin; Dannie, that is where I will bury the M.A.D. medallion."

As Dannie leaned back, she told Sam, "I think also I will put my M.A.D. medallion in a place where a grave used to be, by the railroad track." Sam knew that grave was the place where they found the bones of her father, the place her mother had buried him. Both Sam and Dannie knew that the past could destroy the future, or that you can rid yourself of the past with a strong will, to have a better future. It seemed that a silence had settled into the plane's cabin even the pilots were not talking.

As the plane made its way en route to Langley Air Force Base, the FBI had now entered the container ship in Los Angeles where Koon Hee had left some of the Chinese agents to remove them from the ship. The Pearl Harbor decoy was being towed out of the area towards the place it would become an underwater reef, with many secrets tagged to it that would never be known. Time would tell if any leaks would be given to the news agencies, revealing that this was more than just a ship that had caught on fire, blocking the Los Angeles harbor. But as of now, it seemed like the only two who knew about Mr. Webb were the Chinese CCP and the Intelligence Agencies in the United States.

As the light of the sun came through the airplane window, shining on Sam's face, he opened his eyes, knowing that Langley was now near. He glanced back again at Frank and looked at Dannie, who was asleep. Then, he looked toward Koon Hee and Mr. Webb, who were also asleep. He began to think of the song they always would sing, the one his grandfather loved: "It Will Be Worth It All Someday."

Sam knew that warfare was not a fair or unfair game; it was life or death, and it took strong military might and great spying to ensure your adversary didn't take the greatest thing your country had: its freedom. Freedom that was written and given through the constitutional writers, and the freedom for real democracy, not one that is controlled by communistic dictatorship parties.

As Sam reached up and ran his fingers through the scar on his face, it seemed as though the tension that he once held in unforgiveness was no longer there. He remembered one of the sermons his grandfather had preached: forgiveness is the greatest medication that you will ever find. Sam also knew that his friend Dannie had a lot of darkness and animosity in her heart toward her dad's actions when she was young. He knew that he would have to help her and her mother, who held onto the hidden secret of who it was that was buried by the railroad track.

Sam knew that at one time in his past, he felt unstoppable, and he truly believed that it was impossible for him to lose in any battle or circumstance that he was placed in. But after the last few months, he began to see a weakness in the character that he thought he was, and he knew he could never fathom that the one known as Sam Black the invincible would lie and shake like a child with a fever in a battle zone as important as "War Peace."

As he began to think clearly for the first time in a long time, he realized that the greatest enemy he had to face was himself, and when your enemy is yourself, how will you ever conquer that? So he reached back to the scar on his face and began to run his finger up and down the scar, just to see what his mentality would be or become. He glanced back again to stare at Frank Morgan, in whom had given his life to save his, yet knowing that Frank was the one who put the scar on his face. That scar would always be visible to any person he had to face. But it seemed like the calmness that was in the plane was now him, and the only remorse that he felt was not being able to save Frank's life at the airport or give him a thank you before he passed.

As Sam began to reflect on forgiveness, the word that stood out to him was "given." That's what Frank Morgan had accomplished; he had given his life for Sam, and Sam knew that was a big price to pay — probably the biggest price of all, to give your life for someone else's.

As the plane hit a small patch of turbulence, the shaking woke up the passengers. Dannie turned towards Sam and then towards Frank, asking if they were landing. Sam informed them it shouldn't be long now, that they had crossed some turbulence. Koon Hee stood up, stretched himself, and went towards the restroom. Dannie also stood up, lifting her legs up and down and walking a few steps at a time.

Sam got up out of the seat and turned towards Frank Morgan, checking the suit coat they put over his head and the knot that was tied in the sleeves of the suit coat holding him in the seat until landing. Sam walked over towards Mr. Webb and said, "Sir, I hope you really understand the gains and the losses of this mission." Mr. Webb turned towards Sam, his eyes caught towards the scar side of Sam's face. With a strong stare, Mr. Webb said, "The loss of your comrade is worth more than what this jet is worth, or even every jet put together at Langley. I really don't think that you can put a price on the value of the Star Wars Shield that I've been fortunate enough to develop. It could actually stop the annihilation of millions of people. But even at that, according to the way I think, in the way I write and develop, every individual is important. Even those that have no education or understanding. On that note, I want to thank you, Mr. Black, and your team, for risking your lives. And I am saddened at the loss of your friend's life to save mine. I'm hoping someday you will say that the words of your song were correct, but just with a little touch to the song lyrics saying, 'it was worth it all that day.'" With that, Mr. Webb turned towards a window, looking out, and then closed his eyes.

Sam was puzzled for a moment at those words, especially the wording where Mr. Webb called Frank Morgan his friend.

As Sam turned to look towards Frank Morgan, Dannie stood beside him, her hand on Frank's shoulder. She repeated back what Mr. Webb had said to him: "Your friend Sam and mine." Sam nodded at Dannie and said, "Yes, he was our friend." Then she began to sing Sam's song again, in her soft vocal tone, "It Will Be Worth it all Someday."

"That's how Mr. Webb knew your song, Sam," Dannie said. "On your last breakdown, I was singing your song to you."

As Sam stared toward Frank Morgan, he took the phone out of his pocket and called his friend, K James Bondi. He instructed him to get the information to the right people, that there would be someone there to pick up Frank Morgan's body, and to have an American flag draped over his body immediately after they brought him off the jet. The two extra pilots had overheard Sam talking about the flag, and they offered to help.

"We will help you take the body off the jet if you wouldn't mind," they said. "We could drape the flag over him before we remove him from the jet. It's up to you; we both have fought for our country, and we are patriots."

Sam quickly agreed, appreciating their suggestion. Even though he knew that the main person the government wanted to deal with was Mr. Webb at this point, and for him to be the first one off the plane, Frank Morgan would be the first one to be removed from the aircraft, draped in a US Flag.

K James Bondi assured Sam he would take care of all the landing requests and asked to meet up after the mission was completed. As the jet began to lower its altitude for landing at Langley Air Force Base, Sam walked over to Frank Morgan, checking his seatbelt and the suit sleeves that held him in the seat, preparing him for the landing. Then he returned to his seat with Dannie.

Koon Hee asked Sam if it's all right for him to help carry Frank Morgan off the plane. Sam replied, "Koon Hee, it will be a privilege to have you by my side again, taking our friend and fellow comrade toward his final resting place."

As the plane approached the runway, the pilots were informed where to taxi the plane. What was waiting to pick up Mr. Webb would certainly make the pilots become a little dumbfounded. Waiting for Mr. Webb would be an armored vehicle, with high security, almost like what the President of the United States receives.

As the plane approached the runway, Sam looked out the

Steven Jones

window and saw several military planes. He turned to Dannie and said, "You're only a couple of hours from home, where your mother, I know, is waiting for you. But if you would like to travel with me to see my new grandson, you and Koon Hee both are welcome."

Dannie smiled at Sam and agreed, "It will be a privilege, under one condition. After we've spent time with your daughter and grandson, you and Koon Hee will go with me to check on my mother. Plus, I must get rid of this MAG Medallion. I have a certain spot picked out by the railroad track where I want to put it."

As the plane moved towards the drop-off point where Mr. Webb would be picked up, Sam began to think about Frank Morgan's dealings with gambling mobsters, evidently located in Las Vegas. He wondered if the two men who died in the bombing at Germantown, Maryland, were the ones that poisoned his dog Buck, probably workers for the note writer, Pizza.

He turned to talk to Dannie about the woman she saw walk out of Frank's motel room. "Blondie, there are a lot of unanswered questions that I would like to know. Why would she be working with Frank? What's the reason behind her being in his room and on this mission?"

Given all the information they had received about the woman from those working in a park bench, how she was dealing with undercover agents in drug-infested countries trying to flood their country with drugs, especially Columbia, Dannie wondered. "According to his passport, he had been there several times. Did the government know something about Frank Morgan that they're hiding from us? Was he one of the drug dealers bringing drugs into this country, and did they plant this lady, Miss Martinez, in his surroundings to catch him?"

"Why would Frank blow up a car with only two of them in the vehicle and let the rest live?" Dannie pondered. "That would have to be clear knowledge with the government. They had to know about that bombing in Germantown, Maryland. They were either going to wait until these missions were over and then, through their investigations, arrest the bomber, which no doubt was Frank Morgan."

Dannie began to tell Sam about a few things she had found, mentioning that they had come to her thoughts because of their boating accident at the beaver pond, which had diverted her attention. She spoke about drug cartels in Mexico linked to Colombia, specifically mentioning the Rio Grande Jalapeños cartel. Dannie expressed confusion because Frank had only talked about Las Vegas and the mob, never mentioning anything about a cartel. She noted that most cartels only worked up to the border, employing pack rats or drug carriers with large bags of their drug-making paraphernalia. So, it didn't make sense for them to be involved in gambling or loaning money to gamblers.

"I do believe that Miss Martinez is legit because of The Nest," Dannie said, "and the fact that she was with us, even being mentioned in this mission. Maybe they are training her to be a sniff dog in all other operations from The Nest. Blondie, I am going to have to get to the bottom of this. None of this makes any sense."

Sam replied, "You're forgetting one thing, Dannie. This is your last mission, and you are retired. Let the government deal with this and Miss Mary Martinez, because they are going to have to deal with the body of Frank Morgan too."

Dannie likened Sam's thinking to Polly's cooking, saying, "You're overthinking, and Polly always overcooks and makes enough food for three families."

As their plane came to a stop, there seemed to be a sigh of relief among all passengers and pilots. Sam and Dannie looked out onto the wing of the plane and saw the heavy armored vehicle, along with what looked like tactical force police officers, probably FBI, waiting to receive the package known as War Peace. Sam also spotted someone unexpected, Matthew Marx.

"Dannie, isn't that Matthew Marx?" Sam asked. He seemed to be holding something in his hands as he walked over and gave it to one of the FBI's tactical officers.

Sam quickly realized that K James Bondi had gotten a hold of Mr. Marx about the body of Frank Morgan, as he had just handed that officer a United States flag.

As the FBI officer walked towards the door of the plane, the pilot shut down the engines. As the door of the jet was being lowered, one of the pilots turned to Sam and said, "I will retrieve the flag, be back in just a moment." Stepping out onto the steps leading to the tarmac, a pilot was handed the flag by an FBI officer, then turned and went back to where he was standing at the heavy armored vehicle.

As the pilot returned towards Sam with the flag, Koon Hee stood up, and the other three pilots came to help remove the body of Frank Morgan. Sam removed the suit coat off Frank's face, and for a moment, he knew he was staring into the face of the one he had hated with all his heart. Now, he realized that Morgan had laid his life down for him, and Sam was ending his hatred for him. Frank Morgan had become a real friend and fighting comrade that Sam would never forget. The scar on his face would now remind him of the bullet that Morgan took for him, not the one that came from Frank's gun.

Sam got behind Frank's seat, put his arms through his from behind, to lift him up. Koon Hee and one of the pilots got on each side of his legs to carry him towards the door, where they would lay him on the floor, covering him up with the American flag. All six would carry him off the jet. Sam noticed the bloodstains in the seat from the bullet wound, feeling for the first time what Dannie was feeling and telling him about. He was free from the hate and guilt that almost caused him a total mental breakdown. It seemed possible now that Dannie and he would have a lot to talk about, without the fear of falling to the ground and shaking uncontrollably.

But Sam knew he also had to stand with Dannie's mother and make sure she was kept from looking back in the rearview mirror and seeing her husband dead in the back of that old farm truck. As they laid the body down and began to cover Frank with the flag, Dannie spoke to Sam slowly behind him, saying, "It will be worth it all someday." Sam turned and reminded Dannie that that day had happened a few minutes ago, just like when she explained to him when she looked in the mirror in her room, saying for the first time, "I forgive you, Daddy."

"I can honestly say now, Dannie, with all my heart, Frank, I forgive you," Sam replied. As the four pilots, Sam Black, and Koon Hee lifted the body of Frank Morgan, they began to carry him off the plane towards a stretcher that had now been placed on the tarmac. They all noticed that even the FBI agents standing next to the armored vehicle were giving Frank Morgan a salute for his service in helping to bring back the scientist who had invented probably one of the greatest weapons of their time, the Star Wars program known as "The War Peace."

As they laid Frank Morgan's body on the stretcher, the four pilots, Koon Hee, and Sam stepped back about two feet and gave him a salute. The FBI officers were already on the plane, bringing Mr. Webb off and taking him to his armored vehicle that was waiting. One of the pilots walked over to Sam and said, "I don't know what crime that man committed against our government, but it must've been a hellish crime to have this much attention."

Sam looked at him and replied, "It pays to obey the laws of the land, especially here in the United States. With all the technology they have, most likely they will find you. You can't hide."

The pilot then asked Sam, "Is it possible that you can tell me what crime this man has committed?"

"Well, Sir, I appreciate your service and flying us all the way to Langley Air Force Base, but you know the Constitution: they are innocent until proven guilty," Sam responded, reaching out to shake the pilot's hand before turning to go talk to Matthew Marx.

As Sam approached Matthew Marx, Matthew quickly reached out his hand toward Sam. "I not only want to shake your hand, Sam, I want to thank you for your quick thinking when we were on the container ship. We almost had a little fight at Park Bench; you told them to shut up their mic. I really laughed and thought that was pretty good myself. I knew that you weren't going to leave Dannie behind, and I also knew that your expertise was kicking into high gear to get Mr. Webb off that ship and bring him back to us in safety mode. It came across to me as being very amazing how you figured out the Navy SEALS had been taken out, and those that had picked you up were real Chinese agents; in which you and Frank took control of the situation. I told them at Park Bench it was a shame to even suggest that you leave the hacker behind. I just want to let you know that upfront."

As Sam was talking to Matthew Marx, Jim Logan came over to shake Sam's hand and express his appreciation for Sam's expertise in getting the mission completed. Sam quickly deflected the praise, emphasizing that it was a collective effort involving Frank Morgan, Dannie Browning, Koon Hee, and himself.

"Well, Sam, that proves one thing to me," said Jim Logan. "You don't want to be a hero. You just want to get the job done right."

Sam replied, "I want to get the job done right. My understanding is, your scientist, Mr. Webb, he wants to get the job done perfectly. One thing's for sure about this mission: nothing went perfect. Everything went the opposite direction, and we had to change the guidelines to come out in victory, not in the zero zone. I don't like the zero zone."

As Jim Logan returned to his SUV, Sam asked Matthew

Marx if he could walk with him for a moment, seeking a private setting to ask some questions. Marx agreed, and they walked in a certain direction.

"Of all the ones I've been working around on this mission, Mr. Marx, it seems like you're the one that I can trust," Sam began. "Listen, I have some lingering questions and, in my curiosity as an agent of the past, I need some answers. You know Frank Morgan saved Dannie's and my life in Las Vegas. He took the bullet that most likely I would have gotten, and Dannie the second one. And I understand the secrecy of the agency you work out of. You also know that I've been in the same agency, and I have a lot of secrets hidden in my heart that have never been spoken in the open. But I need to know about Frank's gambling problem and why Miss Mary Martinez was working on this mission."

"Just to let you know upfront, Mr. Marx," Sam continued, "Dannie and I saw her coming out of Frank's motel room before we left on this mission. And we know, and perhaps you know, she's the code name, Chambermaid. What had Frank done that you had sent Ms. Martinez to stay in his presence? To catch him with mobsters from Las Vegas? And why were those two killed in the bombing in Germantown, Maryland? You know, the same that I do, it had to be Frank Morgan who put that type of bomb in that car to keep it contained in such a small area, killing only two in that Mercedes automobile."

As Marx stared down at the tarmac for a moment, he raised up slowly and said to Sam, "If I didn't really know you and trust you, Sam Black, you would never get this information from me. But it just might be possible that you're going to be needing this information in the future, because it might be possible that we are going to be needing you in the future, for the service of your country."

"Frank didn't have a gambling problem, all of that was made up by some bad people in Las Vegas, setting them up to be taken down by the government. We have found a direct flow of major drugs from Columbia in Mexico to certain cartels, not only killing Americans, but they are also starting to move into the cities, setting up their headquarters for major drug movements. Frank Morgan was going to be the undercover fall guy. Miss Mary Martinez happens to be dedicated from her heart, because of the killing of her family. We brought her on this mission because we also have found out that coming in on some of those containers from China is the drug paraphernalia that the Mexicans have been using for a long time, but are now setting up major shops in major cities in the United States."

"So, what you're telling me, Mr. Marx, is that Frank Morgan was a special agent in the DEA?" Sam inquired.

"Yes, he started working behind the scenes even when you were with him in Mexico. He was seed planting for the DEA, FBI, and with The Nest, which only a few know about. But just to let you know this, Sam, every time Frank spoke your name, he always told me, 'He's the best. This man is the best at what he does; there is no one who can beat Samuel Black.' And then he would always say, 'If only I'd been in the right place when he told me, he would never have had that scar on his face to look at the rest of his life.'"

"What about the $5 million that we are going to receive for working on this mission? Who came up with that idea and developed it?" Sam asked.

"That's true, he did have debt, but the debt that he had was what was made through the government, working with him to keep him hidden. To make him look like a real gambler, so we created the scene. Frank Morgan was not going to receive the $5 million. Only you, Sam, Dannie, and Koon Hee. The major company that was helping Mr. Webb in his development of the Star Wars program, in The War Peace, they are the ones, not the government, that are going to be paying $5 million to all three of the ex-KODE Team members. Frank also was a reason behind that, because he knew that you would never take the mission due to your grandson being born in your retirement and your Appalachian Mountain hideaway. And the other reason he said you would never take the mission was because of him. Even when we put the chocolate pudding on the cake, which was the 5 million, you would still have hesitation. But knowing that you had to wear that triangular MAG (Militants

Against Government) necklace, I thought they should offer you 10 million dollars each. That was almost like a man given a death wish because if this mission hadn't gone the way it did, and you all would have been caught on the container ship, you would have become the traitor of all traitors to your country."

"By the way, Sam, what are you going to do with that medallion?" Marx inquired.

"Well, Sir, if it's all right with you, Mr. Marx, there's an old rock on the mountain that I sit on watching the clouds go over. And just to the right of that is an old well that's dried up. I'm thinking about placing it in that old well."

"I must ask you something very important to me, Mr. Marx. I don't think Frank had much of a family. What are you planning on doing with his body?"

"Well, Sam, that's something we didn't plan on; it sure wasn't included in any of the folders about Frank Morgan's death and burial. So, we'll just have to figure that out, ask some questions, and get some answers from some of the higher-ups."

As Marx nodded in understanding, Sam continued, "I have a favor to ask of you."

"Sure, Sam, what can I do for you?" Marx replied.

"When you speak to the higher-ups, tell them that if they

The Kode

don't have a place for Frank Morgan's body, I would like to have his remains or ashes to take to the mountain. I have a place in an old graveyard where I would like to place him. It's next to a hero of mine, my grandfather, who was a mountain preacher and a good man."

"I will do my best, Sam. That's one favor I never thought you would ask of me," Marx responded.

"One more thing, Sam," Marx continued, "just to let you know. Frank found out about the poisoning of your dog. He never said he did it, but we believe he was the one who took out those two in Germantown, Maryland, in the car bombing. Because it wasn't long after that when I saw him; he looked at me and said, 'Two more to go,' and winked and walked off. He knew the investigation would be hidden because of the secrecy of this mission that he was on, and the importance of returning Mr. Webb and The War Peace, so he felt like the real gambler; he had an ace in the hole."

Sam shook his head in disbelief. "Frank never mentioned any of that. He acted like he couldn't care. Now I believe that he was a better actor than Koon Hee was on top of that container."

"We have a helicopter waiting for you, Dannie, and Koon Hee to take you back to the hospital where her car is parked. Just keep in mind, some things are not over until it's over, and that means in the government of security is, there's no heads peeking out of the ground, and no hands reaching out of the dark shadows. The only thing that I'm glad for is that it's over, Mr. Marx. This mission is over. Because I have a family that loves me and a new grandson that's named after me. And I know the work that you do; there are always going to be heads and hands reaching and looking in places they shouldn't be. But I want to place my hands around my little grandson Samuel and hold him close, because I'm not getting any younger."

Marx nodded solemnly. "There is one more thing I have in the back of my SUV I need to give you, Mr. Black."

"Sorry, Mr. Marx, I do not need more missions or folders of planning; my work is done."

"Well, Sam, it's something that we need to give you to take care of. It was Frank's wishes. Follow me, Sam, to the back of my vehicle."

As Sam and Matthew Marx walked towards the back of his vehicle, Matthew pushed the button on his keychain and the tailgate of an SUV came up. Removing a cover over a square object, Matthew revealed a small German Shepherd puppy inside a dog cage.

"Here's all the paperwork, Sam. This little boy is full-blooded and ready for training from one of the best," Matthew said.

The Kode

Sam stood in total denial and surprise for a moment. "Frank was everything that I thought he wasn't. Please let me know about Frank's remains, Mr. Marx. It would be an honor for me and for him to place him on top of that mountain."

As Sam shook hands with Matthew Marx, thinking it was the last time, Marx pointed towards the helicopter that would take him, Dannie, and Koon Hee out of the battle zone.

Before Sam headed towards the helicopter, he opened the dog cage and took out the puppy, holding him close. The puppy started licking the scarred side of his face, and Sam didn't even notice Dannie and Koon Hee walking up beside him. Dannie reached out for the puppy, saying, "Let me hold him, Sam."

As Sam handed the puppy to Dannie, he put his arm around Koon Hee and expressed his gratitude for accompanying him to the hospital to see his grandson.

"Well, think about it this way, Sam," Koon Hee replied, "now you have a son, grandson, and daughter."

"Wait a minute," said Dannie, "he has two daughters, not one."

"Exactly right," agreed Sam. "I am asking my daughter Blondie to give me my dog back."

Dannie smiled and handed Sam his new German Shepherd

puppy. "Are you going to call him Buck?" she asked.

"No, I have been thinking about that, Dannie. I am going to call him Frank," Sam decided.

"That's the perfect name for your new little friend," Dannie remarked.

As Sam placed the dog cage inside the helicopter and prepared to board, he let Dannie get in first. Then he handed her the puppy to hold as he got in. As she handed Sam his dog back, he held the puppy close to his face once more, and it seemed as though it never even moved as it licked the scar left by Frank Morgan.

As the roar of the helicopter's engine increased, it appeared that Sam Black had finally conquered the strongest enemy he had ever faced: himself. Even Dannie, as she watched the dog licking the scarred side of Sam's face, knew that her friend had crossed over the bridge of destruction and mental anguish. It seemed like a wider, brighter smile spread across Sam's face.

As the helicopter lifted off the tarmac, the three remaining KODE team members looked down, seeing Frank Morgan's body being pushed into a hangar. Sam saluted him and said, "I'm sorry, Frank. I didn't really know who you were. You were a true friend in times of trouble and need."

As Dannie saluted Frank's memory and quoted Psalms 23,

she couldn't shake the feeling that Sam would face another trial soon: returning to the hospital to find out his son-in-law, Jeremy, had been shot. She hoped that the word "pizza" wouldn't be on Sam's mind or plate that day.

In the quiet of the helicopter, only the whimpering of the little puppy and Sam's gentle interactions with him broke the silence. Suddenly, Dannie's phone rang. It was Jim Logan.

"Dannie, I need you to keep this to yourself for a few days," Jim instructed. "Let Mr. Black rest and spend time with his family. But I believe you're the only one who can get his attention enough to consider one more mission we need to take care of. I won't give you the details now, but I'll contact you again in a few days."

Dannie took a deep breath and replied smoothly, "I don't need to place that order now; I picked up my shoes at the mall. Thank you anyhow. Goodbye."

After hanging up, she sighed and remarked to herself, "I'm going to have to get a new phone number. Telemarketers just don't leave online shoppers alone." She knew Jim Logan had Sam Black's mountain farm location recorded in his government GPS and had been there before. She decided to let him try to entice Sam with another mission on his own.

As the pilot was setting the helicopter down on the hospital pad, Koon Hee turned to Sam and said, "Instead of taking Dannie's

Camaro to the hospital where your grandson is, how would you like to ride in the helicopter?" He nudged his head towards the pilot seat. Sam laughed because he knew what Koon Hee was gesturing about. He had taken the emergency helicopter in Los Angeles and was able to pick them up and start them on their journey towards Langley Air Force Base.

"We better not at this time," Sam replied. "I feel like I have a little jet lag. I'm going to let Dannie hold my little puppy while I drive her Camaro just a little over 5 mph more than the speed sign says."

As Sam and his two friends stepped off the helicopter and started walking towards the parking garage where Dannie's car was, it never even dawned on any of them that they were five million dollars richer. As they entered Dannie's car, Sam reached her the puppy, and she reached him the keys for the trip toward Washington DC and on to Germantown Maryland. Depending on how the traffic was, it would take them probably an hour and a half before they would arrive where Jennifer was.

Koon Hee began talking to Sam from the back seat, saying, "When you start that new company called The Blackout, Sam, maybe we can ease into China and rescue some of my family who are unloading fish probably even now."

Sam replied, "So what you're asking Koon Hee, for me to do

is go fishing with you in China? How many fishing reels do we need to take or how big a net do we need to take to catch our limit in?"

"I have about sixteen fish, Sam, that we will need to net, making sure they are on our fishing vessel and not theirs, ever again," Koon Hee responded.

Dannie's remark was, "Do you need someone to go with you to help bait the hooks?"

Sam reached over and patted Dannie on the hand, saying, "The number one thing you must do when you go fishing is to have the right bait with you."

Dannie quickly replied, "I'm sure I have the right bait." Sam never even thought that this was another mission. It was a family matter to him because Koon Hee was his son. Even though there was no DNA between them, the love factor was much stronger than any DNA.

As Dannie pondered in her heart whether she should tell Sam about the shooting at the hospital or just wait until they arrived, she decided to get a second opinion from Koon Hee. Dannie told Sam to stop at the next exit where there was a gas station. She said she wanted to go to the bathroom, and probably his puppy needed to potty.

Sam soon spotted an exit off Interstate 95, and he turned off, heading towards one of the gas stations. As he brought the car to a stop, Dannie handed him his puppy and said, "Your dog, you take him for a walk."

As Sam carried his dog toward a grassy area, Dannie asked Koon Hee to walk with her towards the gas station. She wanted to ask him about something. Dannie and Koon Hee were good friends as well, and they were about the same age and had a lot in common. They were both sort of loners. Neither one of them was dating anyone, and Koon Hee had never ever mentioned dating or having a girlfriend in his past. Sam had always told Koon Hee that he was just so involved in his skills with the Kode Team that he had no pleasure or feelings to be dating anyone.

As Dannie and Koon Hee began to talk about Sam, Dannie asked Koon Hee, "What would you do, or what should I do? Should we tell Sam about the shooting at the hospital? Polly has told me that Jeremy is doing great, he is all right."

Koon Hee replied to Dannie, "Has Jennifer received the information yet that her husband has been shot from Polly?"

"I'm not sure," Dannie replied. "Let me call Polly now at the hospital and see all the good and bad that's going on with Jeremy."

As Dannie went inside the gas station, she called Polly's cell phone number. Polly answered quickly, asking about how Sam was doing. Dannie began to tell her side of the story about how Sam had found out about Frank Morgan, also telling her about his new German Shepherd puppy that Sam decided to name Frank. "To be honest with you, Polly, Sam seemed to be a new man and almost like he had a new life; something had resurrected inside his heart." Polly replied, "I am so glad to hear that. Just those words, Dannie, made my day a whole lot better off, and brought my heart some peace."

Dannie began to ask if Jennifer had been told about the shooting of her husband Jeremy. Polly answered back, "Jeremy is sitting right here beside me, next to Jennifer in her hospital room; I will let you talk to him," and Polly reached Jeremy her phone.

"How are you feeling, Jeremy?" Dannie asked. Jeremy told Dannie about the bullet that had struck no vitals, and that he would be going home from the hospital the same day Jennifer would be released.

Dannie asked Jeremy, "Koon Hee and I have been talking, should we tell Sam about your accident, or should we wait and allow him to explain to Sam what happened, and how you are doing just fine?" Jeremy paused just for a moment, thinking about how Sam had been in the past, not even knowing that something in Sam's heart had changed towards Frank Morgan. So, he told Dannie, "I believe you should wait. I will be here in the room with Jennifer when you all arrive. What I will do is, I will get out of my hospital clothes, and

I will put on my street clothes, and he won't even be able to know that I was shot. After he sees Jennifer and holds his little grandchild, I will break the news to him, and I think he will be all right." Dannie turned and told Koon Hee what Jeremy had just spoken to her. They both agreed, most likely that would be the best way to go. It was better to hear from the one that had been harmed about their condition than to have someone else tell you that someone had been harmed, and you had little idea what their condition was like.

Dannie went to the restroom in the gas station, while Koon Hee bought Sam two cups of espresso coffee. He was going to give him both as a joking gesture; he knew that Sam would give one back. They both had a taste for good espresso coffee. He was going to fulfill the promise that was made to Sam on the airplane when he was having one of his nervous breakdown modes. Koon Hee waited for Dannie to come out of the restroom so they could continue their journey with Sam. He also wanted to tell Dannie about his two espresso coffees, and he was going to reach them to Sam when he got back to the car. Dannie loved that about Koon Hee; he was a cut-up at times.

As they started walking back toward the car, they noticed that Sam was kneeling, pouring water into the palm of his hand and letting his puppy drink. Koon Hee asked Dannie with a smile, "I think Sam has what we call a service animal; when you come back from the war zone, sometimes they will give you one." Koon Hee reached Sam the two cups of coffee and turned to walk toward the car.

"What are you doing, Koon Hee? Are you keeping a campaign promise? Come now, get this cup of coffee before I take a belt to your hide," Sam replied, laughing.

Sam reminded Dannie to make sure that Koon Hee had the lid on his coffee very tight and secure. She didn't need to get a second dump of coffee in her Camaro. "Just make sure that you drive normal," he said, "because I'm holding your dog." And remember the last time you dumped your coffee in your pants.

As they entered back on Interstate 95 N. to hit the beltway to go around Washington DC, they all sat silent for a few moments. Until Sam began to sing the words from his grandfather's song from the past, "It will be worth it all someday." Then he paused and started singing the song differently, "It will be worth it all today," he repeated himself, "It will be worth it all today."

Koon Hee reached his hand and touched Dannie on top of her head and said, "It just came to me," he said, "we are all worth five million dollars today." Koon Hee told Sam, "That should be plenty of money to pay The Blackout company to get my family out of China."

Sam turned towards Koon Hee and said, "If that's not enough, I will loan you five million myself, just to help you out."

Sam and Koon Hee were waiting for a response from Dannie. But she had gotten lost in the eyes of the little puppy and wasn't paying any attention to the conversation. Sam tapped the brake pedal a little bit to get Dannie's attention.

"Where have you been, Blondie?" Sam asked. "Koon Hee and I are giving our money to a company to bring his family out of China. We were wondering if you wanted to jump in and be part of it."

"I don't have a clue what you're talking about, Sam," Dannie replied, still enamored with the puppy. "This puppy is the cutest thing I've ever seen."

Sam lost focus on what he was going to say next. "Wait until you see my grandchild. He looks just like me."

"Sam, if he's anything like you, I believe the future of the world will be a better place," Dannie said with a smile.

As they continued to talk among themselves while driving towards the hospital in Germantown, Maryland, time seemed to pass swiftly. Before they knew it, they were pulling into the parking area of the hospital, where Sam's family was waiting for him with open arms. As they got out of Dannie's car, Sam realized he had his dog with him again, at the same hospital where Buck had been poisoned.

Koon Hee picked up quickly on what Sam was thinking and

told him to go into the hospital with Dannie, assuring him that he would watch his puppy dog. He suggested that he and Dannie take turns watching the dog so that Sam could go and see his grandson. Sam agreed, saying, "That will work. But remember this, Koon Hee, you are the guard dog now. But in about a year from now, Frank is going to be the guard dog like Buck was."

As Sam and Dannie entered the hospital, they went to the information desk to ask for Jennifer's room number. As they started towards the elevator, they passed by a small waiting room where they heard a news reporter on the TV talking about the bombing in Germantown, Maryland. Sam raised his arm to stop Dannie, indicating they should listen to what the news reporter had to say.

The news reporter informed his audience that the government had tracked down the bomber, Mike Wilson, who lived by himself below Richmond, Virginia. He was killed in a shootout with federal ATF agents. The two men killed in the Mercedes were identified as drug dealers that Wilson owed money to. The reporter also mentioned that the FBI government officials stated it was a miracle that the small pipe bomb only damaged the Mercedes and harmed no one else.

Sam reached to take Dannie's hand and said, "If you and I had one dollar for every lie that the government tells, that five million dollars would be only a drop in the bucket."

"Yeah, but you must remember something, Sam," Dannie replied, "Matthew Marx said that Frank Morgan had what every gambler wanted, the Ace in the hole. Plus, Frank will be known throughout the government agencies as a hero, not a zero."

As they stepped off the elevator and walked down the hall, entering Jennifer's room, they found Jeremy sitting beside her. Jennifer's face lit up when she saw Sam walking into the room, and she exclaimed, "Daddy, I love you so much, I love you so much, I love you so much." Sam walked around the side of the bed, bent down, and kissed his daughter on the forehead, saying, "I love you more. Jennifer, where is my grandson? I want to hold him now."

"He's in the nursery now. They will be bringing him to my room in a few minutes. Sit over there next to Jeremy; he wants to talk to you about something," Jennifer replied.

As Sam pulled up a seat in front of Jeremy, Dannie walked around and gave Jennifer a hug, saying, "My mother wants Polly, you, Jeremy, and your grandson to come to Thanksgiving dinner."

Jennifer quickly responded, "We accept the invitation without any reservation."

Jeremy began to speak to Sam about his accident. He raised up his shirt, revealing bandages wrapped all around his lower stomach area. "Son, what in the world happened to you?" Sam asked.

"Well, Sam, I had an accident while I was here at the hospital with your beautiful daughter," Jeremy began to explain. He recounted how he got in the way of a bullet that was meant for Frank Morgan.

As Sam stood up in shock, Jeremy pointed back down towards Sam's seat and said, "Sam, sit back down; I'm not done talking." He continued, "The bullet missed all vital areas. I guess you could say I am a miracle." Jeremy informed Sam that he was being released the same day Jennifer was getting out of the hospital, and that they would be going home together to take care of his beautiful grandson.

Dannie and Jennifer watched Sam's actions closely to see how he would react to the news from Jeremy. But it seemed that the only flash that went through Sam's mind was the memory of the blood coming out of Frank's mouth in Las Vegas when he stopped the bullet that would've taken out Sam. Sam reached over and took Jeremy by the hand, smiling, and said, "Any time you're hit with a bullet that misses all vital parts in the body, especially if you're in a hospital when it happens, you are what's called a blessed miracle. I'm glad you're alright, son," Sam replied. Then he turned back towards Jennifer and asked, "How much time is left before little Samuel is brought into this room?"

"Any moment now," Jennifer replied. Just then, the nurse

walked into the room holding little Samuel in her arms. Jennifer pointed towards her dad, indicating that he should have the first hold. The nurse placed little Samuel in Sam's arms and said, "You have something to be proud of." Sam pointed to his daughter and said, "I have a whole lot to be proud of."

Sam sat back down in the chair and began to look down at his beautiful little grandson. He also knew that the only reason he was able to hold this child was because of Frank Morgan, the man he had hated for so long, who had made it possible for him to be with his daughter and family one more time.

After a few minutes, Jennifer said, "Hand him to me, Dannie. I must breast-feed this child." Sam handed his grandchild back to Jennifer and then turned to ask where Polly was.

"She just stepped out for a moment, Dad. I think she went to the concession room," Jennifer replied.

"I'll be back in a moment," Sam said, turning and walking out the door down the hallway towards the restrooms and concessions. He saw Polly coming out and she looked at Sam, raising her hands like she was in a church service, then came running down the hall, putting her arms around him and hugging him tight. "I have missed you so much, Sam, my boy," Polly said. "Listen to me good this time, Sam. That was your last mission. Your family loves you and I love you. It's time for you to settle down, start a new life with Catherine, and be a real man for a change."

Sam hugged Polly again and laughed at her remarks about becoming a real man. He knew what she really meant was to become a family man. But he also knew that she was right this time. He had now come to a place in his life, after losing all the hate and animosity he had against Morgan, to just settle down and enjoy his time on planet Earth.

As Sam and Polly walked back towards Jennifer's room, Dannie went down to relieve Koon Hee from watching Sam's dog so that he could come up also and talk with the family and see Sam's grandson. When they walked back into the room, Jeremy was holding the baby, even though he still had pain from the bullet wound. "It feels good to hold something that you know is a part of you," Jeremy said.

The nurse had pulled the curtain around Jennifer, and she was checking her incisions from the C-section she had to receive during delivery. Everything was going well in the hospital, and Sam was now holding the baby again. As Koon Hee came into the room, Polly grabbed him and hugged him too. "I haven't seen you in a long time, son. Where have you been?" she asked.

As Koon Hee hugged Polly back, he said, "I've been waiting for you to invite me to Sam's house and feed me a good meal. I haven't eaten anything like what you cook since the last time you fed me."

"Well, son, not only am I going to feed you some good food, but we have also been invited to Dannie's mother's house to eat the best Thanksgiving meal you ever have," Polly replied.

Sam asked Polly if she would like to have a hotel room close to the hospital. She shook her head no, saying she was doing just fine there with his daughter. Sam then looked at Koon Hee and said, "Get us a reservation at the Marriott. It's only about five blocks away."

Koon Hee told Sam he would go down and relieve Dannie from watching his puppy and that he would give her the information, and she would be glad to take care of that for all three of them. As Koon Hee started towards the car where Dannie was with Sam's dog, he began to think about his family that was in China and how he was already making plans before he had ever spoken to Sam. But now that he knew he had Sam's help in the future, the task of removing his family would be a whole lot easier.

As Koon Hee approached the Camaro, Dannie was standing on the outside holding Sam's dog as if it were his grandchild. He gave her the information about reserving them a room at the Marriott, and Dannie handed him the dog so that she could make the reservation.

The Kode

As Dannie reached Koon Hee the dog, she said, "Tomorrow is a new day for all of us." She told Koon Hee how Sam acted when Jeremy told him about the shooting at the hospital. "I believe that there is a 100% change in him," Dannie said.

As Koon Hee stared into Dannie's eyes, something seemed to sparkle in his heart. "Dannie, tomorrow would you like to have lunch with me?" he asked.

Dannie replied, "Do you know where Sam wants to go for lunch? I'm not talking about Sam, Koon Hee. I'm talking about you having lunch with me. You know where Sam's going to be. He's going to be here at the hospital, to see if they are going to be checking his daughter out to go home."

"Are you asking me out on a date?" Dannie asked.

Koon Hee smiled at Dannie and took her hand. "We will call this our first dinner date."

Dannie quickly remembered how she looked in the mirror in her bedroom and how it felt like all the pressure was gone from her past. She was quick to accept Koon Hee's offer. "Yes, I will go to lunch with you, with one attachment," Dannie replied. "Who is paying for the meal?"

Koon Hee smiled and said, "Uncle Sam is."

"In that case, we will have dessert also, Mr. Koon Hee,"

Dannie said with a giggle. "You do know that I'm talking about the government, not Sam Black, right?"

"It makes no difference to me who pays," Koon Hee replied.

As Dannie was making the reservations at the Marriott, she received a call from her mother. Her mother told her that the Sheriff had just come by again and would like to meet with them, if possible, tomorrow evening at 5 o'clock. Dannie recognized the worry in her mother's voice. She also knew that her mother had no knowledge that Dannie also knew about the killing of her dad. Dannie tried to push aside thoughts of what the Sheriff might tell her, saying, "I want you to fix Sam and Koon Hee a good old-fashioned dinner. I will get them to come with me tomorrow also when we talk with the Sheriff."

As her mother hung up, Dannie's mind began to race backward again to that night when she heard the gunshot and looked out the window, seeing her mother dragging her dad's dead body in the old farm truck. She vividly remembered staying at the window, waiting for her mother to return from the burial site by the railroad track. She recalled how one of her mother's eyes was swollen at breakfast the next morning, probably where he had hit her. She remembered Psalm 23, which her mother had often quoted, particularly emphasizing the part "thou art with me," repeating it three or four times before continuing with the whole Psalm.

The Kode

Dannie walked back over to Koon Hee and said, "Is it possible that we can have a dinner date also tomorrow evening? Because I am going to need you and Sam to come with me to my mother's house for an appointment at 5 o'clock. My mother is going to fix us one of those dinners that you don't forget about. If you don't mind, Koon Hee, would you watch the dog for a minute while I go up and talk with Sam about something?"

"Sure, Dannie, it will be a pleasure to eat your mother's cooking," Koon Hee replied. As Dannie walked back into the hospital, she decided to take the stairs to Jennifer's room instead of the elevator. She knew that the news her mother had received from the Sheriff had to be devastating to her. With each step up the emergency exit stairway, it felt like a weight pressing down on her shoulders. She knew that Sam would help her with this burden, and between the two of them, they would figure out how to tackle or cover up this problem if it was her dad they found in the grave.

Entering Jennifer's room with a smile, not wanting anyone to see the sadness in her heart, she asked Sam to come out in the hallway for a moment so she could go over with him the reservations at the Marriott. Sam excused himself for a moment, telling his daughter, "I'll be right back."

As they started walking down the hallway, Dannie began to tell Sam about the message her mother had received from the Sheriff to meet with her and her mother tomorrow evening at 5 o'clock. Sam assured Dannie that her mother would be in the clear.

"The other thing is, Dannie, you don't have the information on what the Sheriff is even wanting to talk about. My thought is, he is going to announce to your mother that is your dad and her husband that they found in that grave. That's the reason why he wanted you to be there with your mother before he made the announcement to her," Sam suggested.

"I never thought about it that way, Sam," Dannie replied.

"The other thing is, Dannie, if he thought your mother was involved, wouldn't he be asking her questions without you being around?" Sam reasoned.

"I suppose so, or maybe he wants to try to read our faces to see if there's a common guilt look," Dannie mused.

Sam looked at Dannie and said, "Regardless of what the Sheriff has to say, you must have evidence in a court of law. There are no bones about it, and Sam Black knows how to remove evidence, even if it is bones. Don't forget the bombing in Germantown, which we know was committed by Frank. Just like Matthew Marx said, he had the Ace in the hole. And it just so happens I know someone very personal that works at the coroner's office. They used to work at The Nest, and you know how obvious, sometimes, it is. It's always best when you know the right people."

Dannie told Sam about the dinner date she and Koon Hee were going to have. Sam laughed and said, "Am I invited?"

Dannie replied, "I don't want to take my daddy on my second date. I will be glad to go with you tomorrow to your mother's house, even if they check my daughter out. Polly would take care of her and Jeremy; they will be in good hands."

"Dannie, all of this will be over soon, and we can all then get our lives on track, to enjoy the sunrise every morning with our family every day," Sam reassured her.

"Let's go back to Jennifer's room, spend a few moments, and then we'll go to the motel to get some rest," Dannie suggested.

As Dannie and Sam went into the room, they gave everybody hugs and kisses. Sam said he would call earlier the next day to see if Jennifer was going to be released. Dannie turned and invited Polly to go with them the next day to have dinner with them and her mother, knowing Polly was very close to her mother and could provide comfort. "Be sure, Polly, if Jennifer has to stay another day, please come with us," Dannie requested.

As they started to leave the room, Jeremy asked Sam about bringing him his gift in the morning. Sam turned and said, "I don't have any get-well flowers, but I can go and pick up you and Jennifer some."

Jeremy replied, "That's not what I'm talking about. Bring me a good coffee espresso."

"I think I can handle that, Jeremy, my boy. We'll see you all in the morning," Sam promised.

As they started towards the car, Sam said to Dannie, "You can drive to the motel since I won't have any coffee that you can dump in my lap. I'll have my little puppy dog."

Koon Hee told Sam, "After spending time with your dog, I think that may be my next mission, to get me one also."

As they pulled into the parking lot of the Marriott, Sam told Dannie to check if they would allow dogs at the motel. She made a call to the front desk, and the receptionist told her that all the rooms were taken, and they had no more rooms available where dogs could stay. Dannie shook her head and said, "All rooms have been taken where dogs are allowed to stay."

Sam told Dannie, "You know what we must do," and smiled. "After we check in, I'll go through the side door. I'll put a cover over Frank's cage, and in the morning, you can give me the keys to the Camaro, and I'll go out through the side door when we're ready to leave."

"I've got a better plan, Sam," Dannie said. "It just so happens I have an old duffel bag in the back, and that cage will fit in perfectly. It looks like a piece of luggage, and that way, if somebody's watching the camera when you come to the side door, they'll never know the difference."

All three began laughing in the car, saying, "It seems like our sneaking in and out of places will never come to an end." Dannie went into the motel to sign in and get their keys to the rooms. Sam turned to Koon Hee and said, "You know, Dannie has had some hard things happen in her past when it comes to dating. And I don't know if she would want to sit down to explain all of it to you because of the horror of the memory. We'll give her a day or two to see, and if not, you and I can talk about her situation from the past."

"Thanks, Sam. You know, Dannie and I have been good friends ever since we've been working together. And maybe that's all the future will hold, is that we will be just good friends. But whatever happens, always stick by her through thick and thin," Koon Hee replied.

As Dannie returned with the keys to the motel room, she handed each one their room key, saying, "It's time to get some sleep." She took the duffel bag out of the trunk of the car and handed it to Sam. "Don't forget, Sam, Frank has now become part of the Kode Team, because he must sneak in also."

As Koon Hee and Dannie went through the main entrance of the hotel, Sam went to the side door with his new friend. As the three members of the past and present Kode Team entered their rooms for a night of rest, Mr. Webb had been taken to a secure location where extreme secret service members were in charge of his protection and his family. They realized now that no matter where he went, he was like the President of the United States; protection had to be always available.

As the night passed, it seemed that Sam Black, Dannie Browning, and Koon Hee were sleeping with a little bit more ease than in the last few days. About 6 AM in the morning, Sam began to be awakened by whimpering sounds from his puppy, Frank, in the cage next to him. As Sam raised up, he could hear people talking in the hallway as they walked by his room. As he stared at his dog, he realized that he hadn't brought him any food.

Sam got up, took a shower, and while putting his clothes on, he received a knock at his door. It was Dannie with a cup of coffee and something rolled up in a napkin. Sam finished putting his clothes on, and opened the door, saying, "Dannie, come on inside."

"Here, Sam, I have you an espresso from the breakfast room they have downstairs in the motel. I also have something for your dog. It dawned on me this morning when I woke up that we forgot to buy the dog some food."

She handed Sam the napkin, and inside were pieces of turkey sausage that Dannie had cut out to feed the puppy. Sam was quick to ask Dannie why she got up early, as he usually woke up first.

"I got a call from my mother this morning, Sam. She was doing a double check to make sure we were coming to have that dinner with her. Her voice didn't sound good, Sam, it sounded weak," Dannie explained. "I told her that Polly might be coming if Jennifer wasn't checked out of the hospital today, and that seemed to excite her. She loves Polly like a sister."

Dannie handed Sam the keys to her Camaro and said, "I'm going to go back and lay down for a while. They have a good breakfast down in the cafeteria. After Frank eats, go and enjoy yourself, Sam. I'll see you a little bit later."

As Sam began to feed his puppy one piece of sausage meat at a time, he hoped that Jennifer would have to stay one more day in the hospital for Dannie's mom's sake. Sam took one of the paper coffee cups that were in the room and ripped it in half to give his friend some water.

Sam placed his dog back in the cage and then the duffel bag to go to the car. He received a call from Polly at the hospital.

"Sam, everything here at the hospital is good. Jennifer has just fed the baby, and the doctors have decided they need to stay one more night at the hospital and probably would be checked out tomorrow around noon," Polly informed him.

"That'll be all right, Polly. In fact, I want you to go with us. We'll only go down to Dannie's mother's home to have dinner this evening. It'll only be for about three hours, and then I'll bring you back to the hospital," Sam said.

"There's one thing that I've found out, Sam, trying to rest and sleep in a hospital room with all the activity going on, it's almost impossible. So, tell her I'll come, but I may be doing a lot of yawning," Polly replied.

"Well, Polly, if you're sitting at the table, every time you yawn, you can put a piece of that good ole cornbread in your mouth," Sam chuckled.

"If that's the case, Sam, I'll eat the whole pan full, and you will get none," Polly teased.

"I'll be by the hospital to pick you up, Polly, about two o'clock."

"I'll be ready, Sam. Love you," Polly replied.

Sam reached the car with his dog, took him out of the cage, and placed the cage in the back seat. He walked towards a grassy area to give the dog his potty break. Spotting Koon Hee walking out of the motel entrance, Sam waved for him to come over. Koon Hee wanted to know if Sam had eaten breakfast yet.

"No, son, only Frank has eaten his breakfast," Sam replied.

He asked Koon Hee to go to the reception desk and extend their rooms for one more night, explaining that they were going to keep Jennifer an extra night at the hospital.

"Will do, Sam," Koon Hee said. "I'll be waiting for you in the breakfast area after you're done with the dog."

Sam placed his dog back in the cage, set the cage in the back seat, and drove the car to an area with shade. He opened the windows a little bit and started back into the motel to the cafeteria area. As he entered the room, he saw Dannie and Koon Hee sitting off to the right next to a window. They waved at each other as Sam went to the coffee espresso machine to get his second cup of morning brew. He walked over and set his coffee on the table, saying, "Keep a good eye on this. I am going to get me some oatmeal and yogurt."

"Sam, I can't guarantee the coffee will be there when you get back," Koon Hee joked.

"It will be there if you keep an eye on it, and not a hand," Sam retorted as he walked towards the food bar.

As the three of them sat and ate, they talked about the mission of getting Mr. Webb out of the container and laughed about how the fallen door might have knocked some sense into Dannie. After they finished their breakfast, Sam reminded them of their lunch date and told them he would be waiting in the room. They could pick him up about 2 PM to go and pick up Polly at the hospital and have dinner with Dannie's mother.

Sam told Dannie she would have to put his dog back in her duffel bag when they returned to the side door of the motel. He said, "Knock on my door when you get ready to leave, and you can have your keys back." Sam knew they had to make some kind of newsbreak about the death of Frank Morgan so that Pizza wouldn't be trying to find him.

As Sam and his dog entered back into his motel room, he called Matthew Marx and told him what he thought should happen with the death of Frank Morgan. They decided to come up with the idea that Frank Morgan had been killed on the street outside one of the casinos in Atlantic City, New Jersey. Marx said he would take care of that, making sure the big networks would get footage from the made-up police scene. He also told Sam that he could have the ashes of Frank Morgan, along with the flag that had draped his body. The higher-up officials said it was an honor to let Sam have his remains. Sam told Matthew Marx he would call him the next day to make the arrangements for picking up Morgan's ashes.

Marx knew that Jim Logan had called Dannie about a new mission that he wanted them to do, but he never brought that up with Sam Black, wanting to give him some time to deal with everything that was going on with his family and the birth of his grandson.

Sam set his puppy's cage on the bed and called Polly back at the hospital to double-check everything about his daughter's extra night's stay. He told Polly he would come in and walk her to the car for the trip in the afternoon.

As Sam laid back on his bed with his puppy next to him, he fell asleep. His next awakening would be when Koon Hee knocked on his motel door to pick him up to go to the hospital to get Polly. Startled, Sam realized he was still in the motel room and had fallen asleep. He saw Koon Hee through the peephole and opened the door, saying, "Come in, son. Let me wash my face; I must have fallen asleep." Koon Hee said he would get the puppy ready and put him in the duffel bag. Dannie was waiting at the exit door they had been using.

As they came out of the exit door towards the car, Dannie handed Sam the keys and said, "Sam, you drive us. I'll hold the pup." As they drove out of the motel parking lot towards the hospital, Sam began to hum the song he loved, "It Will Be Worth It All Someday." He told them that Matthew Marx had agreed to let him take Frank's remains back to the mountain to be buried in the old graveyard next to his granddad. Sam said in a low tone, "I never thought in a million years that someone would be buried in that grave site other than myself. In fact, I'm going to let Jennifer know that if something ever happens to me, to put Frank and me in the same grave."

As Sam parked the car next to the hospital's main doors, he

left the engine running and said, "I'll be back in a few minutes with Polly, and we'll make our journey." As Sam started down the hallway towards the elevator to go up to Jennifer's room, he walked by a waiting room where he saw a major news network reporting about a murder near a casino in Atlantic City, New Jersey. It just so happened to be the same TV where he saw news about the bombing in Germantown, Maryland. As he stopped to listen to the news, he saw one of the police officers speaking to a camera operator. He recognized the man as one of the agents from The Nest. The officer mentioned that the man murdered was Frank Morgan, claiming they had been called into a casino earlier about him arguing over table money. Sam knew without a doubt that it wasn't Frank Morgan in the body bag. The Nest knew how to manipulate situations, keeping their enemies guessing. Sam thought about Frank, realizing that appearances could be deceiving. Just like his dad used to say, "You cannot judge a book by its cover."

As Sam walked into Jennifer's room, Jeremy asked where his gift was. Sam apologized for forgetting his coffee espresso but promised to bring one later when he brought Polly back to the hospital. Jeremy insisted he'd hold Sam to his word. Sam kissed his daughter and Jeremy on the shoulder and reached to take Polly by the hand.

As they walked towards the car, Polly suggested Sam to go into the cafeteria, buy his son-in-law the espresso coffee, and take it to him. "I will wait for you on the first floor by the nursing station, just pass the elevators," Polly told him. Sam shook his head in the yes motion and went towards the cafeteria to get Jeremy the espresso coffee he had promised to bring that morning. After a few minutes, Sam arrived at the nursing station and smiled. He took Polly by the hand and said, "Let's go; you are a needed woman for Dannie's mom." When Polly saw the puppy, she became like a little child, holding it and loving on little Frank.

As they started down Interstate 95 S. toward Dannie's mother's home place, it seemed that the car was full of joy and happiness. Even Dannie seemed to have lost her train of thought about the Sheriff's visit that evening and was laughing over Polly's and Sam's stories. As they pulled onto the old sand gravel road going down towards the home place, they had to stop at the railroad track because the Amtrak was passing by. That's when Dannie began to look towards the right where the old road was going down to where the grave of her dad might have been found. It was as though she was peering under the train, trying to see if there were any Sheriff's cars down the road.

Sam spotted her in the mirror and said, "Blondie, how did the three blondes get killed hunting, when they came out of the woods and found some tracks and started following them to see what they were?" Dannie stuck her tongue out at Sam as he was watching her through the mirror and said, "I already know the answer to your joke, Mr. Black; the train ran over them." Polly began laughing, "I thought maybe it was a grizzly bear."

As the train passed by, they crossed the railroad track driving by the soybean fields. Dannie was quick to glance again to the right in the area of the grave where she thought her mother buried her dad. As they pulled into the driveway, Dannie spotted Big Willie, her favorite place to play as a child. It seemed like it was part of her whole life. Sam blew the horn a couple of times as they began to exit the car; Mrs. Browning came out on the porch waving at them as though they had been gone for five years.

As they all entered the old farm plantation house, there were hugs and kisses. Dannie's mom led everyone into the living room, pointing to everyone to sit down, while she was finishing the dinner, which would be ready shortly. Dannie got up and walked over into the kitchen and gave her mother another hug, "Mom, I'll help set the table." Polly also was quick to move into the kitchen, telling Mrs. Browning, "I will get the big bowls out so we can pour the food in out of the pots; you've already worked hard enough. Just make sure that you put that cornbread on my side of the table, away from Sam."

As Dannie's mom called for Koon Hee and Sam to come on in and sit down at the table, everything was ready. Polly told Mrs. Browning, "Please sit down, and I will serve all because you've done all the cooking." She said, "Polly, I'll make an agreement with you.

I will let you serve the table if you will come down and stay a couple of days with me before Thanksgiving, and you and I will prepare the meal together." "I will take you up on that deal if you will fix that good banana pudding, and I will bring that potato salad that you've always liked," Polly replied.

Sam said, "That is enough about future cooking; you are making us all hungry twice as much."

As Polly was serving the table and pouring homemade lemonade and coffee, she knew she was right at home. They hadn't paid any attention that when they started eating it was about 4:45 PM and the Sheriff was supposed to be there at 5 PM; but it seemed as soon as they started laughing and talking among themselves, they heard the knock at the door. Dannie looked at the time on the clock above the old China cabinet. She knew it had to be the Sheriff; she said, "I'll get the door, mother."

Dannie opened the door, the Sheriff was standing there with two of his deputies. "Is your mother home, Dannie?" "Yes," she said, "we are eating dinner." By this time, Mrs. Browning was coming towards the door also, telling the Sheriff to come on in the house that she had enough food for everybody. He said, "This will only take a few minutes, Mrs. Browning, of your time." Polly and Sam also came in to be supportive.

"What was found in that grave by the railroad track was your husband that you thought had left the state. With a little luck some of his things had not deteriorated. We found a Social Security card and a picture of you and him standing in front of this house. We also found a piece of paper that was folded in what was left in one of the pockets of his pants. It said he owed money to a man called Bill Thornton and that he had three days to pay up or else. We had some police records on Thornton from his past; he was in a little bit of everything to make money, in most cases illegal. After some investigating, we found out he was killed in Baltimore Maryland two years after your husband went missing. We just wanted to let you know that you can pick up the remains from the coroner's office. Most likely he was killed by Thornton or someone that work for him," the Sheriff explained.

Mrs. Browning began to weep, Dannie ran and put her arms around her mother and said, "You'll be all right, mother." Sam stepped up and started talking to the Sheriff and said, "Take what's left of the body to a crematory. She'll probably want to have a special service at her church, The Church of the Brethren."

The sheriff turned, walking out the door, he said, "I am sorry Mrs. Browning for your loss." Sam followed them out, walking with the Sheriff and his deputies to his car; Sam wanted to plant a seed in the thoughts of the Sheriff, "Every time that I visit Mrs. Browning, she would always tell me, 'Sam, I hope he comes home this week, I'm missing him so much.'"

The Sheriff turned to tell Sam, "Well maybe now she can put it to rest."

"I don't know if that's possible," Sam replied, "I have been trying to do Ola that way, for a long time."

The sheriff reached to shake Sam's hand and said, "I can say that I understand, I really don't, because my wife is still alive."

As the Sheriff was getting in his car preparing to leave, Sam said, "Let me know when you want to come up on the mountain with me and do some hunting."

"Thanks Sam, I might take you up on that this fall."

The next morning, when Sam woke up, he looked over to check on his dog, which was next to him in bed in his cage. "Frank, it won't be long before you have your first trip to the mountaintop house that you and I will be spending a lot of time at. I just hope you are a good listener like Buck was, and I believe you will be," he murmured.

After Sam took a shower and changed his clothes, he turned the TV on. An advertisement caught his attention; it was about jewelry and rings that you give to the one you love. He pondered in his heart for a moment, "Maybe it's time to ask Catherine to become my bride."

He went down to the motel cafeteria and noticed Dannie and

Koon Hee laughing at the table by the window as they were eating their breakfast. This time they didn't even recognize him as he walked in; their eyes were fastened on each other. As he went to the coffee machine to get his espresso coffee and a bowl of oatmeal and yogurt, he decided to go to a jewelry store and buy the ring that he should have bought a long time ago for Catherine. They didn't even seem to notice Sam until he sat down next to them at another table.

"Hey Sam, when did you come in?" Koon Hee asked.

"I thought I would just slip in because it looked like you two were having a lot of fun," Sam replied. "Well, now comes the real fun," Sam said, "because we are going to have to drive through that nasty traffic around Washington DC to get home."

Koon Hee reminded Sam that he did not live in either area of Sam or where Dannie lived, that he was just along for the ride right now to get some good food from Polly's cooking and Dannie's mom. "Sam, Dannie and I were planning on going ahead and leaving a little early and driving to your house and waiting for you there. We were going to stop along the way somewhere and have lunch again; it would be our second lunch date."

"Well, there's something I would like for you to do with me before you all head out," Sam said.

"Sure Sam, what would you like us to do?" Koon Hee asked.

The Kode

"Well, what I want you to do, Koon Hee, is to drive Dannie, follow me. You two finish eating; I will go up and get my dog and meet you at the truck in a few minutes," Sam explained.

Koon Hee told Dannie, "That's a strange request. He knows I have never driven your Camaro, so I'm wondering what he's up to."

Dannie shook her head, saying, "I don't have a clue. Well, let's get up and go, and we will find out."

As they waited for Sam at his truck, they saw him coming, carrying his dog cage in Dannie's duffel bag. Sam opened the front door on the driver's side, placing the dog on the seat. Dannie handed Koon Hee the keys to her car and said, "Let's just do what he says." As they followed Sam out of the parking lot of the motel, he then turned right, going towards the hospital. He drove to the first red light and turned left, heading towards the big mall. As he pulled into the mall's parking lot and parked, Koon Hee pulled beside him in Dannie's Camaro. They got out of the car and walked over to Sam's side of the truck and knocked on his window. Sam was working on the dog cage to get it open. After getting his dog out of the cage, he opened the door and stepped out onto the pavement. He handed the dog to Koon Hee and said, "I want you to take him for a potty walk and watch him until Dannie and I get back."

Sam reached and took Dannie by the hand and said, "Follow

me, I have something I need you to help me with."

They walked through the mall and Sam stopped at a jewelry store and told Dannie, "Here it is, this is what I'm looking for." They entered the store, Sam turned and told Dannie, "I'm looking for the perfect engagement ring that I'm planning on giving to Catherine." It looked like Dannie's face turned ten shades of happy.

She grabbed Sam and hugged him, saying, "It's about time, Sam Black. You have been lingering behind for a long time."

They walked over to the counter and Dannie asked where the engagement rings were located. The lady behind the counter led them to the end and pointed down. As Dannie looked over the rings, she asked Sam, "How much do you want to pay for your engagement?"

Sam said, "Nothing, I will let the government pay for it. And that means I get to pick her out a very big stone."

Dannie turned and asked Sam, "Have you ever noticed any kind of rings that she wears?"

Sam said, "The only rings I've noticed that she wears are silver-looking."

"Then I have found the perfect ring, Sam, here it is," Dannie exclaimed. "This ring is called the eternity diamond engagement ring, in white gold and almost 4 carats; look, Sam, the big diamond in the middle is cut like a heart."

As Sam held the ring and looked at the heart-shaped diamond, he knew that there had been a lot of changes in hearts. And after this mission, he felt he had the biggest change of heart. "Blondie, I think you have picked the best one," he said. The price tag of almost forty thousand dollars didn't change Sam's thoughts.

The lady behind the counter, working in the jewelry store, said to Sam, "She must be a very special lady."

Sam told the woman, "This lady must become the love of my life because I lost the last one. Let me rephrase that," said Sam, "She has become the only love in my life since I lost the last one."

As Sam was paying for the ring with his credit card, he noticed Dannie was still looking at the engagement rings. "Your time will come, Blondie, I promise you; your time will come." As they left the jewelry store and came out of the mall, they noticed that Koon Hee was sitting on the tailgate of Sam's truck with the dog in his lap.

"Thanks, Koon Hee, for watching my dog. You and Blondie can leave now if you would like. I am going to go pick up Polly, Jeremy, and Jennifer at the hospital. I will meet you all at the house later this evening, and you know Polly, she will be cooking us another meal."

"We're on our way, Sam. Tell Polly I will be looking forward to her good cooking," replied Koon Hee.

As Dannie and Koon Hee drove off, Dannie began to laugh and clap her hands. "He's finally going to do it. Do what Koon Hee asked. He is going to ask Catherine to marry him; he bought her a beautiful engagement ring."

Sam took the ring out of the bag and opened the box it was in. When the sunlight hit the diamond, it was blinding. The heart was a beautiful cut precious gem, just like Catherine.

As Sam returned to the hospital to pick up his family to start the journey home, he began to think about his favorite song and said within himself, "The someday has now happened."

Polly called Sam, letting him know they were ready to leave the hospital, that she had a car seat for the baby specially delivered to the room, and that it was time to go home. "I'm almost there, Polly," Sam replied.

"Then pull to the front doors, and that is where we will meet you; they will bring Jennifer out in a wheelchair. That's hospital policy."

Sam pulled to the front door and stopped. He took his puppy out of the front seat and placed it in the back of the pickup. He secured a strap across the cage so that it couldn't move and closed the tailgate. Leaning over the side of his truck, Sam spoke to his dog, when he heard Jeremy speaking his name as they came through the doors. Jennifer held the baby, pushed out in a wheelchair, while Polly carried her bags and the new infant car seat.

As the Sam Black family loaded up and started towards home, it felt like a new beginning had begun in each life. Sam and Jeremy sat in the front two seats; Sam explained to him the best way to trout fish in a small mountain stream. Jeremy, not a big hunter like Sam, loved to go fishing with him. In the back, Polly and Jennifer's conversations shifted between changing baby diapers, breastfeeding, and ensuring the child was lying correctly in the crib. It had been planned beforehand that Jennifer would stay with Polly until she was totally well enough for her and Jeremy to return home.

As they pulled into the driveway, Dannie's Camaro and Catherine's SUV were already there. Catherine knew the door combination, and they were in the house. They saw Sam pull in, and they all came running out. Catherine came around to the side where Jennifer was sitting, opened the door, and said, "Pass me that beautiful little child." As Jennifer took the baby out of the car seat, she handed little Samuel to Catherine. Polly came around to help Jennifer into the house. Koon Hee and Dannie gathered the luggage from the back where the dog was. Sam undid the strap holding his dog cage and took his little friend Frank out of the cage, making him sit on the ground.

After they had all entered the house, Polly suggested, "I think we should have a prayer of thanks for the birth of little Samuel and the safe return of his grandfather, Dannie and Koon Hee." As Polly gave thanks and all bowed their heads, when the prayer was over, they noticed that Sam was on his knee as though he was praying.

"There is one more request," Sam said. Every head turned towards Sam, wondering what his prayer request was. He took the box out of his pocket that contained the ring. Looking up at Catherine, he said, "Should have done this a long time ago. I would like for you to be my wife, Catherine. Will you marry me? I pray your answer is yes."

Catherine walked over in front of Sam and said, "I have been waiting for this moment for a long time also. Your prayer is answered; yes, I will be your wife and marry you." Everyone in the room was overwhelmed with joy, and the loud laughter seemed to get the attention of Frank, because the little pup began to howl.

Sam put the ring on Catherine's finger and gave her a kiss. Everybody began to clap their hands and started asking when the date of this marriage was going to happen. Sam was quick to say,

"Catherine, I will work on that; it's time for Polly to fix us one of those wonderful, country dinners."

As the celebration continued at home, Sam Black, Jim Logan, was on his way to Sam's home to speak to him about something. As the family finished their dinner and little Frank ate scraps beneath Sam that he had dropped for him, it was as though Sam was right about the song that he loved. It will be worth it all someday.

Dannie and Koon Hee sat in the swing on the porch, while Sam and Catherine walked the pup in the yard. Sam noticed a dark SUV with dark windows pulling into his driveway with government tags. He kissed Catherine on the cheek and said, "Stay here just for a moment and let me see who this is." As he walked over to the vehicle, he noticed that it was Jim Logan.

Jim opened the door and stepped out, extending his hand to shake Sam's. "I want to thank you again, Mr. Black, for your service to the country. With the way everything went south, you and your team were able to bring it North."

"Sorry, Mr. Logan, I don't want what you have. What I want is behind me in the house, and that's my family," Sam replied firmly.

"Don't get me wrong, Sam. What I have for you is what you asked for," Jim insisted. He walked towards the back of the SUV, raised the tailgate, and handed Sam a chrome-like suitcase. "Inside that suitcase that I just gave you, is the flag and the ashes of Frank Morgan that you had asked Matthew Marx about."

Sam held the suitcase in his left hand as Jim reached out to shake his hand again, thanking him for his service to the country. Sam briefly held Jim's hand. "It's been a pleasure working with you also. Just do me one more favor and that is keep a good watch on Mr. Webb, the War Peace."

"Don't worry about that, I think we have control of that now," Jim reassured Sam as he got into his vehicle.

As Dannie and Koon Hee walked towards the vehicle to speak to Jim Logan, Dannie pondered what was inside the suitcase. Perhaps it was the mission they wanted her to encourage Sam Black to take. After speaking and shaking hands, Jim Logan left to go back to The Nest.

"Tomorrow we have one more mission to finish. I will tell you about it in the morning; right now, we continue our family celebration," Sam announced to Dannie and Koon Hee as they returned to the porch swing.

As Sam walked back over and took Catherine by the hand to begin their walk, he held the case in his left hand. Dannie informed Koon Hee about the possibility of another mission to convince Sam to take. Regardless of what it was, they trusted Sam and would wait for his orders.

The Kode

Catherine never even asked Sam what was in the briefcase; she would wait until he spoke about it. She didn't even realize how big the diamond was in her engagement ring until the sun hit it, catching her attention. "Oh my gosh," she exclaimed, "that's the biggest diamond I have ever seen.

"Sam, I'm not worth this much," Catherine said.

"No, you're not Catherine. You're worth a whole lot more than that to me," Sam replied.

As the day ended at the Sam Black home, everyone seemed happy and at peace.

The next morning, Polly was already up early and had a big breakfast cooked, complete with her famous biscuits and French toast. After breakfast, Sam announced that he would be taking Koon Hee, Dannie, and Catherine to his mountaintop farm. He instructed Polly to take care of Jennifer, Jeremy, and little Samuel, assuring them that he would return the next evening. Sam informed everyone that they would be leaving around 10:30 that morning. He reached down and picked up his little pup Frank, saying, "I'm taking him for a potty walk. All of you get ready for the trip."

As Sam opened the coat closet, they noticed he took out a silver briefcase and carried it with him along with his dog. Polly walked over to the kitchen window and watched Sam place the briefcase in the back seat of his truck. She, too, wondered what was in the briefcase and why Sam had said nothing about it. But she knew that Sam had a change of heart, and it seemed like whatever it was, had no effect on his emotions.

When everyone was getting into the truck, Sam asked Koon Hee to place the briefcase between him and Dannie in the back seat. Sam had already placed his dog in the cage in the back of the truck. During the five-hour trip, no one asked Sam about the briefcase; they simply talked about family matters and the upcoming marriage between Sam and Catherine.

They started up the dirt road towards the farm when Sam pointed out the old coal tipple where his daddy had worked for many years. He also shared the tragic story of how his dad's older brother had been killed when he was crushed between two coal cars.

They reached the top of the mountain. The road turned left, passing by the graveyard towards Sam's house. When they came to the graveyard, which was on the right side of the road, Sam stopped. "Everybody out of the truck," he said. "We have a mission to complete." Sam reached in and took the metal briefcase, then walked to the back of his truck and opened the tailgate, taking out a small military-type pick and shovel combination.

He started walking through the old graveyard, Sam said, "Follow me." They came to a place of old gravestones, some made from rocks. Carved into one of the old stone rocks was the name,

Rev William J Black. To the right was a stone carved with the name Laura Black. "This is my grandfather and my grandmother where they are buried. My dad decided not to be buried next to his, so this space is open," Sam explained. He pointed out his daddy's brother's grave, carved on the stone was Lee Black, who was killed in the train accident.

Sam reached out to Koon Hee, handing him the briefcase, and said, "Hold this for a moment while I dig a hole." Sam dug a square hole about 2 feet wide and 2 feet long and about 2 feet deep. Dannie and Koon Hee had now figured out what was in the briefcase; it was the remains of Frank Morgan. When Sam had finished digging, he asked Koon Hee to hand him the briefcase. After Sam had placed the briefcase in the hole, he started filling it up with the dirt that he had dug out. He turned to Dannie and said, "If you don't mind, would you start quoting Psalms 23?"

As Dannie quoted the requested Psalms, Koon Hee asked, "Can I place some dirt in the grave also?"

"Sure, son, here is the shovel," Sam replied.

As they finished filling the grave, Sam walked over the hill and found a flat limestone rock. He walked back and placed it as a headstone. While Sam was over the hill, Dannie explained to Catherine what was in the case and what Frank Morgan meant to Sam Black - a total change of heart.

As they left the graveyard and headed to Sam's mountaintop cabin home, very few words were spoken. It seemed like a time of reverence. The memories of the past and future would always be buried on that mountain, the mountain of Sam Black.

About the Author

Steven Jones hails from the scenic town of Bluefield, West Virginia—a place famously shared with Nobel laureate, John Nash, whose life inspired the film "A Beautiful Mind"—and has led a life as vivid and compelling as any narrative. Once a golden gloves boxer who braved the demanding life in the coal fields, Steven found his true calling far from the shadow of his early ventures. After dedicating years to the electric trade within the depths of coal mines and navigating the complexities of managing a store and restaurant, he ventured far beyond his roots. Drawn to his mother's familial ties south of Washington D.C., Steven's journey took an international turn, leading him to various countries on missions that tested the limits of his resilience.

His adventures read like a novel: From being kidnapped at gunpoint in one country and miraculously released to a tense stop in Nigeria amidst an attempted coup en route to a meeting with the President. These experiences, ripe with danger and intrigue, did not deter him. Instead, they inspired Steven to pen "THE KODE" while immersed in the cultures of Asia. Steven Jones's life story encapsulates the essence of a man who, through trials and travels, discovered his passion for storytelling, capturing the spirit of adventure and the resilience of the human spirit.

Made in the USA
Columbia, SC
01 July 2024

c3eb8963-9e12-43d0-9a1f-8df2bea90b2cR01